I0762213

Under A Fallen SUN

John Coon

SAMAK PRESS

UNDER A FALLEN SUN

Samak Press
ISBN: 978-1-7324871-3-0

Book Cover Design and Interior Formatting by 100 Covers

AUTHOR'S NOTE

Writing a story is like painting a picture with words. You open the door to a new world by recounting scenes and characters and invite readers to come inside and explore that world.

Under a Fallen Sun took many brushstrokes over many years for me to craft a full picture for my readers. It began as a simple short story in college and eventually morphed into a novel that will serve as a gateway into a larger fictional universe.

I am indebted and grateful to many people for helping me realize this vision. Jeff Keyes and Spencer Durrant deserve special mention for their efforts in reading earlier drafts of this story and offering valuable suggestions on plot and character development. My Dad offered valuable input in crafting key scenes. Finally, my Mom read the original short story before she passed away. She offered encouraging feedback that helped me shape *Under a Fallen Sun* into what it is today.

– JC

SCATTERED NOISES OUTSIDE the house drew Todd's attention to the boarded-up window. He gently laid the photograph down on the end table and pressed his eye against a knothole near the middle board. No sign of anyone on the driveway or in the yard.

Good. The lights did the exact job they were meant to do.

Todd didn't feel ready for another fight with what lurked in the shadows just yet. His left arm still sported a crude splint from the last encounter. Only electrical tape held the metal, padding, and cloth strips together at this point. Much of the swelling subsided since he popped his wrist back into place. Those nerves still reminded him how inflamed they were each time Todd made the mistake of bumping against any solid object.

The end table captured his attention a second time. Todd picked up the photograph where he left it. He gazed at the photograph with an unbroken stare, studying it like a map to hidden treasure. His eyes traced Caroline's red hair, freckled skin, and broad smile.

Todd closed his eyes and bit down on his lower lip. Only three weeks since Caroline had been stolen from him. It felt like another lifetime now. He longed to feel her breath caress his neck in the early morning hours. Her infectious laughter burrowing into his ears would offer a perfect antidote to the pain he felt right now.

Those monsters ripped Caroline from his life. Since that moment, they watched and waited. Their sole purpose, it seemed, centered on bringing the same fate to him.

One light flickered. Another did the same. His eyes snapped open. He ripped his gaze away from the photograph and glanced at the ceiling.

Every light extinguished with a suddenness mirroring a candle's flame blown out. Darkness flooded the entire living room. Todd sprang to his feet. His eyes darted first to the boarded-up window, then to the front door.

"Damn! The lights!"

Scattered noises outside the house grew in strength and number. Growls soon permeated the entire living room. Those awful creatures were drawing closer. No matter how many times Todd heard it, their low shrill sounds sent a chill rippling through his entire spine. He sprinted out of the living room and through the kitchen.

Glass shattered, followed at once by a loud thud. Todd couldn't help wondering how large of a stone they tossed against the boarded-up kitchen window this time. It sounded big. Too big. If he didn't fix the lights soon, their attacks would only grow worse.

Todd yanked open a door leading into the garage. Banging sounds from creatures trying to break down the garage door greeted him. More unsettling growls accompanied the banging. He ripped open the circuit panel and shut off the main circuit breaker. Then, just as quickly, Todd threw the transfer switch to a standby generator.

Lights snapped to life on every side of the house. One light popped on inside the garage. Multiple screams ripped through the air. Todd closed his eyes and let out a relieved sigh.

No doubt those creatures began their retreat into the shadows where they belonged. He slumped down against the wall. Nights like this one made him wonder how much longer he could hold out.

This marked the second such attack in three days. Their boldness increased as they became more convinced of the weakness of his position. These monsters kept testing his defenses. Now one figured out how to cut power to the house. Todd felt fortunate this place had a backup generator. Still, it only felt like a matter of time before they pinpointed the right weakness to breach his defenses and drag him away.

Todd couldn't let them do it. For Caroline's sake. She would want him to keep fighting and hang on as long as he still possessed the strength to do it. He only wished she could be here by his side. Her spirit drove him to fight. Still, her warm body pressed against him and her voice in his ears alone could fill a chasm of loneliness carved out in his soul.

A spasm shot through Todd's right leg. He clenched his teeth and rolled up his dark blue jeans. The fabric concealed a large wound. Where blood once oozed, now a scab sealed fluid inside. Pebble sized bony growths started to press against the underside of his skin in the surrounding area.

Todd scrambled to his feet. He stumbled again and crawled up the steps. Breaths escaped from between his lips in short heavy bursts.

He needed light.

Unfiltered light. Applied directly to the leg.

As Todd reached the top step, he glanced over at a shelf set against the wall on his left. He stumbled off the side of the stairs. His knees banged against the cement floor, and he winced.

Todd crawled toward the shelf and grasped onto the side. He pulled himself to his feet and wrapped his fingers around a flashlight. Spasms kept surging through the injured leg. Each wave came in greater intensity than the one before it.

Now almost doubled over, Todd turned on the flashlight. He planted the beam squarely on the festering scab. Each bony growth began to twitch and shrink under the light. Todd shouted and clenched his teeth. His knuckles turned white from clutching onto the shelf.

Searing pain gave way to a dull throb until, at last, muscle tissue in Todd's leg returned to normal. A cloudy fluid oozed from under the scab and trickled onto the cement. Steam arose from the fluid as it made its descent. He dropped the flashlight to his side and panted. Melting bony growths grew more difficult each time, but he had to do it. Todd had to prevent these changes from occurring as long as humanly possible.

Human remained the keyword there. Todd did not want to become like others he encountered in this town. Deep in his heart, though, it felt like a losing battle.

Hopes for escape dwindled even as days he spent trapped here morphed into weeks. Todd's tolerance for unfiltered light grew progressively weaker each day. Searching for a way to shut off the barrier had proven too dangerous to do at night. By day, sunlight now sapped his strength much too quickly for him to cover any substantial ground. It continually forced him to return to this same spot and prepare for the night ahead.

Todd always wondered what Hell felt like to its inhabitants. He now had a pretty good idea.

STEAM RUSHED OUT once Jason popped the hood. He waited a few seconds for it to dissipate, then hunched over and unscrewed the radiator cap.

Jason gave a low whistle.

"Bone dry."

This wasn't news Paige wanted to hear. Her idea of celebrating spring break with her boyfriend and their friends did not involve breaking down on an isolated Texas highway.

"How dumb do you have to be to let a radiator run out of coolant?"

Jason raised his head and peeked over his shoulder. He greeted the question posed to him with a frown and a squint.

"Piss off, Rich."

Rich laughed.

"Not exactly a gear head, are you?"

Paige pushed back a blond lock from her eyebrow and took a turn greeting Rich with eye daggers.

"You heard, Jason. He said, 'piss off.'"

Rich threw up his hands and smirked. "Fine. You tell me what we're gonna do now with an overheated car besides marinate in the sun."

As much as Paige hated to admit it, Rich had a valid point. The high plains heat already beat down on her, extracting every last drop of water from her exposed arms and legs in real time. A half-full water bottle would only last so long in this situation. Her crop top and shorts didn't keep Paige as cool as she hoped and expected.

Jason continued to lean over the radiator. He stared at it as though fluid would suddenly condense and fill the radiator if he thought about it long enough. Paige joined him in front of the bumper and draped her arm over his shoulder.

"Anything I can do to help fix it?"

Jason shook his head.

"Not really. There's not a whole lot anyone can do now except call someone to come give us a tow."

Paige toyed with his cropped red hair. She trailed her fingers in a circular pattern on the back of Jason's head.

"It'll be okay," she said. "We'll figure this out and get back on the road soon enough."

Her reassuring tone did not line up with Paige's actual feelings. She couldn't help wondering if they created some serious trouble for themselves here.

"I don't think we're gonna find anyone out here who can tow us."

Heather poked her head out of an open backseat window. She brushed back an ebony curl matching her glistening skin and held up a smartphone.

"I can't pick up a signal in these parts."

Paige wiped beads of sweat from her forehead and squinted at the plains stretching endlessly before her on the horizon. She wondered how far away Las Vegas was from their current location. Hell, she wondered how long crossing the border into New Mexico would take at this point. They couldn't even make it out of West Texas without running into trouble.

Looking at the surrounding vista didn't raise much hope of finding help. Dry grasses, pockmarked with scraggly bushes and sandy patches, lay in all four directions. Only a fence running parallel to the highway, along with intermittent electrical poles, interrupted an endless sea of grass on either side.

Paige turned to Jason again as her boyfriend slammed down the hood.

"How far do you think that highway goes before it reaches the next town? If we start walking now –"

He shook his head more emphatically this time.

"I'm not dying to find out what dying from heatstroke feels like."

"Didn't we pass a gas station a while ago?" Heather asked.

Paige's eyes followed the sound of a car door opening. Heather crawled out of the backseat, adjusted her bra strap, and walked toward them. She glanced down at her smartphone and then out at the stretch of highway extending into the horizon behind Paige and Jason.

"I could have sworn I saw one a couple of miles back there," Heather said. "If we start now, maybe we can reach it inside of an hour."

Jason turned and gazed in the same direction. A frown became etched on his face with a depth equal to cracks in the white and yellow lines running down the asphalt.

"I think it's a lot further back than a couple of miles," he said, turning and facing the girls again. "Staying with the car is the best call."

Rich barely held back a laugh as he leaned against the side of the car.

"Best call? Not hardly. I don't see anyone around here coming to the rescue, do you?"

Paige pursed her lips tight for a moment and released them into a deep sigh.

"This is I-40. People do travel this highway, you know. I'm sure a trucker or someone else will come along to help sooner or later."

"I wouldn't count on one of those people stopping to help us."

Paige glared at Rich. He pushed away from the car and held up his hands in a defensive position.

"I know. I know. 'Piss off, Rich',"

Rich's tone parroted how he thought Paige's voice sounded when she was angry. It only made her angrier whenever she heard him do his impression.

Heather glanced back at Rich as well and shook her head. A deep frown also carved out a spot on her face. She turned to Paige and shrugged.

"As much as I hate to say it, Rich has a point about one thing. We can't just stick around here and take our chances, hoping some kind soul will come along to save us."

Jason closed his eyes and rubbed his hands down his cheeks. They popped open again and he fixed his gaze on Heather.

"I don't like the idea of abandoning my car to chase down mirages."

"Do you have a bottle of coolant lying around in the trunk?"

"No."

"That settles it. This car isn't going anywhere until we fill the coolant tank back up. Even then, you might be spending a few hundred bucks to get that radiator fixed."

Jason gnawed on his lower lip. His fingers tapped the back pocket of his jeans holding his wallet.

"Thanks for bringing that up. Obvious information always makes me feel so much better."

Heather flipped him off.

"No need to be an ass about it."

She turned and stomped down the asphalt toward Rich. Paige licked her lips and gazed at the lonely highway. Her eyes trailed yellow and white lines, first in one direction and then the other. Her hopes some traveler would miraculously appear on the horizon, to save them in their hour of need, dimmed as the sun grew hotter and brighter.

IT DIDN'T SEEM fair. Todd wondered what he did to deserve this curse.

Their original plans did not include making a pit stop after leaving Amarillo. Caroline noticed the road sign almost by accident. She decided it would be fun to take a detour and grab a bite to eat for lunch. Todd smiled when he thought back to her enthusiastic suggestion. His wife never passed up a chance to try out some local cuisine. The more off the map it was located, the more her curiosity drove her to take a "taste-cation" as she termed it.

Caroline's food blog even carried that same word she coined in the title. She relished going on her taste-cations. Each blog post contained almost as many photos as actual words. She always spent a few minutes before each meal at a new restaurant snapping photos from different angles – making sure the lighting was exactly right – so her blog readers could see the true color and texture of each menu item she ordered.

"I hope you plan to take as many photos of our kids one day."

Todd's words from the last taste-cation they took together popped up into his mind as clearly as though he said them only seconds ago.

So did Caroline's reaction. She simultaneously pinched her green eyes and crimson lips shut and gave him a broad smirk.

"That depends on if their behavior rates five stars or not," Caroline said, after her lovely face bounced back to its normal sunny demeanor. Todd thought her usual smile could light up an entire room with the irresistible happiness it conveyed. "If they're being little monsters, I might have to settle for fewer photos and a lower rating."

Monsters.

Todd shuddered. The happy scene vanished faster than a Texas torrent in the summer. Glass tables. Cushioned chairs. Warm sunshine just outside the beige canopy shading a medium-sized patio. Like it or not, that cozy outdoor cafe had morphed back into an aging boarded-up house illuminated by every light he could scrounge up.

Monster seemed like such an innocent word not so long ago. If only he knew at the time what would have happened to him and Caroline, he would never have agreed to take a new job in Albuquerque. Certainly, at the very least, he wouldn't have made a hasty decision to pack everything they owned into their SUV and drive from Humble to New Mexico – just to save a few bucks on shipping their belongings to their new place.

Todd closed his eyes tight, frowned, and pressed his right fist against the hardwood floor. He finally relaxed his hand and latched onto the edge of the countertop to pull himself to his feet. Todd glanced sideways at a door, only a short distance from the refrigerator. It lay open a crack. A simple crack that exposed a swath of darkness hiding behind a wooden rectangle adorned with faded off-white paint.

Did he have to venture into the basement again? Todd silently cursed the fact he already knew the answer before asking that question. No other choice remained. His circumstances robbed him of a better option. He had to face that thing again – whatever the hell it was.

Todd threw open the door. A distinct thud from the knob striking sheet rock greeted his ears. Light from the kitchen splashed on the darkened stairs. He hesitated at the top of those stairs and turned back to the kitchen. Todd scanned the counter-top and spotted a UV flashlight. He snatched it up and started down the stairs again.

A lone wooden chair sat near the middle of a cramped living room. The flashlight beam bounced off assorted boxes and plastic bins lining the walls. No lids on any box or bin. Each one overflowed with random goods. Some still sealed in their original packaging.

Todd selected this house for that reason alone. He combed an entire block until he found the right place. It did him no good to hole up somewhere where without enough supplies to survive while putting his escape plans into action. No such problem existed along those lines in this particular spot. The former owner of the house stored enough water, food, clothing, tools, and other necessities to meet Todd's needs. It gave him some leverage for dealing with monsters infesting this town stuck smack dab in the middle of nowhere.

The chair was turned away from him. It faced a boarded-up basement window embedded in the east wall. Shadows shrouded the chair. An outline of an individual stood out against the darkness. Todd approached the chair from behind and held his flashlight at eye level.

Creaking wood and clanking metal signaled to Todd his return to the basement did not go unnoticed. A low growl greeted his footsteps when he reached the chair. A vigorous rattle of chains followed. Clanking metal reverberated through the small room.

"You cannot keep me locked down here forever," Each word dripped venom as a hoarse voice spit them at Todd. "The others will come for me soon. Then I will be free to put an end to your miserable existence."

Todd shook his head and shifted the flashlight beam down to the floor in front of his prisoner.

"Your threats mean nothing to me. Which one of us is in chains? And which one of us is free to come and go as they please?"

"Circumstances can change without warning."

A deep frown overtook Todd's lips.

"You and your kind have seen to it, haven't you?"

He dragged the flashlight beam upward. It washed a distinct blue hue over the chair's occupant. The beam revealed a naked arm. It bore pale skin that grew paler under the blue light. Todd centered his flashlight directly on the whitened forearm.

Soon, wisps of smoke climbed toward the ceiling. Pale pigment grew red where light met skin. A low wheezing groan greeted Todd's ears. The metallic clank of the chains returned, soon joined by chair legs thumping against the floor.

"It doesn't have to be like this." Todd squeezed the flashlight handle harder as if this action could somehow focus the beam like a laser. "You can end it right now by telling me exactly what I want to hear."

A painful groan mingled with another low growl escaped the prisoner's lips. No words followed. Skin directly under the UV light began to blister and peel. Then, finally, his captive couldn't hold back any longer. Groans and growls turned into an ear-piercing scream.

Todd immediately pressed his right palm against his right ear. Then he tilted his head downward and mashed his left ear against his shoulder. This kept him from dropping the flashlight on the ground. Todd let the screams linger for a few seconds longer until he saw tears leaking out from his prisoner's black oval eyes. This persuaded him to swing the flashlight away and let the beam fall off to the side.

"You're one tough nut to crack."

Tough nut or not, Todd had no intention of admitting defeat. This wasn't his first time dealing with an adversary who wasn't forthcoming with critical information.

His thoughts drifted back to that cramped cell in Kandahar. Todd could feel dust and sweat mingling on his face as though he still baked in the desert heat on a typical Afghanistan afternoon.

A prisoner lay before him on a narrow horizontal table. One set of thick ropes bound his arms to the tabletop. Another set stretched tight across his legs and held them in place. A black cloth covered the prisoner's entire face.

Todd nodded to another man dressed in fatigues and a bullet-proof vest who stood on the other side. He grabbed a small bucket and approached the table. The other man tilted the bucket over the black cloth until a steady trickle of water splashed over the lip.

At once, the prisoner thrashed at the ropes holding him down. Todd silently counted off 60 seconds before finally waving off the other man. Upon getting the signal, he pulled the bucket away and backed up a few steps from the table again.

Todd leaned forward and ripped away the now damp cloth. Widened eyes and clenched teeth greeted him.

"Please, as Allah as my witness, I do not know anything."

The prisoner's words exuded as much pain and fright as his face showed. Todd pressed his eyelids together for a moment and frowned. He opened them again and let out a deep sigh.

"Why do you insist on lying to us? We saw you transporting at least one suspected bomber to the market. Closed circuit cameras don't lie."

"I am a simple taxi driver. Please."

"No, you aren't. You're a murderer."

"I have shed no blood from another man."

Todd pounded his fist on the table. It struck the wood close enough to the prisoner's cheek to make him flinch.

"You're a lying son of a bitch! Who are you trying to protect?"

Images flashed in his mind.

An explosion. Flames engulfing the lead vehicle in their convoy. Screams and smoke choking the air at an equal rate.

They sent two good soldiers home to be buried after that attack. Two others were discharged from their company with a single leg left. Todd ended up being one of the lucky ones.

"Answer me," he demanded. "Answer me!"

A jolt raced through Todd.

He blinked.

That cramped cell in Kandahar faded back into the background of his subconscious. A darkened basement greeted his eyes again. Heavy breaths escaped from his mouth and his nose.

His current prisoner lifted his head and thrust out his chin in a defiant fashion. A thin smile crawled over his equally thin lips.

"I will tell you nothing."

Todd answered it with a shout and struck the butt-end of the flashlight handle against his adversary's head. Both black ovals disappeared behind a pair of pale eyelids and the head slumped downward until chin met chest. Todd flipped the flashlight back to its normal position.

"If you won't talk, then you've lost the right to stay awake."

He grasped the chains circling the prisoner's chest and tested them to see if they remained tight against both chair and prisoner. Todd figured his prisoner would be out cold for a while, but he didn't want to risk an escape. This one could not find its way back to the others at any cost.

Todd started back up the stairs. At once, a spasm shot through his right leg. His leg locked up on the stair and he stumbled forward. Todd planted his right hand on the stair in front of him to keep from falling on his knees.

He clenched his jaw and grunted. Todd turned around and sat on the stair under him. He yanked up his right pant leg. Bony knobs appeared again – in the same place as before.

Todd swung the UV light onto the bony growths below the long scab. Smoke wafted up from his leg as the beam did what it was supposed to do. He bit into his lower lip to suppress screams and grimaced while squeezing his eyes shut. When the pain finally lessened, Todd opened them again.

His wound still looked awful, but no trace of bony growth remained. Each one melted and gathered into a small puddle of cloudy fluid on the stair below his feet.

This offered only a stopgap solution. Time did not favor Todd. He couldn't prevent his body from undergoing a terrifying metamorphosis indefinitely. Todd had seen enough to understand what became of the others in this town.

Something needed to be done. Soon.

PAIGE BECAME CONVINCED her thumb had turned invisible to passing motorists. She stuck it out and waved in both directions. The effect remained the same eastbound or westbound. Half a dozen cars and trucks drove past since Paige and her friends started walking east along the highway.

None slowed down. Not even for a second.

Heather and Rich finally crossed over to the narrow median. It alternated between patches of sandy dirt and grass. The median divided eastbound and westbound lanes, creating two fully separate roads from a single highway. They made a goal to draw attention from motorists traveling east back to Amarillo. This approach didn't yield better results for Heather or Rich. If drivers in any of the vehicles whipping past the group saw or cared about the foursome, they did nothing to indicate it.

"Tell me again why we didn't fly to Vegas?"

Paige glanced sideways at Jason and frowned when he said these words. A glare sprouted on his face after seeing yet another car zoom past. It softened once he noticed her worried expression.

"I know. Flying is tough for you." Jason's terseness softened. "I'm just feeling frustrated. I thought at least one person would have given enough of a damn to stop and help us out by now."

Paige gazed down at her feet. A fear of flying didn't keep her on ground. She wanted to share with him exactly why she insisted they spend a couple of days driving out to Nevada from Louisiana. But she convinced herself Jason wouldn't understand her reasoning. Paige had to travel this road. Sure, it seemed like a desperate gamble. Then again, she had run out of options.

Nearly a month had passed since her family's world turned upside down and inside out. Her brother had to be out here somewhere. Paige knew it. Whether or not Jason, Heather, or Rich also possessed the same knowledge did not seem as important at the moment.

"Have a little faith," Paige finally told Jason. "Somebody will stop soon. I'm sure of it."

Empty words. They felt empty leaving her mouth. In her heart, she had a tough time envisioning anything but a grim fate.

"I said no!"

Paige and Jason simultaneously whipped their heads toward the median. Heather shielded her face with her hands and backed away from Rich. His smartphone pointed straight at her.

"Get that phone out of my face," she snapped. "I don't wanna be in your damn video."

Heather sounded exactly like she would toss a rock at him if she had one available. Rich laughed and kept his phone locked on her like a rifle scope.

"You'll love this video once it goes viral."

"I don't care if you get 10 trillion views. Leave me out of it."

Typical Rich.

All he seemed to care about these days was posting a bunch of new videos to his YouTube channel to entice more subscribers. His smartphone could be put to much better use. Like checking to see if he had a signal. Then they could call for help instead of trying to flag down random vehicles passing by the group.

"Hey Rich, how about looking and seeing if you got any bars on that thing?" Jason had no reservation about vocalizing thoughts he obviously shared with Paige. "It would sure speed up getting out of this predicament."

Rich pulled down the phone and swiped the screen with his index finger. He glanced up at Jason and Paige and shook his head.

"No bars. No 4G. Nothing. Same as usual."

Paige stopped in her tracks. She closed her eyes and lowered her head.

"You got a headache?"

Tangible concern arose in Jason's voice. He wrapped an arm around her shoulders.

Paige nodded.

"Something like that."

She pinched the bridge of her nose between her fingers to let Jason think he correctly diagnosed her body language. Paige didn't want to reveal what actually cluttered her head at that moment. Her thoughts focused on a desperate prayer.

God, if you're there and listening, please help me out, Paige pleaded in silence. *Don't leave us stranded here on this highway. Don't leave me to die out here.*

Once those words rolled through her mind, Paige's eyes popped open again. She scanned the highway in both directions. Nothing. Not even the sound of a car or truck engine in the distance.

Paige kicked at a patch of grass and scowled. Her parents celebrated prayer as a miracle solution to all of life's problems.

"God is watching you," her mom always told her. "If you talk to him, he'll take on all your burdens."

How would Mom feel if confronted with breaking down and ending up stranded countless miles from civilization? Would she be so quick to parrot whatever platitudes the pastor dished out in his Sunday sermon? Paige smirked while she pictured her mom sitting in the passenger seat screaming and hyperventilating. This same woman freaked out when Peanut, their family cat, scratched up a leg on a brand-new sofa – only a few hours after her parents bought it and brought it home.

A gust of wind kicked up from the east and sent locks of Paige's hair into her eyes. She brushed unruly blond strands back into place. Feeling even a small breeze brought welcome relief from the sun relentlessly beating down on her.

Paige and Jason continued walking forward, sticking out their thumbs and waiving. Rich made random goofy comments as he kept filming. A couple of things he said made her smile. Paige turned away so he couldn't see it. She didn't want Rich to take it as a sign to crack more jokes. The ratio of bad ones to good ones wasn't worth it.

A blaring horn pierced the relative quietness of the surrounding plains. Paige flinched and snapped her head toward the source of the sound. A semi-truck approached from the west.

"This one isn't passing us. I'll make sure of it."

True to his words, Jason set himself up as a human roadblock. He strolled out onto the asphalt and straddled the white dotted line separating the two eastbound lanes. Jason waved his arms with the same vigor of an air-traffic controller signaling to a plane approaching a runway. The truck horn blared at him again as the semi-truck closed on his position. It didn't intimidate Jason into budging from his spot on the highway.

"Are you out of your mind?"

Paige's first instinct was to dart up, grab Jason's arm, and pull him to safety. She couldn't force her legs and feet into following through with that action.

"We're getting someone to stop one way or another. I'm so tired of this shit."

Paige swallowed hard. Her lips trembled. Why did Jason have to be this way? She desperately wanted someone to help them too, but not at the expense of her boyfriend's life.

A low rumble ripped through the air. Paige plugged her ears when she heard the engine brake. The others all followed suit. The semi slowed and rolled to a stop only a few yards ahead of Jason.

A husky bearded man, sporting a flat-brimmed cap, poked his head out of an open window.

"Damn, son! You got a death wish? You're gonna cause an accident standing out in the road like that."

Jason grinned. "I got you to stop."

The trucker scratched his beard and answered with a hearty laugh. "That's just because I'm a charitable man."

Rich and Heather sprinted across the median to the passenger's side door. Paige approached the driver's side door.

"Thank God you stopped."

The trucker cocked his head downward and flashed a broad smile. His teeth bore the same shade as the coffee he downed at the last truck stop.

"You bet, honey. Now what can I do for you?"

"Our car broke down a few miles up I-40. We're hoping you can give us a ride into the nearest town, so we can get a tow truck out here."

The trucker glanced down at his wristwatch for a moment and then closed his eyes. Paige tried to read his lips while he mumbled a few words. He appeared to be weighing if he had enough time to make a quick detour.

"We can give a little money for your time if that helps," Paige offered. "We really need your help. We've been stranded out in these parts for most of the day now."

The trucker popped his eyes open again and shook his head.

"Y'all don't need to pay me. I can drop you off in Travis. Just a few miles southeast of here. Won't be a problem at all."

Paige's smile threatened to break out of the boundaries of her lips. She motioned to Jason and pointed toward the passenger's side door. They finally found their lifeline out of this awful situation.

"Thank you so much, sir. You're a lifesaver."

"The name's Randall. And I'm happy to help."

Heather popped open the door and they all filed into the semi-truck. Jason and Rich joined her on a long seat in the back of the cab. The seat also flattened out into a small bed where a driver could sleep when needed. Paige took the cushioned leather seat up front. Once they closed the door, Randall shifted gears and started down I-40 again.

Hearing the steady hum of a diesel engine soothed Paige's nerves. Things looked more promising now. With any luck, they would get a tow truck out to their car, get it all fixed up, and then be back on the road before dark. Paige didn't want to spend a minute longer than necessary in Travis. They already lost so much valuable time they couldn't get back.

Randall cast a glance over his shoulder at Jason's McNeese State Football shirt. He gave a low whistle.

"What are a bunch of Louisiana college kids doing out in this part of Texas?"

Jason shrugged.

"Spring break road trip. We decided it would be fun to drive to Las Vegas from Lake Charles."

Randall let out another hearty laugh.

"You're serious? Haven't any of you kids heard of airplanes?"

Jason answered him with an icy stare. Heather crinkled up her nose and held the corners of her mouth tight. It was her way of restraining nasty words resting on the tip of her tongue. Rich had a much different reaction. His head bobbed up and down with extra vigor.

"I've read about them on Wikipedia," he said, glancing at Paige and adding a chuckle. "Maybe one day, I'll get to be inside one."

Rich's sarcasm elicited no change in expression from Randall. The trucker simply laughed again.

"They did it for my sake," Paige explained, turning to face the trucker. "I don't deal so well with flying."

"Fair enough."

The semi turned down a narrower road cutting through grassy plains. Paige retrieved her smartphone from her handbag. She unlocked the screen. A couple of bars finally registered. Paige swiped the screen, clicked on her contact list, and immediately dialed.

One ring. Two rings. Three rings. No answer.

The next thing Paige heard was a man's voice.

"Hey, if you're hearing this message, then you know what to do."

"Why haven't we heard from you for so long?" Her words spewed out in a rushed frantic tone. "Call me. Please. We're all worried sick about you."

Paige ended the call and glanced up from the screen. Four sets of eyes locked on her and faces adorned with suspicious expressions greeted her.

"Isn't that your brother's number?"

Paige looked away and stared down at her smartphone again. She didn't know how to answer Heather's question without inviting other unwanted questions.

"Just a hunch, but I'm willing to bet that your fear of flying hasn't got a thing to do with why y'all decided to drive to Vegas," Randall said.

Paige's eyes stayed glued to her smartphone. Her heart pounded as she searched for the right explanation.

"Is there something you're not telling us?"

Heather reached out and touched her shoulder. Paige finally glanced up and turned to face her friend. She pursed her lips before releasing them into a worried sigh.

No reason to keep the truth hidden now.

"I thought he'd be out here somewhere."

"Your brother?"

Paige nodded.

"The last time anyone heard from him he was driving down I-40 to Albuquerque. I know it's a long shot, but I thought maybe I'd find some answers."

Jason grasped the seat edge. Deep grooves formed in the upholstery around his fingers.

"You're telling me the whole reason we turned this into a long-ass road trip is so you can look for your brother?"

His unsympathetic tone earned a fresh stony glare from Paige.

"We haven't seen or heard from him or my sister-in-law in three weeks. I need to know what happened to them."

"So, naturally, you make up a bullshit excuse to drive to Vegas instead of flying there?" Jason's voice climbed a few decibels while he pondered their current unnecessary ordeal. "Why not tell me the truth? I tried to help you track him down. I shared photos on Instagram and Twitter. You didn't say he was lost along I-40 somewhere!"

Paige sucked in her lower lip and closed her eyes. She knew she screwed up big time in trying to keep it quiet. Jason had done what she asked of him so far, like any good boyfriend would do.

"What did you think a drive through Texas would accomplish that couldn't be done with emails and phone calls? It doesn't make a lick of sense to me."

"Jason has a fair point. This feels like a huge waste of time."

Rich had a habit of offering up his thoughts when they weren't wanted. Paige never considered it an appealing personality trait, but it annoyed her more than ever at the moment.

"I had to see for myself what happened." Her voice grew crisp and cold. Each word matched the attitude she sensed from Jason and Rich. "Don't you follow the news? People are disappearing in this part of West Texas all the time."

Heather rolled her eyes.

"I sympathize with your loss, Paige, but now you're starting to sound a little paranoid."

"Paranoid?" Paige shot back. "What makes you think I'm paranoid?"

Heather shrugged. "If even a few people around here were vanishing without a trace, don't you think the FBI, or the military would be all over it by now?"

Paige scowled and turned away from the other three. She stared straight ahead. A few houses and other buildings began to pop into view on the approaching horizon. They passed a sign indicating Travis was only three miles ahead.

Randall turned and glanced at Paige.

"I don't mean to pry about your brother –"

"Then don't pry."

An equally curt expression accompanied those words. Randall gave her a half-smile and shook his head before returning his gaze to the narrow road.

An uncomfortable silence formed inside the cab and settled everywhere like a heavy blanket of fog. Paige fiddled with the fabric on the right sleeve of her crop top and refused to make eye contact with anyone. She kept staring out the window, as though searching were the only thing that still mattered. Searching for anything. She never intended to act deceptive about coaxing her boyfriend and her friends into driving to Vegas. On the other hand, she didn't believe they would have agreed to do it if they had known her true purpose.

Paige didn't want to travel through this lonely part of Texas all alone.

Why didn't her brother call or text or do something to let everyone know he was fine? That's all she wanted. That's all her parents wanted. One simple action to make it all feel better. Even a brief message would make all those posts on Instagram, Facebook, and Twitter over the past month feel like they were not shared in vain.

"I have a feeling this day will start looking up for y'all. We're finally here."

Randall's enthusiastic declaration cut through the silence. Paige saw a large square sign welcoming visitors to Travis. It wasn't your typical street sign. The sign had been carved from wood and mounted on a pair of thick posts. Bright green lettering spelled out each word. Paige enjoyed the rustic design.

Once the cab moved parallel to the sign, a loud whoosh blasted through her ears. At that same moment, Paige's entire body tingled from the crown of her head down to her fingertips and toes – like a bolt of static electricity surged straight through her. She sat up straight and her eyes popped wide open.

"Did anybody else feel that?"

Paige turned around. Jason, Heather, and Rich showed signs they experienced the same sensation. Their expressions mirrored her own.

"What the hell just happened?" Heather leaned forward and peered through the windshield. "I feel like I just touched an electric fence."

Randall laughed.

"You college kids worry too much. It's probably nothing. We'll get you to an auto shop here and then you can get back on the road."

Paige hoped the trucker was right. Breaking down in the middle of nowhere felt stressful enough without adding other problems into the mix.

TRACES OF SUNLIGHT filtered through cracks between boards covering the living room windows. Todd sat on the floor and leaned back against a small sofa. He rested his elbows on his knees and buried his face in his hands. Whatever energy or desire he once possessed to prepare for the evening ahead had fled from him.

What purpose did trying to last one more day serve? Nothing he said or did to his prisoner seemed to make one bit of difference. That thing had proven as obstinate as anyone he'd ever interrogated. It possessed a pain threshold he'd never seen in any human.

That was the problem. It wasn't human. Not one bit, as far as Todd was concerned.

When it came right down to it, he wasn't sure how to classify that thing in his basement. Todd settled on simply calling it a monster because of everything that had happened to him since he and Caroline first set foot in this hellish town.

The sign welcoming visitors seemed inviting enough at the time. A wooden square mounted on top of twin thick wooden posts. Green wording popped out from inside the square. Caroline made a comment about how neat it looked and wasted no time snapping a photo with her smartphone. No doubt the sign would end up being a lead image on her next taste-cation blog post.

An odd sensation gripped Todd's entire body as their SUV passed the sign. Something akin to static electricity surged from his head to his toes. Todd didn't give it much thought at the time. Caroline became too wrapped up in snapping photos to say anything about it. Driving such a long distance robbed him of energy and the rumbling in his stomach didn't help matters. Todd chalked up the strange feeling to an overdue need to get out from behind the wheel and stretch his legs again.

He drove only a short distance down the town's main street before Caroline pointed out a small cafe sign. She had an eagle eye for finding these things.

"It looks like we can park in front." Caroline turned to him and flashed one of her patented broad smiles that Todd loved so much. "And we're just in time for lunch."

Todd pulled up along the sidewalk and parked the SUV directly in front of the cafe. It seemed a little emptier than he anticipated. An open sign hung on the front door, but blinds were drawn on both front windows. No other cars were parked on the street near the cafe. A small adjacent parking lot on the side of the building contained only two cars.

"Are you sure you want to try this place?" Todd turned and glanced at Caroline. She unlatched her seat belt. "It doesn't look like much of a culinary hot spot to me."

"This does seem to be a sleepy town." Caroline opened her door and bounced out onto the sidewalk. "Maybe Humble isn't as boring as we thought."

Todd laughed as he exited the SUV. Boring suited him just fine. He cast his eyes up and down the street after closing the door. Caroline hit the nail on the head. He didn't see another car or truck anywhere on the street. Todd expected to spot at least one or two random vehicles. No one drove past in either direction. It felt out of place, even for a rural community.

Did they take a detour into a ghost town by mistake?

Caroline turned the knob and popped open the cafe door. Sunlight streamed into the dining area. She gasped and whipped her head back at Todd.

"Something bad happened in this place."

Todd quickly joined her in the doorway. The cafe interior echoed a different era. A jukebox stood against the opposite wall. Booths covered with brown leather upholstery jutted out from walls to their left and their right. A small counter surrounded a kitchen area only a short distance from the jukebox. Those things didn't stand out to Todd as much as the rest of the cafe interior itself.

Bar stools were scattered across the room. Tables and chairs had been overturned. Three chairs were little more than shattered pieces of wood, as though someone smashed each chair over another object or a person. Plates, glasses, napkins, and silverware lay strewn about over the floor. Remnants of food had been trampled into light brown carpet.

Todd glanced back at the cafe windows and, for the first time, saw a giant diagonal crack running across one window. Smaller cracks spread out from the bigger one, forming a pattern resembling a broken eggshell. Chips and chunks of glass peppered the floor below where the cracks originated.

"What in God's name do you think could have happened here?"

Caroline glanced at Todd again. Her smile had yielded to tightened lips and eyes as wide as plates.

"I don't have a clue. But I'd like to find out."

Todd took a couple of steps forward. Caroline at once tugged on his bicep to pull him back.

"Are you nuts? I don't want to poke around in here. We need to hop back in the SUV and get out of this place as fast as we can."

Todd gently patted the top of her hand with his opposite hand.

"I need to know what's going on. No sense running if you don't know what you're running from and where you need to run."

Caroline closed her eyes and dipped her chin to her chest. She let out a sigh.

"Can we let someone else handle this? You're not in Afghanistan anymore. This isn't part of your job description now."

"Apparently, it doesn't fit the job description for anyone else in this town either."

Todd brushed her hand aside and approached the counter. He avoided eye contact with his wife and kept scanning the layout of the room. As much as Todd didn't want to admit it, Caroline had a point. Things were much too quiet in the cafe. An intense fight or struggle must have taken place at some point before they got there. No other explanation fit for the scene that lay before them.

Todd bent down and scooped a slice of toast and a browned sausage link off the floor. The bread felt as hard as a rice cake between his thumb and fingers. The sausage had grown cold and stiff. A small glass lay on its side a short distance from the spilled food. The juice it once held had since dried up, leaving behind an orange film inside the glass.

"Whatever happened here, happened quite a while before we showed up."

Caroline glanced over her shoulder and stared through the open door leading back outside to their SUV. Her expression remained a frozen snapshot of concern.

"I really don't like this. Todd, honey, we need to get out of here and back on I-40 right now."

A metallic clank, equally loud and sudden, greeted them from the kitchen. Todd tossed aside the food. He raised his hand and signaled for Caroline to crouch down.

"Stop that." she hissed while dropping her voice to a whisper. "We're not in the military."

Todd bent down and snatched a steak knife off the floor. He crept around the counter, trying to stay low to the ground. Caroline followed a few steps behind him, occasionally glancing back toward the SUV. It seemed like, to Todd, she feared their vehicle would vanish as soon as she wasn't paying attention. Todd pressed his fingertips into the kitchen door and nudged it open.

A similar chaotic state unfolded before them inside the kitchen. Ingredients, pans, and utensils were scatted across the tile. Charred bacon and sausage lay on top of the grill. Stale scrambled eggs filled the air with a pungent aroma. Oil had congealed into a yellowish sludge inside an adjacent basin. A fry basket hung there suspended halfway into the sludge.

Caroline scrunched up her nose and lips.

"This greasy spoon definitely wouldn't have gotten a good rating on my blog."

Todd allowed himself to enjoy a brief grin before the corners of his mouth snapped back into serious mode. He scanned the kitchen area but had no solid idea for what caused the earlier clank. Then, out of the corner of his eye, he noticed the walk-in freezer door hung slightly ajar.

"Can we leave now?"

Todd glanced over his shoulder at Caroline. She swung her head side to side, giving a once-over to every visible nook and crevice inside the kitchen. Her fingers wrapped around her purse strap tight enough that her knuckles bulged out.

"I just wanna check one more thing out. Then we can go. I promise."

He grasped the handle and pulled the freezer door outward. A pair of boxes had fallen from the shelf. Packages of once-frozen meat were strewn across the floor. Their rancid smell made Todd's eyes water. Todd stepped inside the freezer and immediately stopped in his tracks. Blood had pooled near a floor drain just a few inches from his sneakers. Todd's eyes followed the dried blood back to the source. A burly man clad in a white shirt, apron, and hair net lay face down on the floor. His head was turned away from Todd, but he could tell the blood had flowed out from under his head and neck. Todd's mouth dropped open when his eyes drifted toward the back wall.

A lower jaw lay on the floor between the body and the wall.

Todd's breath escaped his lips in jagged bursts. He stumbled back outside the freezer.

"Oh God! Don't look at it, Caroline. Whatever you do, don't look at it."

"What's in there?"

"An extremely dead cook."

Caroline's eyes widened like plates again. She pressed her hand to her mouth to stifle a scream. Todd quickly slammed the freezer door shut before any temptation to glance at the mangled corpse got the best of her.

"I should have trusted your first instinct. I owe you an apology."

"You can make it up to me later. Let's get out of here while we still can."

Caroline and Todd sprinted at an equal pace back to the SUV. He dug his keys out of his pocket and clicked a button to unlock the doors. As Todd flung open his door, he froze in his tracks. He looked up and down the street. His eyes traced trees, buildings of all shapes and sizes, and the sidewalk on both sides of the street.

"What are you waiting for?" Caroline's voice rose in pitch as rapidly as each breath escaped her lips. "We gotta get out of here and find help."

"Do you hear anything?"

"What do you mean?"

"Birds. Cats. Dogs. Vehicles. People. Do you hear anything?"

Caroline's eyes narrowed and she poked her head outside the open car door. She tilted her head and mirrored Todd in scanning the immediate vicinity.

"I don't hear a thing."

"Neither do I."

Todd's throat tightened as he said those words. There should have been some random background noise around them. Only stillness and silence.

It felt so wrong.

A thud against cement echoed in Todd's ears. Caroline, the SUV, and the surrounding street fled from before his eyes. The living room with the boarded-up windows returned to fill their place.

Todd wrenched his head up from his hands. His eyes popped wide open. That thud sounded like it came from the basement.

Todd scrambled to his feet and grabbed a large metal flashlight. He flung open the door leading to the basement and charged down the stairs. The flashlight beam bounced off each stair ahead of him. When he reached the bottom stair, it revealed an overturned chair.

His prisoner remained partially chained to the back of the wooden chair. One arm had slipped free. The long, pale limb tugged at a section of chain. It bound the other arm against an armrest on the other side of the chair. Then, at that moment, the chain slackened.

The other arm emerged from the chain.

Todd's own arms and legs stiffened. His fingers clasped the flashlight even tighter. He swung the beam toward the chair. The light landed on his prisoner, tearing their face from basement shadows. Their black oval eyes glowed for a bit like a cat's eyes in dim light.

A weak cry emerged from Todd's prisoner. He threw up an arm as a shield to protect his eyes from the light. Todd's heart pounded in sync with each breath escaping from his mouth. He could not let this thing get free. His faint hopes for escape and even his survival depended on keeping this monster trapped in this basement. Holding one of their kind as a prisoner gave him a valuable bargaining chip. Something to hold the others at bay if the generator failed.

Two long arms reached out across the cement. Todd's prisoner dragged body and chair forward from under the flashlight beam. The creature snarled at Todd as it neared his legs.

Todd swung the flashlight, so the beam fell lower on the floor. It blinded his prisoner a second time. Another whimper escaped from the creature's lips. Todd set down the flashlight on the ground in front of his feet, keeping the beam pinned on the creature. He whipped out a pocketknife and seized one of the forearms belonging to his prisoner.

Todd sliced the blade across his prisoner's wrist. The creature howled as sharp metal severed a tendon. Todd let the creature draw its wounded limb close to its body. Dark blood trickled out from under the fresh wound and pooled on the cement immediately around the wounded wrist.

"You gave me no choice."

"Let me go." His prisoner's defiant tone faded from their voice for the first time since Todd captured him. "I don't want to die down here. Let me return to my people."

Todd's sympathies were not aroused. He snatched up the flashlight once again and pinned the beam on the creature. Pale skin began taking on a redder hue under continued exposure to focused incandescent light.

"Trust me when I say we're far from finished down here. When you start giving me answers, then I'll make a decision on your fate."

Before his prisoner could even think to respond, Todd flipped around the flashlight and struck the butt end against the side of their head. Both black oval eyes faded behind pale eyelids.

Todd picked both chair and prisoner from off the ground. He secured chains around each arm again. Then, Todd bound a strip of cloth around the injured arm. He couldn't have his prisoner bleeding out while he was away.

THIS PLACE SEEMED rather lifeless to Paige, even for a small town out in the middle of nowhere. The main street cutting through downtown Travis featured a dearth of cars beyond Randall's semi. At a minimum, she expected to see a vehicle or two either traveling ahead of the big rig or going in the opposite direction.

Unsettling thoughts crowded their way into Paige's mind. She didn't want to entertain those thoughts, but they hung around like unwanted party guests camped out at the snack table.

What if this is a ghost town?

Did the trucker bring us here on purpose?

Oh no! What's he gonna do to us?

Paige pressed her hand against her chest and took a deep breath. She needed to find a way to stay calm. It didn't make sense to let her imagination run away with her. She chalked it up as a side effect of a stressful day. Besides, there were four of them and one of him. Even if he had ulterior motives, Randall wouldn't be foolish enough to try anything while so severely outnumbered.

"Everything okay? You seem a little nervous."

Randall glanced over at Paige as if he sensed her thoughts. She glanced back out the window. Houses and other buildings seemed completely deserted. The whole town gave off a creepy vibe.

"Are you sure this isn't a ghost town?" Paige asked. "I'm getting an odd feeling driving through here."

Randall squinted for a second as he thought about her question. He cracked his usual broad grin, gave a chuckle, and nodded.

"It's a bit quieter than the last time I came here; I'll grant you that. I haven't been here for a year or so. Guess they've fallen on hard times."

"I hope this is a ghost town! That would give me some sick video for my channel and something cool to talk about on my next podcast."

Paige whipped her head around and glared at Rich. Her tightened scowl and narrowed eyes mirrored similar reactions from Heather and Jason. Did he ever think before blurting out whatever popped into his head?

Rich threw up his hands.

"What? It would be kind of cool."

"You know what would be cooler?" Heather said. "Finding someone in this backwater town who can fix our car."

Rich smiled and nodded. "I'm just saying ..."

Heather pressed her index finger against his lips and shook her head.

"Don't say it."

A loud horn ripped through the stillness outside the truck. Paige and the others nearly jumped out of their skin. Randall answered their worried looks with a chuckle.

"Just letting these folks know we're here."

He turned off the street into a parking lot in front of a combined auto repair shop and service station. Randall pulled up along the furthest outside pump and parked his semi in front of it. His horn did not draw any attention to their arrival. The parking lot remained as empty as before the semi pulled into it.

"Now let's see what we can do about getting y'all back on the road."

Randall opened the door and hopped out of the cab. Paige opened the passenger door and followed the trucker. Jason, Heather, and Rich were a step behind her. Paige immediately veered off toward the garage on the right side of the store entrance. It housed a pair of bays where mechanics worked on cars. Both bay doors were closed. A car sat perched on a lift inside like a mechanic was working on it only a short time ago. Still, no one popped into view. The place looked deserted.

Paige marched up to the nearest closed bay door and knocked on the glass.

"Hello? Can somebody help us?"

Her eyes surveyed the garage from one end to the other. Tools and various auto parts, along with containers of oil and transmission fluid, were strewn about on the floor. Did a fight or brawl break out at this place? No one seemed to be around to confirm or deny that theory. Her questions elicited no voices nor movement inside the auto shop.

Paige persisted and beat her fist on the door much harder a second time.

"You have customers. We need a tow. Can somebody come out here?"

Jason leaned against the glass and surveyed the same places as Paige did moments earlier. He didn't get a different result. Jason turned to her and frowned at facing the prospect that their situation hadn't improved after all.

"I don't get it. Are these people out enjoying a late lunch? Where is everybody?"

Paige shrugged.

"I don't know, but this is starting to piss me off."

Randall plucked off his cap and wiped some sweat from his forehead with his other hand. He gave a low whistle and shook his head.

"Damn! I thought for sure someone would be here. You kids have just gotten a big dose of the wrong sort of luck today."

Paige turned and stared at him with a half-frown. The trucker annoyed her for pointing out the obvious. Then again, it wouldn't be polite to yell at him when he made a special detour to help them out.

"I've had better days," Paige finally said in a terse tone. She forced herself to skip over two or three things she actually wanted to say.

Randall hurried toward the front door of the convenience store.

"Well, I gotta go in and drain the lizard and then get back on the road," he said. "I'll go see if there's a bathroom in here. Best of luck to y'all."

The trucker opened the door and sauntered inside. As soon as it closed, Heather squinted and stuck her tongue out.

"Why do some people insist on announcing when they're going to the bathroom?" She said, opening her eyes again. "I don't wanna know about it. I prefer not to get a mental image of them dropping their pants and then standing over or sitting on a toilet."

Rich laughed. "Maybe that's a redneck flirt."

Heather scowled at Rich's remark. She didn't see the humor in the bathroom talk like he did. Paige said nothing. She continued to gaze at the door and watched Randall approach an empty counter and then turn down an empty aisle. The store appeared as equally deserted as the garage.

"Is it just me or does it look like this store needs a serious remodel?"

Paige turned to Jason, and he pointed to some windows on the far side of the store. She noticed the same thing that drew his attention. Long, deep cracks ran across the face of one window. A giant eggshell fracture covered the middle portion of another one as though some massive object struck the glass at some point.

"Wait a minute! Did that trucker say he was gonna hit the road and leave us here?"

An awful realization washed over Paige once Heather said those words. Randall had no intention of bringing them back with him. He planned to leave them here in Travis to fend for themselves. The same light clicked on for Jason and Rich. They were not at all pleased with that potential scenario unfolding.

"Like hell he is," Jason replied.

"He owes it to us to help us find some actual help – you know, like a tow truck – before taking off," Rich said.

Paige decided she wasn't about to let Randall hop back in his semi and leave the rest of them to rot here in Travis. She marched up to the door and flung it open. The other three followed hot on her tail.

Once inside, Paige found no sign of Randall anywhere. She peered down a hallway. It led to a unisex restroom and a janitor's closet.

"Randall? Where did you go?"

At once, Randall popped up from behind the counter. He clutched a key on a block of wood. All four of them jumped when the trucker emerged so quickly without warning. Randall grinned like a fisherman who landed a trophy bass on his line.

"Found what I was looking for. They hid this bugger real good. I had to drop down on my knees to locate it."

Paige walked over to the edge of the counter. She stood before him with arms folded, blocking his exit.

"You weren't planning on leaving us here in this deserted town, were you?"

Randall gave her a funny look. He glanced over his shoulder. Jason barricaded himself in front of the other exit from behind the counter.

"We have no intention of getting left behind." Jason said, giving the trucker eye daggers.

"Are you kids trying to Shanghai me? I've got a delivery to make to Fort Worth. I really don't have time to run all y'all all over West Texas just so you can get a tow."

"All we're asking is for you to help us find a real live person who can fix our car, so we can get back on our way," Paige replied. "We obviously haven't done that yet, so it would be nice if you could hang around just a bit longer."

Randall pinched his lips together, looked down at his groin, and then back up at her.

"Fine. You win. Now can you let me get to the can before I make a mess of myself?"

Paige nodded and finally stepped aside. Randall continued past her down the hallway, jangling the key on the end of the wood block as he walked. He whistled an off-key tune to some song she did not recognize.

Jason picked up a bag of unopened potato chips off the floor and examined it.

"What gives with this place? It looks like a tornado ripped through the inside of the store."

"It's peculiar," Paige replied. "That's for sure."

She glanced down the hallway again. Randall stuck the key in the doorknob and turned it. He cracked open the bathroom door.

A low growl came from inside the bathroom.

"Is someone in here?" Randall said. "My bad."

The growl suddenly morphed into a terrifying roar. A clawed hand sprung out of the darkened bathroom. Randall shouted and threw up his arms in front of his face. It grabbed both arms and dragged him inside the bathroom.

Terror washed over Paige's face. Her lips trembled. She couldn't move either leg. Jason, Rich, and Heather rushed up to her side.

"What the hell's going on in there?" Jason shouted, turning to Paige. "What happened to the trucker?"

The trucker's shouts escalated into screams. Those screams stopped almost as quickly as they emerged, replaced by sounds of tearing flesh and gurgling. Paige searched around for a weapon to protect herself from whatever lurked inside the bathroom.

Randall stumbled backward through the open bathroom door. He staggered into the wall and finally fell forward. What remained of his throat had become a shredded bloody pulp. A pool of blood spread out from under the trucker and his vacant eyes stared up at Paige.

She screamed and stumbled backward.

"He's dead! Oh God! He's dead! Something just murdered him!"

Jason rushed forward and caught her before Paige fell to the ground. All four turned and sprinted for the exit. When they reached the main door, Jason spun around and raced back toward the spot in the hallway where Randall's corpse fell.

"What are you doing?" Paige screamed.

Heather waved at him frantically. "Come back! You're gonna get killed."

Jason disappeared around the corner. Paige started forward, but Rich and Heather each grabbed an arm to stop her. She struggled to free herself from their grasp, but their grip remained firm.

"We need to get out of here now," Rich said. "With or without Jason."

It became a moot point. Jason rounded the corner again. His left hand clutched a set of keys.

"I figured we wouldn't get anywhere without the keys to his truck," Jason said. "Now let's get the hell out of here."

The foursome sprinted out into the parking lot. They hopped in the cab. Jason got behind the wheel. Paige joined him up front. Heather and Rich climbed onto the seat-bed in the back.

"Have you ever driven one of these things before?" Heather asked.

She felt around trying to locate her seat belt. Jason glanced over his shoulder and shook his head.

"There's a first time for everything."

"Oh God! We really are going to die."

Jason glared at her.

"Thanks for the vote of confidence."

He started the engine, shifted into drive, and floored it. The semi peeled out of the parking lot as Paige finished strapping her seat belt in place. She refused to take her eyes off the side mirror as the convenience store and auto shop shrank in the distance. Paige had to see for herself that whatever murdered Randall had not pursued them. Nothing emerged from the store. Only when it finally disappeared from her line of sight did Paige finally allow herself to let out a relieved sigh.

She reached out and smacked Jason in the shoulder with the back of her hand. He flinched.

"Don't scare me like that again! I thought that thing – whatever it was – was gonna kill you too."

"I didn't see anything."

"What do you mean you didn't see anything?"

"Whatever attacked the trucker stayed in the bathroom. It wouldn't come out into the light."

Heather leaned forward as far as her seat belt permitted her to move.

"It wouldn't come out into the light? What in God's name did they lock up in that bathroom?"

Jason gnawed on his lower lip and glanced out at the side mirror.

"Your guess is as good as mine. But I'm not itching to go back and find out."

The semi approached the welcome sign marking the town border. Paige gazed ahead at the lonely stretch of asphalt with a smile forming on her lips. She never felt so relieved to be getting out of a town in her whole life.

A curious shimmer rippled across the air in front of the road. Paige squinted, a crease forming on her forehead. It resembled traces of a mirage, but that did not make a lick of sense. The temperature hadn't climbed high enough to produce any such visual mind tricks.

She quickly glanced over at Jason again.

"Did you see that?"

"See what?"

"We better slow down. Something about this isn't sitting right."

"I've got a better idea. Let's keep going and not look back until we're on I-40 again."

Paige's worried frown deepened. She didn't want to hear Rich's input on the matter. Jason squinted at the road and came to the same conclusion as Paige.

"I think you're right."

He mashed down on the brake. The wheels squealed as the semi started to reduce speed. Then, the grill of the cab made contact with the shimmer.

Metal instantly buckled.

Paige's head and neck whipped forward and then slammed back against the seat along with her torso. An electrical charge surged through the engine and dashboard. It resembled long fingers of lightning attacking the truck. The shimmer spread out from the truck in an enormous ripple.

Glass shattered across the windshield and both windows on either side. Everyone inside the semi ducked down to avoid numerous flying shards.

Jason flung one arm up in front of his face as a makeshift shield against broken glass. With the other, he cranked the wheel hard to the left and swung the cab off the highway. The trailer behind the cab couldn't handle the sudden, sharp turn. It became unbalanced and tilted to the right. Then the trailer jackknifed behind the cab and pushed it off the road. The cab skidded sideways for several feet before finally coming to a stop.

Steam and smoke billowed out from the front of the semi. Paige pinched her eyes shut and rubbed her hands down her face. She pulled them away and saw blood. That ended up being the final image she remembered seeing before everything went dark.

PAIGE COULD NOT tell how much time had passed when she opened her eyes again. Her neck had grown stiff. When she tried to turn her head, an invisible hand squeezed every muscle and nerve like an orange. She let out a sharp cry.

"What the hell happened?"

Jason's voice sounded as groggy as Paige felt. He leaned forward and turned toward her. Multiple cuts from glass shards dotted his face and forearm. Jason also sported a swollen lip.

He reached out and touched Paige's cheek.

"You're bleeding."

Jason brought away an index finger tipped with crimson, confirming his observation to her.

"How bad is it?"

Paige wasn't totally certain she wanted to hear the answer. Still, she needed to know how severe her injuries were from the crash.

"The cuts look mostly superficial. It looks like you didn't catch any glass in your neck. Thank God."

Paige tried to smile at that welcome bit of news but moving the muscles under her face almost made her cry out again. She didn't remember a time where she suffered whiplash this bad.

"You do have a nasty gash on your forehead, below your scalp. A piece of glass sliced you pretty good there."

"Heather? Rich? Are you guys, okay?"

Neither one had said anything yet. Paige immediately assumed the worst.

"I hurt like hell." Heather let out a groan to add extra emphasis to that point. "Good job, Jason. Congrats on crashing a semi on a deserted road in sunny weather."

"It wasn't my fault." Jason's tone perfectly matched his scowl. "It felt like we slammed into an invisible wall. I don't know what the hell happened."

Another groan filled the truck behind Paige, this time from Rich.

"Do me a favor, Jason. Warn me before you get behind the wheel next time, so I can flag down a ride from someone else."

"Piss off, Rich!"

"I think you should do that. God, my entire body feels like it got pounded with a hammer."

Paige closed her eyes and drew in a sharp breath. A twinge of pain attacked her ribs. She bit down on her lower lip until it subsided.

"It wasn't Jason's fault," Paige finally said.

Rich answered her with an aggravated sigh.

"Of course. Jump to your boyfriend's defense. Let's not forget you're the reason why we're in this fucking situation in the first place!"

"Rich! Just shut up and listen to me. There was some weird shimmer across the road before we crashed. I think it prevented the semi from leaving the town."

"Weird shimmer?" Heather's tone changed dramatically. "You mean like a force field?"

Rich laughed. "Force field! That's hilarious. There's no such thing."

Paige wished she could turn around without experiencing blinding pain in her neck. She wanted to smack Rich upside the head so bad.

"Okay, Rich. You offer a better explanation for what happened."

"It's simple. Jason's driving sucks ass."

Jason unbuckled his seat belt and turned to position himself so he could smack Rich. Paige held up her hand to stop him from moving out of his seat.

"Whatever," she said. "Let's focus on getting out of this wrecked truck before it gets dark."

Paige gazed out toward the horizon. The sun hung much lower in the sky now. Streaks of yellow, orange, and red mingled in scattered clouds flanking the fiery orb. She realized they needed to find a safe place to hide and rest from their wounds before what remained of the day transformed into night.

Paige tried the handle on the passenger's side door, and, to her relief, the door popped open. All the front-end damage did not extend back to either door. They wouldn't need to try to kick out what remained of the windshield or dislodge broken windows on either side of the truck.

Jason popped open the other door. Paige turned her entire body at a snail's pace. She kept her neck as immobile as possible. Practically every movement brought a new burst of pain. It reminded her of an invisible hammer striking her neck. Paige slid off the seat and dropped to the ground. She let out a sharp moan as her feet struck a patch of grass and grabbed her neck.

Feet dropped to the ground behind Paige. A hand gently clasped her shoulder a moment later.

"Is your neck going to be okay?" Heather asked. "You look like you're in some serious pain."

Paige snapped her eyes shut and clenched her teeth. She gently rubbed her neck with both hands for a minute before slowly exhaling.

"I think so. I hope so. I never realized whiplash hurt this bad."

"I'd suggest we go find a doctor, but our track record for getting help today isn't so good."

Heather and Paige made their way around to the backside of the jackknifed trailer. They came face to face with Jason and Rich. Both boys stood on the road directly in front of the spot where the invisible barrier repelled the truck backward with such force.

Rich had fewer cuts than Jason, but he also sported a couple of huge bruises on his left hand and on his forehead. He squinted at the stretch of road ahead of them. Rich held out his hand and waved it back and forth in an exaggerated manner.

"So, where's this so-called force field?" he said. "I'm not seeing what y'all seem to be seeing."

Jason gave him a sideways glance.

"You can't actually see a force field. It's like made up of energy or something."

"Prove it," Rich replied.

Paige sighed. This really wasn't the best use of their time. They needed to find shelter. It didn't take a genius to realize something had gone deeply wrong here in Travis. She began growing anxious to go somewhere safe, so they didn't have to find out how much worse things could get.

"Y'all need to settle down. We need to find a place where we can hide and recover from our injuries while we figure out what's going on here."

Jason turned to Paige and pointed at the road.

"First things first. I'm gonna find out exactly what's blocking the road."

He scoured the side of the road and snatched up a fist-sized rock. Jason wound up his arm like a pitcher standing on the mound and let the rock fly. After sailing a few yards, it stopped dead in mid-air like it struck an invisible wall. An electric ripple spread out in all directions from the point of impact. It resembled water rippling on a pond after skipping a stone across the surface.

Jason's rock dropped straight down and bounced on the asphalt. Paige turned to Rich. His mouth now hung open wide enough to fit an entire sandwich inside.

"How in the hell is that even possible?"

Rich looked back at Heather and Paige like they held a key to shedding light on this mystery. Paige answered him with a blank stare.

"You're asking the wrong person," she said.

Heather pulled out a smartphone from the handbag hanging off her shoulder.

"Maybe we can call for help."

"Who?" Rich asked. "And how are they going to get us out of here when they do arrive?"

"We managed to get in here," Jason replied.

"Yeah, and in case you haven't noticed, we can't get back out," Rich scoffed.

Paige decided to interrupt before Jason ordered Rich to piss off again.

"Someone can probably fly in with a helicopter and get us," she said. "If that is some sort of force field, there's no way it can go high enough to block out the entire sky."

Heather swiped her phone and punched in a pin number to unlock the screen. A dejected moan escaped her lips seconds later. Paige pivoted her whole body around. Heather's face – sporting the same assortment of cuts and bruises as the others – said it all. Her lips curled into a deep frown while her brown eyes settled into an unblinking stare at the out of service area notification on her phone.

"I'm not getting a signal at all." Heather glanced up from her phone. "I think that force field – or whatever it is – is interfering with my phone's reception."

"I guess that settles that," Paige replied. "We have to go back into town and find a safe place to rest and hide until we get this thing figured out."

Everything about the walk back to downtown Travis along that lonely stretch of road gave off an odd vibe. The breeze Paige enjoyed earlier on Interstate 40 had disappeared. In fact, the air now seemed as still and controlled as air circulating inside an office building. A distinct lack of noise created an equally unsettling feeling. No sounds of engines from passing cars. No chirps from birds nesting in trees or flying above their heads. No barks from a random dog or meows from a random cat. By all outside appearances, they were the only living things in the entire town. Paige already knew that wasn't the case.

She was not alone in finding the deafening silence so unsettling.

"This place is really starting to freak me out," Heather said. "It's too quiet around here."

"We're probably living out one of those urban legends you're always talking about," Jason said.

He turned and gave Rich a knowing smirk.

"Go ahead and dismiss it as a joke. That stuff is real shit." Heather's voice grew more animated. "Unexplained things happen all the time."

"Now you're the one getting paranoid."

"Oh yeah, Jason? How do you explain what happened to Annie Desmond – that country singer you're always listening to on iTunes?"

Jason cast his eyes down.

"I don't 'always' listen to her. I mean she's hot and all, but –"

"When's the last time you've seen or heard from her? Supposedly, she took sick before a concert a year ago and abruptly retired. Afterward, she vanished without a trace."

This specific urban legend spread around campus like wildfire. Paige lost count of how many times someone shared it with her. Annie Desmond, as the story goes, participated in a botched anti-aging drug test. The drug destroyed her face and forced her underground so she could hide from unscrupulous drug manufacturers. Paige never bought the tale. Heather was a different story. No would ever convince her these urban legends were only an exaggerated version of a more boring truth. The girl lived for sensational stories.

Paige could not blame her at the moment. After all, if they were stuck inside this "force field," who knows what else might be real?

"Well, I doubt we'll find her out here," Paige said. "I'll settle for meeting somebody – anybody – who can help us out of our current mess."

The sun hung low enough in the distance that it appeared to almost touch the ground. Shadows started to spring up in place of fleeing sunlight. A streetlamp lit up ahead of them. It seemed dimmer than normal. The light produced a vaguely red tint. Seeing that sight struck Paige as really odd.

Why would a small town use red lightbulbs of all things in the streetlamps?

The foursome crossed to the other side of the street to avoid the service station. Paige saw no sign of the thing that attacked and murdered Randall earlier in the day. A twinge of sadness gripped her as she thought about the trucker's dead body still laying inside that store. Did Randall have a family? A wife and children who waited for him to come home? Paige never thought to ask him about it when she had a chance. She felt deep empathy for that family – if they existed. Not knowing what became of a loved one produced a gnawing pain she understood all too well.

"Did anyone else see that?"

Paige froze in her tracks and turned her whole body to avoid jarring her neck. Heather had stopped in front of the window of a barber shop.

"See what?" Paige asked.

"I could have sworn I saw something moving behind those blinds."

"Whatever it is, we probably don't want to go in there," Jason said.

Paige shrugged.

"Maybe someone's in there who can help us."

Jason couldn't hide a fresh shudder that raced through his limbs.

"That line of thinking didn't work out well for our trucker friend. I'm not eager for us to share his fate."

"Only one way to find out."

Rich marched up to the door. He grabbed the knob and started to turn it. Heather seized a handful of his polo shirt sleeve and wrenched him backward. Rich let go of the doorknob and stumbled back a couple of steps.

"What are you doing?" Her voice barely climbed above a whisper. That didn't make it sound any less cross and panicked. "You trying to get us all killed?"

Paige spotted movement behind the blinds a second time. Four fingers poked out between slats in the middle of the blinds. She drew in a sharp breath. The blinds snapped back to their former position.

Footsteps.

The doorknob started turning.

Paige cast a sideways glance at the other three. The same fear overtaking her also staked a claim on their faces. Paige wanted to run. She wanted to hide. Both legs refused to budge even an inch. Each limb had become rooted to the sidewalk.

Her lips trembled as the door opened. A hand emerged from behind the wooden frame. Long skinny fingers beckoned to them, inviting each of the foursome to draw closer.

"You may enter."

Paige and Jason exchanged worried glances. No one took a step forward. Even Rich's bravado which he conjured up only moments earlier fled from him. For Paige, it became difficult to not think about what happened to Randall when he got pulled inside a darkened bathroom. Listening to the stranger standing behind the door may only set the stage for springing a similar trap on whoever dared to enter.

"You may enter," the voice repeated.

This time, the tone grew a bit sharper. Paige wasn't sure what to make of the voice. It sounded calm and forceful, but also possessed a whisper-like softness that would fade away amid a crowded and noisy room.

Rich shook his head and approached the door a second time.

"To hell with just standing here. I'm going inside. What have we got to lose at this point?"

Jason's eyes darted between Rich and the opened crack revealing a glimpse into the barber shop's darkened interior.

"Possibly some body parts," he said. "I'm not stoked to find out."

"Suit yourself."

Rich pressed his hand against the door to push it open. The hidden figure drew it back before he had a chance to move the door. Paige's eyes trailed Rich as he entered the shop and settled on what lay beyond the door. It appeared normal, compared to what they had seen earlier in that other place. Nothing strewn about across the floor. Several chairs lined the wall on one side. A pair of tables sat in front of the chairs. Multiple magazines lay scattered across each table. Four cushioned chairs were bolted to the floor on the other side of the shop. A mirror, countertop, and drawers stood behind each chair.

Paige took a deep breath and finally followed Rich's lead. She turned her head as much as her sore neck allowed. Heather and Jason also reluctantly joined them inside. The door clicked shut behind the group once they had all moved a few feet inside the barber shop.

"Your presence here is unexpected," the voice said. "None of you look familiar to me."

Rich turned toward the source of the voice. His face scrunched up and he shook his head. Paige couldn't help cracking a smile.

"Why would we?" Heather's bemused tone matched Rich's expression. "We're not from here."

"So why are you here?"

Paige finally turned to the side so she could put a face with the voice. An individual stood before her unlike anyone she had ever seen. They wore what a long dark blue coat – almost resembling a duster – that wrapped around their body. Long locks of reddish hair sprang from their head and fell to their shoulders. Their face featured pale skin and thin lips. Gloves adorned each hand. Strangely, the person before her also wore a pair of sunglasses. Their eyewear made no sense to Paige. Seeing anything, with the sun setting outside and blinds drawn inside the barber shop, had grown increasingly difficult.

Her lips formed into a half-frown. Paige refused to look away from this mysterious person.

"We're here to find help," she said. "Our car broke down outside of town. We need a tow."

"That is indeed a problem."

"Can you help us out?"

The red-haired stranger's head remained stiff and silent for a moment. Paige wished their eyes weren't covered up with sunglasses. Unease gripped her, not knowing where those eyes looked. Paige could not shake a sensation that the stranger's eyes were focused on her alone like they were trying to drill a hole right through her mind and body.

"I will take you to Barber," the red-haired stranger finally said. "He will know what to do."

Paige wasn't sure she heard them right.

"You mean one of the barbers that work here?" she asked. "Aren't they here in the shop?"

"No. I will take you to Barber." the red-haired stranger grew alarmingly blunt while emphasizing the word Barber again. "He will take care of this situation."

With those words, this individual turned and marched toward the door. The red-haired stranger threw up a hood that covered much of their head. Upon reaching the door, they turned back and faced Paige and the others again.

"Please follow me. I will take you to see Barber."

Paige licked her lips and turned to Jason. He simply shrugged. Still, he couldn't conceal the fear also welling up inside him. Jason's eyes kept bouncing from Paige back to the red-haired stranger standing at the door.

"I guess we don't have a choice." Jason leaned over and lowered his voice. "We gotta get out of this town somehow. Maybe they can help."

Paige glanced at the red-haired stranger out of the corner of her eye.

"Something is unsettling about all of this," she said. "What if they're the ones responsible for whatever caused the semi to crash?"

Rich barged past Paige. He turned and stabbed his index finger at her.

"I don't wanna hear it. You got us into this mess in the first place. I'm done listening to you."

Paige's mouth dropped open a little. She glanced at Heather and Jason as they each walked past her. Their tight-lipped smiles told Paige they also weren't on her side.

"You must follow now. Time is running short."

Paige felt the red-haired stranger's gaze focusing on her alone. She lowered her head, closed her eyes for a moment, and gnawed on her lip. This really didn't strike her as the best thing to do. Something about the red-haired stranger's odd appearance and mannerisms made her skin crawl. The others didn't seem to share the same concerns at this point. They were all hurt, tired, hungry, and thirsty – just like her. Perhaps it would be better to roll the dice and see what path lay ahead.

She opened her eyes again and joined the rest of the group at the door. The red-haired stranger opened it and led them out to the sidewalk again.

EVERY SINGLE MUSCLE in Todd's neck grew tense as sunlight dimmed on the flattened horizon. He peered through a crack in the boarded-up window, scanning the street for any signs of trouble. These monsters usually emerged during the twilight hours. He forced himself to stay alert and focused. Their numbers were small, but attacks upon the house had increased in frequency and intensity as the week progressed. He could not afford to let his guard down, even for a split second.

It was a prison.

Todd banged his fist on the windowsill as the thought crossed his mind. This boarded-up house started as a refuge. Now it had become a virtual prison. He couldn't risk leaving at night and opening himself up to an easy attack as a lone target. And now, he grew increasingly weaker during the day. This only made it a growing struggle to replenish diminishing food, water, and supplies in a town with so little left.

Todd gazed down at his bare arms. A reddish hue tinged his skin from where sunlight enveloped it earlier in the day. He stepped out the door for only a few minutes. That's all he needed to feel a burn. No amount of sunblock could protect his skin. Seeing a sunburn only created further alarm for Todd. No doubt remained in his mind his condition had worsened. Todd's skin grew more photosensitive by the day. Even with extensive survival training, he felt limited in his ability to fight off changes attempting to overtake his body.

Why can't I figure out how to shut down that damn barrier? Todd repeated a thought that had crossed his mind countless times. *I'm running out of time. It shouldn't be this hard.*

It turned out to be more difficult than Todd ever imagined. Caroline discovered the barrier almost by accident on the same day they fled the deserted cafe.

The young couple both jumped into the SUV after encountering that corpse in the freezer and the unsettling stillness outside. Todd made a U-turn, floored the gas pedal, and peeled down the main road toward the town limits. The front wheels of the SUV nearly hopped on the sidewalk in his zeal to get out of there.

Caroline snapped her head toward him. Her nails dug into the hand grip over the door.

"Don't wreck the car! I don't wanna get stuck in this awful place."

Todd nodded. His eyes remained fixed on the road in front of him.

"I'm sorry. I just want to get back to I-40 and across the state line into New Mexico before whoever murdered that cook decides to come after us."

The welcome sign at the edge of town soon popped up on the horizon. Caroline peered out the window. At that moment, her eyes grew as wide as plates again. A small mockingbird flying just ahead of the SUV suddenly froze in mid-air. A shimmer rippled out in every direction from the bird. Small electrical bolts wrapped around its equally small frame for a couple of seconds.

The mockingbird plummeted to the ground.

Dead.

Caroline screamed.

"Stop the car! Stop the car right now!"

Todd slammed on the brakes. Their SUV did a 180-degree spin on the asphalt. It finally came to a halt facing back toward the town. Caroline unlatched her seat belt and flung open the passenger side door. Todd quickly followed her and finally saw for himself what spooked his wife.

A few feet from their back wheel, the bird's small body lay on the ground. Smoke wafted up from amid its gray feathers.

Todd gave a low whistle.

"It looks like that bird got cooked real good."

Caroline cast her eyes toward the stretch of road in front of the lifeless bird. She wrapped her arms around herself.

"Mockingbirds don't randomly fall out the sky dead and burnt. It dropped as fast as a mosquito getting caught inside a bug zapper."

Todd opened the rear door on the SUV. He grabbed a tote bag and unzipped it. Todd pulled out a nylon rope and a kitchen magnet. He tied one end of the rope around the magnet.

Caroline raised a brow. She gave Todd the same look she always gave him whenever she caught him tinkering around with malfunctioning appliances inside their old apartment instead of calling the landlord.

"What are you doing?"

"Testing out a theory."

Todd tossed the magnet at the same spot where the bird fell. It also slammed to a halt in mid-air and bounced back toward the SUV. The magnet changed directions with the force of a boomerang. Caroline and Todd both ducked. He released the rope from his hand and the magnet fell to the ground before reaching their position.

"We're dealing with some sort of electromagnetic field here," Todd said. "It's repelling everything that tries to cross through it."

"What does that mean?"

"We're not going anywhere."

Caroline gnawed on her lower lip and glanced down the road leading back into Travis. Todd didn't need to be a mind reader to understand what fearful thoughts now sprang up inside her head. Those same thoughts also began to bombard him.

"We'll find another way out of here," Todd said, trying to reassure her. "This can't be the only road in or out of this town."

Finding another escape route ended up being an impossible task. Todd and Caroline journeyed down one street after another. An identical scenario played out on each potential exit they tested out. The same magnetic field or force field prevented them from leaving the town in each instance. The only results their efforts brought were fuel and hope dwindling in equal portions.

Todd whipped out his smartphone at one point thinking he could reach out to some old military friends. Perhaps, they would be able to tell him and Caroline what to do or send help. It proved as useless as their exit route scavenger hunt. His phone's signal wasn't strong enough for him to place a call and connect with an actual living, breathing person elsewhere.

Todd's thoughts drifted back inside the house he currently occupied. What would it take to get that creature downstairs to spill the information he needed? It resisted all previous efforts to extract the right answers to his questions. A week later, Todd still knew as little as he did when he first ambushed that thing. He drew in a weary breath and cast his eyes toward the basement door.

"Time for another round of this garbage."

He decided to employ a different tactic this time. Todd took a detour into the living room and approached the coffee table. An assortment of odd-looking gadgets lay before him across the tabletop. They varied in size and shape. Some were metallic in their look and feel. Others reminded him of a soft plastic. Todd didn't have a clue what function each device served after confiscating them from the creature in his basement.

There was a definite way he could find out.

Todd snatched up a device that resembled a long square rod with three uneven tines jutting out from the top. Each tine doubled in length from the previous one. The tines were tipped with transparent glass bubbles. A small clear panel was buried in the center on the lower half of the square rod.

He flung open the basement door. Todd carried this new device in one hand and his UV flashlight in the other. He switched on the flashlight midway down the stairs, scattering a blue glow ahead of him.

A determined scowl washed over Todd's face.

This time, I'll make this monster crack, he reassured himself without words. *This time, it will finally tell me what I need to know.*

The prisoner had not moved since its ill-fated escape attempt. Chains remained taut against their body and the chair sat upright on the cement. Todd's entrance did not stir the creature. It hung its head and refused to break eye contact with the floor.

A low voice finally broke the silent darkness.

"The others will come for me. When they break through your defenses, your time will meet an end."

Todd's nails dug into the flashlight handle, and he bit down on his lower lip until he tasted a hint of blood. Taking the knife he used to hobble this creature and finishing the job would feel so good. Nothing would give him greater pleasure than to see the last of its life bleed out before his eyes.

He couldn't do it. For Caroline's sake, Todd had to keep going. He had to make this thing talk while he remained unchanged.

"What? No boast about how you will break me?" The creature's voice dripped with a smug satisfaction. "No assurance you will make me tell you everything you want to know? Perhaps you have finally accepted the futility of your situation. Your world will soon be our world."

"The only thing I've accepted is that I need to move from Plan A to Plan B."

Todd lowered his hand until the bulk of the UV light blasted his prisoner directly in the eyes. It let out a short growl and jerked its head out of the beam's path. Todd shifted the beam again so that it followed the same path as the creature's head.

"Look at me. Don't make this harder on yourself."

It finally raised its head a few seconds later. Black ovals locked on Todd. Thin lips revealed a seething hatred. His prisoner hungered to wrench free from the chains and attack him without restraint. Every line etched into the creature's face told him as much.

"Now I've decided to take one of your gadgets here and test it out. I'm not sure what kind of weapon it is. But I'm willing to bet it is a weapon."

A partial smile graced his prisoner's lips.

"What makes you so certain that gadget is what you think it is?"

"Here's the fun part: I'm going to test it out on you, and we'll find out together."

Todd set the UV flashlight on a nearby shelf. He angled it so the beam kept the backdrop behind his prisoner partially illuminated. Then he pressed the center panel on the square rod.

The glass balls affixed on the end of each tine lit up. A red light blanketed the tip of each tine inside the glass. Todd stuck it out in front of him and pointed the gadget at the creature.

"How do I shut down the barrier surrounding the town?"

"Even if I reveal this information, escape is not an option for you. This is our home now."

Todd strolled over to his prisoner. He jammed the end of the gadget against the creature's neck. Pale skin glowed red where tines made contact. The prisoner's face contorted, and its jaw clenched tight.

"Stop! Please stop!"

Todd did a silent count to ten before pulling back the gadget again. His prisoner panted.

"How do I shut down the barrier?"

"I will tell you nothing. Little time remains before you change. Exactly as all others in this place have done before you."

Todd mashed his lips together and clenched his jaw. He jabbed the gadget harder into the creature's neck a second time. The red glow from the tines began to spread across the skin. It resembled strands from a spider web. His prisoner stiffened against the chair. A low growl escaped its lips and it panted hard again. Todd held it in place a few seconds longer this time. The glow spread into his prisoner's cheek, exposing each vein, before he finally pulled the gadget away again.

"How do I shut down the barrier?"

The creature swallowed hard and cast its eyes toward the floor again. Those thin lips curled into a defiant sneer.

"I will die before I ever disclose the path out of this place."

Todd pressed the panel on the gadget. The red glow dissipated from the tines. He jammed it into his pocket and marched over to a window high on the wall behind his prisoner. Todd pulled a lower board loose and positioned it so an obvious crack between that board and an upper board now showed. It would be enough to permit a few rays of sunlight to barge into the basement and fall upon the chair once the sun rose again.

"You better pray you find some extra strength sunblock before morning,"

With those words, Todd snatched the flashlight from its perch and stomped back up the stairs.

EVERY STREETLAMP LINING the main road through Travis shone with a distinct red hue. It struck Paige as rather odd. Were things always this way around here? She never traveled to another place where streetlamps produced anything other than normal white light. It gave Paige one more bullet point to add to her growing list of reasons for why she felt troubled after departing the barber shop.

Paige wondered if her friends, amid their stubborn bravado, entertained similar misgivings. Heather dropped back a pace behind Jason and Rich when she noticed Paige trailing the rest of group. She leaned in close enough so she could whisper to Paige without drawing the others' attention.

"What's up with the lights?" Heather gestured at a nearby streetlamp. "If I didn't know any better, I'd think they were trying to pass red traffic lights off as streetlamps."

"I have no idea. But I do know one thing. It's only making this whole situation creepier."

"Paige, we don't really have a choice. This is the first person we've found in this town. We have no vehicle, so we're limited on options for getting help."

As much as Paige didn't want to admit it, Heather made a valid point. They had no working vehicle and no way out of town. Worse yet, Paige had not made any actual progress on locating her missing brother since leaving Louisiana. Concocting this spring break road trip to double as a covert search for him backfired in the worst way imaginable.

Laughter interrupted Paige's thoughts. Her eyes drifted to a bright light emanating from Rich's smartphone. Jason faced the phone as they walked, dispensing mock documentary-style narration as the group passed by each building on the main road.

Their antics finally caught the attention of the red-haired stranger. This mysterious individual stopped in their tracks and wheeled around to face Jason and Rich. That same pair of sunglasses remained on the stranger's face. Paige wondered how in the world anyone could see out of those things in such dim light.

"Please turn that off." The stranger's voice came across as polite but firm. "For your own sake."

Paige turned and glanced at Heather again. This time, the same concern gripping her had finally washed over her friend's eyes.

Jason whipped out his own phone and tapped the screen. It lit up.

"Last time I checked, it's a free country," he said. "Rich can record whatever the hell he wants."

"So you believe. Does not mean it is true or a smart action to take."

"Are you threatening us?"

His other hand balled into a fist. Paige cringed and stepped forward. Someone had to intervene before this escalated out of control.

"Guys, please turn the stupid video recorder off, so we can keep moving."

Jason's lips twisted into a scowl. Rich beat him to punch, however, in voicing his displeasure.

"Why the hell should we?"

Paige positioned herself between the red-haired stranger and the two boys. She grasped Rich's arm holding up the phone.

"Just listen to me, Rich. We're all tired, injured, hungry, and thirsty. Let's not antagonize the one person who's in a position to help us out."

Rich held the phone rigid. Paige refused to break eye contact with him. If he insisted that she listen to the stranger at the barber shop, Rich needed to follow suit now. Finally, he relented and switched off the video app. Rich lowered the phone to his side.

"You win. Happy now?"

Paige sighed and pushed away his arm. She turned to face the red-haired stranger, who gave an approving nod.

"Thank you. We can continue on now."

The stranger resumed a brisk pace down the sidewalk. It suddenly dawned on Paige she didn't know where they were going or why they were walking to this destination. Her feet throbbed from walking around in flats virtually all day.

"Why are we still walking?" she asked. "We need someone with a car or truck who can give our car a tow. That's the whole reason we came here."

Quick breaths interspersed Paige's words as she labored to match the stranger's long-legged strides. The stranger stopped in her tracks. She cast a confused glance at Paige.

"A car?"

"That's what I said."

"I do not have one."

"What do you mean you don't have a car? Why in the hell didn't you say anything about it back at the barber shop?"

Paige received only a silent stone-faced stare as an answer. The other three began to grumble about it behind her.

"Can you tell us why in God's name we should keep following you?" Jason finally opened the lid on thoughts he kept sealed for the last few minutes. "What's in it for us? You don't seem to be much help at all."

“I promise we will take care of your problem.”

“Is that a fact? We don’t even know your name or what you’re doing in this place. You could be trapped here like us for all we know.

“I am Melody.”

The stranger had a lyrical sounding name. How it rolled off her tongue, though, didn’t feel all that lyrical to Paige. Then again, everything she said sounded weird the way she said it. Paige wondered at first if English was Melody’s second language with how she talked. Now, as she thought more on it, Paige couldn’t imagine a part of the world where anyone spoke with a similar accent.

“I come from a distant place,” Melody explained. “What I am doing here is not your concern. All you need to know is that you are in the right hands.”

Paige studied her face. The sunglasses helped mask all traces of obvious emotion. Still, Melody’s voice betrayed a growing annoyance bubbling to the surface from inside her. Not that Paige cared. She had grown weary of taking things on blind faith. This started to feel too much like reliving another useless Sunday sermon from the family pastor.

Melody turned and continued her brisk march ahead of the other four. A town square appeared on the horizon. The main road merged into a horizontal cross street running in front of the square. Beyond the cross street lay a small immaculate plaza. It took up an entire city block.

A large statue stood in the center of the plaza. A hip high stone wall formed a rectangular border around the plaza, leaving a few feet of open space between the statue and the wall itself. Trees dotted the plaza. Paved trails led up to the wall from the east and the west. Each trail cut through a small opening in their respective section of the wall.

The plaza seemed to be the group’s destination, but Paige saw no one else in the vicinity. It didn’t make any sense. Before she made up her mind to challenge Melody again, an excited shout from Heather broke the silence.

"Look over there."

Paige turned suddenly, forgetting about her neck for a moment. A renewed burst of pain offered a quick reminder of what happened in the semi earlier. Paige rubbed her neck as her eyes trailed where Heather's finger pointed down a side street. Her eyes stopped on a ranch house surrounded by lights of all shapes and sizes.

Nothing would seem all that remarkable about the ranch house under normal circumstances. Right now, though, it fit like a square peg in a round hole compared to the rest of the neighborhood. The house featured more lights than Paige had ever seen on any other house. Floodlights were mounted at every corner. Lamp posts lit up both sides of the driveway. Lights illuminated every inch of the porch – both from the ceiling and the railing. It rendered the whole property brighter than a Christmas light display on steroids.

"One of these isn't like the others," Paige said.

The foursome turned off the main street and started walking toward the well-lit house.

"Wait! You must come back here at once."

Melody's voice betrayed an unusual frantic tone. Paige raised both brows and her lips twisted into a confused expression.

"Someone is obviously home here," she replied. "We'd be foolish to pass by without seeing if they can help us."

"Barber is not in that place. We must stay on the main road."

Rich smirked and answered Melody with a dismissive hand wave.

"I think I'm gonna take what's behind door number two," he said. "Go tell your friend Barber that we found a better option."

Paige glanced back over her shoulder one more time as the foursome drew closer to the well-lit house. Melody did not budge from the crosswalk at the top of the street. She drew out a small dark gadget from her clothing. Paige had never seen anything like it before. The gadget resembled a phone charger plug without a USB cord connecting it to the phone. A pair of tines extended like antennas from the top.

Melody pressed her thumb against the gadget, near the two tines. The entire face of her device lit up as a holographic screen emerged. At once, Melody began speaking words that sounded unlike any language Paige ever heard before.

"I don't think Melody is from around here," she said, turning to the others.

"Neither are we," Jason replied.

"I'm not talking Texas. I'm talking Earth."

Rich clapped his hands together and let out a big laugh when she made that declaration.

"Sounds good, Paige. Hey, maybe she's on an interstellar spring break and her spaceship broke down here too. So now she's trying to phone home."

A smile spread over Jason's lips. He mashed them together to keep from bursting out laughing. Paige glared at both boys.

"See for yourself, you idiots."

Both Jason and Rich glanced over their shoulders as Paige had done. Heather followed suit. Each set of eyes narrowed to a squint, then widened again a second later.

"What in the hell is that thing in her hand?" Jason finally asked.

"I don't know," Paige replied. "But I have a feeling we shouldn't stick around here on the street so we can find out."

Upon nearing the end of the driveway, Paige heard distinct rustling in some nearby shrubs. It didn't come from any of the landscaping in the yard belong to the well-lit house. These noises emanated from shrubs in the neighboring yard, beyond a wooden fence marking the boundary between the two yards. Paige's curiosity got the best of her. She veered off toward the shrubs.

"Where are you going?" Heather asked.

"Checking something out in the bushes. I heard some rustling over there."

"If you hear a strange noise, you should stay away from it. Don't go toward it."

Paige halted just before reaching the fence line. What Heather said made a ton more sense. Her inclination to wander off and check out some random noise started to feel dumb. They needed to stick close together, especially after what happened to Randall and what happened with the semi.

She turned away from the fence and started walking back toward where the others stood in front of the driveway. At once, a distinct growl pierced the air. It came from the shrubs behind the fence line. Paige froze. She didn't dare turn to see what lurked behind her.

"There's some kind of wild animal in those bushes, y'all." Her voice quavered. "I think it caught my scent."

The other three turned to face her. Heather unleashed a scream.

"That's no wild animal."

Jason's voice carried the same level of extreme fear as Paige's did.

The growl grew louder and closer. An angry snort followed. Paige's hands trembled. Tears started to trickle down her cheeks. Every muscle and nerve in her body tightened. Paige wanted to run more than anything right now. But she didn't like her chances of out-running whatever emerged from the bushes behind her. Images of Randall's violent demise clawed their way back into her mind. Would she suffer the same fate as him?

Paige found herself starting into a desperate silent prayer for the second time today. At that same moment, the front door to the well-lit house flew open. She opened her eyes and glanced up. A man emerged in the doorway toting a hunting rifle.

"Stay perfectly still," he ordered.

Paige's ears perked up. She recognized that voice.

It couldn't be. It wasn't possible.

A shot rang out from the rifle. The creature behind Paige howled. She heard a loud thump against the asphalt.

"Now you can run. Hurry! Get inside!"

No one needed to tell Paige twice. She bolted across the front lawn as the others sprinted up the driveway. They dashed inside the house ahead of her. As Paige neared the porch steps, the growling behind her intensified. The creature grew closer with each growl. It put every ounce of energy into running her down before she reached the front door.

"Duck!"

Paige obeyed the familiar voice and stooped her head as she ran. A second shot rang out from the rifle. The creature trailing her let out the most awful squeal she had ever heard. Paige's handbag banged against her ribs and her own frantic breaths soon drowned out everything else.

Once Paige reached the doorway, she felt a gentle push on her back and the door slammed shut behind her. Bolts locked a second later. Paige bent over with hands on knees, trying to catch her breath. After a few seconds, she finally straightened up and turned to look at the door.

Her mouth dropped open when Paige finally got her first clear look at her rescuer's identity.

"Todd?"

A small smile sprouted on his face, but then faded away as quickly as it emerged. His lips twisted into a confused expression and his sky-blue eyes soon flooded with tears.

"Paige!"

Todd flung his arms around her, and they shared a deep embrace. Tears streamed down both faces.

"You two know each other?" Heather asked. "How in the hell is that even possible?"

Paige opened her eyes and pulled away from Todd again. She brushed away lingering tears with her hand.

"This is my missing brother."

IT HAD TO be a hallucination. Todd told himself he was caught up in the midst of a vivid dream and he would soon wake from it. That had to be the only rational explanation. No other reason why his baby sister stood before him entered his mind. Todd shuddered at the thought that Paige now faced the same predicament as him.

He set the rifle down next to the sofa and started pacing back and forth in front of the closed door.

"This is a nightmare. How could this happen? God, why did you let this happen?"

Todd cast his eyes at the floor. Paige frowned.

"I can tell you're really thrilled to see me."

Todd stopped in his tracks and glanced up at her. He tried to paint a smile on his lips again, but he could not hide the pain in his face. Yet another cruel twist of fate had fallen on his shoulders.

"Of course, I'm happy to see you again. But I'm horrified you're trapped this hellish place with me."

"What are you doing here?"

"I was going to ask you the same thing."

Paige turned away and closed her eyes. Words to adequately express every emotion flooding into her head fled from her. The trauma of the past month resurfaced all at once. Every plea through Twitter, Facebook, and Instagram. Paige posted pictures of Todd and Caroline that friends and family shared non-stop. She begged for any scrap of information she could gather and chased down every possible lead on their whereabouts.

One new question hit her mind with the force of a salty ocean wave spraying her face.

"Where's Caroline?"

Todd withdrew from eye contact this time when she turned to face him again. His hand gripped the armrest belonging to a nearby sofa and his nails dug into the cushion. Fresh tears sprang from Todd's eyes, and he sucked in his lower lip. Paige's friends gazed at the siblings in awkward silence. She realized they didn't know what to say. Not saying anything was probably the best choice to make right now.

"I'm so sorry, Todd. I can't even begin to imagine what you're going through."

Paige finally connected the dots. Tears emerged in her eyes a second time. His reaction told Paige what she needed to know concerning her sister-in-law's fate. Todd sniffed and brushed away his own tears. A determined scowl washed over his stubble covered face.

"Why did you come here?" he snapped. "Don't you realize what you've done?"

"We kind of ended up here by accident."

Heather's eyes darted between Paige and Todd. She wanted to deflect some of the attention away from Paige and defuse the tension in the room.

Todd jerked his head toward her as soon as she spoke up. His blue eyes bored into Heather.

"What do you mean?"

Heather retreated a couple of steps from him.

"Paige has never been to Vegas. So, we thought it'd be fun to head out that way for spring break –"

Todd held up his hand.

"I know."

He immediately glanced at Paige again.

"The question is do Mom and Dad know?"

Paige stomped right up to Todd. Her eyes grew cold, and a scowl now crossed her lips.

"Who cares if they know? I'm not a little kid. I don't have a curfew. I'm a college student. I don't need to give them the 411 on where I'm going and when I'll be back."

"They worry when they don't hear from you."

Paige rolled her eyes and shook her head as she backed up a few steps again. Todd could see her rebellious streak hadn't faded a bit since the last time he hung around his sister.

"Ironic coming from the guy who disappeared off the face of the planet for almost a month and didn't bother to tell anyone where he went."

"I couldn't do anything about it."

"Did you even try?"

Todd punched his fist into the sofa armrest. It made Paige and the others jump.

"What kind of question is that?" He glanced back up at his sister with a steely gaze. "Of course, I tried! Every damn day. I searched for a way to reach the outside world. I prayed my guts out that I'd get a hold of you. Or Mom. Or Dad."

Paige wrapped her arms behind her head and closed her eyes. Jason started forward, intending to wrap his arm around her shoulders, but stopped in his tracks when Heather shook her head at him.

"We feared the worst, you know. Texas rangers scoured I-40 searching for any sign of you. Nothing. It's like you vanished without a trace."

Her eyes popped open again. Paige stabbed an index finger at her brother.

"And now here you are. Why no calls? Why not even a simple text?"

Todd fished out his smartphone from his pocket and tossed it to Paige like he flipped a basketball to her. She snagged the phone with one hand. A large crack crossed the middle of the screen and smaller cracks spread out along the edges. Paige turned it on. The phone incredibly still had a little juice left in the battery. When the home screen popped up, she noticed it had no bars. They were still apparently not in a service area.

At that moment, Paige realized it wasn't just a problem with her phone or her friends' phones. No one else could get a signal in Travis. Did it have something to do with the force field they encountered earlier?

"I didn't realize you couldn't reach me," she said, looking up from the phone.

"Why did you come here?" Todd probed her again with his question from earlier. "Do you realize how much danger you've put yourself in?"

Paige stormed out of the living room without saying another word. Todd looked away and gazed at one of the boarded-up windows.

Rich rose sharply from his chair and pinched the bridge of his nose. He sighed deeply and shook his head at Todd.

"If you're done being a jerk for a second, we'd like to point out that Paige set this whole road trip up so she could find you. Now that she's succeeded, you're trying to make her feel like absolute shit for it. Bravo. Well done."

Todd hurried into the kitchen after Paige. He caught her by the arm. She shook his hand off and jerked her arm away.

"I'm sorry," Todd's voice shed all the earlier sharpness. Rich's revelation humbled it right out of him. "I had no right to lash out at you."

"I searched for you because I love you." Paige spoke barely above a whisper. She still refused to turn and look at him. "You're my big brother. I didn't want to lose you. I didn't want to give up hope."

Todd tenderly touched her shoulder.

"I'm grateful you never gave up hope. That's one of your greatest qualities. You never give up."

Paige wheeled around and finally managed a half-smile. They shared an embrace a second time. When she pulled away again, Todd's eyes were awash with renewed concern.

"Where did you get all these cuts and bruises? What happened to you?"

Paige brushed back a blond lock. She turned and gazed at the boarded-up kitchen window.

"It happened when we tried to flee on the main road out of town. We got to the welcome sign at the edge of Travis and –"

"And you crashed into the barrier."

Paige jerked her head around and faced him again. A second later, she winced and grabbed her neck. When she opened her eyes once the burst of pain subsided, Paige nodded.

"How did you know what happened?"

"Caroline and I encountered the same barrier when we tried to leave."

"What is it?"

"It could be some sort of electromagnetic field. I don't really know for sure. I do know it lets people and cars inside the town, but nothing can get back out again."

"How is that possible?"

Todd crossed his arms and took a turn gazing at the boarded-up window.

"I have no idea. We tried so hard to find a way around it or find a different way out."

Paige hung her head.

"Does that mean what I think it means?"

"There's no way out." Todd confirmed the fear welling up inside her. "That barrier – whatever it is – surrounds the entire town. No chance of walking or driving out of here."

Paige's heart sank when she heard this piece of news. She held out some hope they would find an alternate route out of town.

Whoever created the barrier was determined to not let anyone or anything inside Travis escape. That conclusion raised other questions in her mind.

What was Melody's true agenda? Who was this Barber character she talked about so much? Were they the ones who were responsible for putting the barrier in place?

Still, those were not the first questions that popped out of her mouth.

"What were those things behind me?"

Paige's curiosity tore her up inside. A part of her wanted to return to the front door and peek outside to see if corpses of the creatures who pursued her still lay in the road. It might prove useful to get a better look at the threat that menaced her only a short time earlier. On the other hand, Paige wasn't sure she had the stomach to handle what she might see outside.

Todd rubbed the nape of his neck with his right hand and pinched his eyes shut.

"They used to be human. I don't know what in the hell they are now."

Those words sent a chill down Paige's spine. Melody must have sprung those creatures on them when they took a detour down that street against her wishes. What fate laid in store for them if they kept following her? Paige shuddered when she realized how close she and her friends came to walking right into a trap.

"What do you mean they used to be human?" Absolute fear wrapped around each word in her question. "What's going on here?"

"Something changed what's left of the people in this town. They don't look the way people are supposed to look. They don't act like them either."

Paige drew in a sharp breath. She was afraid to ask what that entailed.

"They've become monsters." Todd answered the question as though he sensed her thoughts. "Ugly ferocious creatures that would sooner rip you apart than look at you or talk to you."

"Can they talk?"

"I suppose. I can't say I've been in a mood to attempt a conversation with one yet."

"Who or what did this to them?"

"Isn't it obvious?"

Todd's tone sharpened considerably at her naive question. Paige realized the answer stared her in the face the whole time. Melody and the mysterious Barber had to be the driving force behind all these strange and frightening things.

Paige walked over to the sink and stared at one of the boarded-up windows.

"I don't think they're from Earth – the ones responsible for all of this. I think we met one of them. She used an odd gadget."

"You met one?"

"She wanted to lead us to someone she called Barber. I think they were going to do some really bad things to us."

Her throat tightened. Paige closed her eyes and pressed her palms down on the edge of the sink. For a moment, she felt a distinct urge to vomit. How could any of this be happening? Why were these aliens doing these things? It didn't make any sense to her. More importantly, it terrified her to think anyone would journey across the stars only to lay siege to a town in the middle of nowhere.

Now she was trapped here with those beings.

Paige looked up from the sink at her brother again. Todd didn't say anything. He simply stared at the boarded-up window as though gazing at someone or something in the distance. No words were needed. His hardened eyes and clenched jaw told Paige he felt an identical mixture of fear and anger as her.

"That's a nasty gash on your forehead." Todd finally sliced through agonizing silence building up in the kitchen. "We need to get you cleaned up."

"I survived one hell of a wreck." Paige replied. "How do I look?"

"You've got some minor cuts and bruises. And your hair is a bit unruly."

"Gee … Thanks."

Todd's lips twisted into a wry smile.

"You're the one who asked."

Paige squinted and stuck out her tongue at him. Jason, Rich, and Heather were carrying on an animated conversation as she entered the living room again. Paige kept her focus on Todd. She followed him into the bathroom and sat on the edge of the bathtub. He opened a first aid kit from a nearby cabinet and poured rubbing alcohol into a gauze pad. Todd dabbed the gauze across the gash on her forehead. Paige clenched her teeth and let out a sharp cry.

"I know it stings. Hold still."

Todd cleaned the wound. He applied some antibiotic ointment to another gauze pad and taped it over the gash.

"That should heal in a couple of days."

Paige stood up and walked over to the sink. She turned on the faucet. Water pooled around the outer edge of the sink as she splashed it until droplets ran down all sides of her face. Paige wiped the remnants off with a hand towel. She examined the cuts from the glass in the mirror. Without little streaks of blood accompanying each cut, they didn't stand out as badly as she expected from the rest of her face.

Todd and Paige soon rejoined the others in the living room. He planted himself on the arm of a larger sofa directly across from the small one. Her stomach rumbled and her throat felt parched. For the first time since leaving their car on the side of the highway, hunger and thirst returned in full force.

Paige wasn't alone. Jason rose from the small sofa and started making his way toward the kitchen.

"What do you have to eat around here? I feel so hungry right now I could chew my own arm off."

"Mostly canned stuff in the basement," Todd replied. "Pasta. Tuna. Maybe a little –"

Jason stopped in his tracks. He turned back and gave Todd a sideways glance.

"Really? That's it?"

"What were you expecting? Have you taken a look around the town?"

Jason shrugged.

"I guess eating gross food is better than eating no food at all."

His expression shone a different light on his feelings. Jason had a tough time not mirroring a kid who had been told they had to wolf down a plate of broccoli before getting any dessert. He turned and approached the basement door. Todd sprang to his feet and thrust up his hand. Paige shot him a puzzled look as he charged toward the same door.

"Hold on a second!" Todd said. "You better let me go down there."

Jason snapped his head toward Todd again.

"I'm pretty sure I can handle getting some cans of tuna fish. Thanks anyway."

He turned the knob and the door popped open a crack. Todd smacked his hand against the wooden frame and immediately slammed it shut again. Jason glared at him and backed up a couple of steps.

"What the hell are you doing?"

"I can't let you go down there alone."

"Get out of my way."

Jason grabbed the doorknob again. Todd pressed his hand against the door to prevent it from opening.

"I said no."

Heather rose from her seat and walked over there with the intention of diffusing rising tensions again. She latched onto Jason's shoulder and pulled him away from the door. Jason glanced down at her hand and back at Todd. His lips were now drawn into a fierce scowl.

A similar frown spread over Heather's lips.

"Why can't he go down there?" she asked. "Are you trying to hide something from us?"

"This isn't your house. You can't go wherever you feel like going."

"It isn't yours either."

"I've been here longer."

Heather laughed and rolled her eyes.

"I don't give a shit how long you've been here. We're all tired, hungry, and thirsty. I just want to eat something."

A crease formed in Paige's brow, and she rested her hand in her chin. What was Todd trying to hide from them exactly? Why did he want them to stay away from the basement? This seemed out of character for her brother to be confrontational over something so petty and stupid.

"Todd, what's going on here?"

Paige grabbed her brother's other arm.

"If something is down there," she said. "You need to come clean about it right now."

Todd closed his eyes for a moment and let out a sigh. He opened them again and fixed those blue eyes squarely on Paige.

"I captured one of those alien creatures."

Her blue eyes widened and her breath quickened.

"What? Are you serious?"

"It's chained up down there."

Rich popped up from the sofa. A crooked grin plastered his face.

"I call bullshit. There's no such thing as aliens."

Todd's steely eyes fixed on him like a detective getting ready to interrogate a suspect.

"Wanna bet? I don't make up things like this, Bubba."

Rich squinted at him and smirked even harder.

"Okay. Prove it."

Paige nodded.

"Let's see it."

Todd pulled his hand away from the door.

"Fine. I guess you should know what you're up against. But stay behind me."

He marched over to the kitchen counter and snatched up a long black flashlight. Paige had seen one like it before. A cop shined the same type of flashlight in her face the last time she got pulled over for speeding in downtown Lake Charles.

Todd cracked open the door and plodded down the stairs. Paige and the others followed closely behind him, mimicking his tiptoeing. When they reached the bottom, Todd raised the flashlight beam. It fell on a figure chained to a chair in the middle of the basement.

Paige and Heather both gasped. Jason let out a low whistle.

The creature in chains possessed arms almost twice as long as the average person. Paige noted both limbs were similar in length to Melody's arms. It had black ovals for eyes, deathly pale skin, and an egg-shaped head. Shaggy red hair adorned the prisoner's head. When it saw four new faces in the basement, the prisoner bared two rows of sharp teeth and greeted them with a low growl.

"What in God's name is that thing?"

Rich's usual smug skepticism yielded to subdued terror. His voice barely climbed above a whisper.

"That is your alien," Todd replied. "In the pale and ugly flesh."

No one argued the point. Paige knew one thing for certain. Todd's prisoner resembled no human she had ever encountered.

MELODY HESITATED. A flurry of thoughts crowded into her head all at once. Each one alone jarring enough to give her pause. Barber would be displeased. She knew as much. Even if Melody hoped for a different outcome, he would quickly extinguish those hopes.

"We must leave now. Barber wishes to meet with you at once."

A guard stood before her and beckoned for Melody to get inside the open transport.

Melody nodded.

"I am aware of his wishes."

Her tone showed a flicker of annoyance. Barber already ordered Melody to report back to their observation center when the four humans escaped her grasp. She didn't crave a reminder – no matter how good the intentions were behind it – from a simple guard.

Melody stepped up inside the transport and took a seat. A metallic whoosh echoed through the interior as a door sealed behind her. At once, Melody removed the gloves protecting her hands and the glasses adorning her eyes. She wiped a black oval with a long pale finger. Away from her face, the glasses revealed amber-like lenses. Melody struggled to adjust to these glasses, no matter how much she tried. The frames settled on her petite nose all wrong compared to the ones she used to wear back home.

They were a necessary inconvenience. The glasses opened an enhanced visual field in twilight and at night. She could see enough to do what she needed to do. Their whole team had so much work still left to carry out. Melody fidgeted with her glasses as trees and buildings flowed under the transport in a steady blur.

Perhaps that's why nervousness over speaking with Barber gripped her down to her bones. These humans could turn out to be a major problem – now that they joined with one still bent on resisting her people's presence.

The transport came to a sudden jarring halt. Melody nearly stumbled out of her seat. It felt like an invisible hand yanked her entire body forward during the braking process. She would request a new driver – if she got sent back out in the field again.

Doing more field work was no certain thing for the moment.

A metallic whoosh greeted her a second time. The guard beckoned to her to join him outside. Melody complied as she re-gloved her hands and put back on the amber glasses.

"Thank you for bringing me back so soon."

He answered her with a stiff nod and sealed the door behind Melody.

"It is my honor to serve."

Melody turned and marched up to the outer door. A sensor flickered from the top of the door and a red light washed over her face. It crawled down the front of her body while Melody stood motionless.

"Bio code scan complete," an electronic voice told her. "You are now permitted to enter."

The outer door dissolved like boiling water turning to steam. Melody stepped through the opening and the door quickly reappeared, as solid as before, behind her a few seconds later.

Melody stared down a long corridor. Small red lights embedded in the ceiling lined both sides. Lights in Barber's office were active. Melody secretly hoped to not find him in there. She yearned to draw the good fortune of dealing with an underling. The sort who could be easily intimidated.

Barber definitely could not be intimidated.

She drew in a sharp breath and closed her eyes for a second or two. Melody opened them again and marched straight up to his office before she had a chance to think about it longer. A metallic whoosh greeted her once again and she entered. Near the back of the office, a colleague stooped over a workstation and punched data into a console. He wore similar clothing to Melody, apart from a coat. Numbers and formulas popped up onto a display screen in front of him.

"I am here as you requested."

Her colleague straightened up and wheeled around to face Melody. She added a nervous gulp once she confirmed Barber stood before her.

A deep frown crossed his lips.

"So you are. I wish it were under better circumstances."

"Again, I regret what happened. I tried to warn them away from the house with lethal lights. I did not anticipate –"

"You should have anticipated that scenario before it unfolded and called in a transport."

Barber crossed over to an adjacent workstation. He punched a couple of buttons on the console. A three-dimensional image flickered on the screen. It showed a head shot of the human who occupied the house with lethal lights. His head turned on the screen as though pinned to a turntable. Rows of bio data ran across the screen directly to the left of the human's head.

Barber glanced up at her. His black oval eyes narrowed into a stony gaze.

"Each one of us knows where the one called Todd is hiding," he said. "You were irresponsible to think you could journey past his dwelling and still bring this new batch of humans here on your own."

Melody looked away from his intense eyes and stared at her own feet.

"They were injured and requested my help. I thought if we rendered aid and sent them on their way, they would be none the wiser."

"Render aid? Do you think that is wise?"

"They are young and not from this place. I see them posing no true threat to us."

Barber rubbed his long pale fingers down his cheek and shook his head at her.

"Each one of these humans is a threat. How can you so easily forget what the one called Todd has done to some of our own? Do you remember how the town leaders first reacted to our presence? Do not be so willfully blind."

Melody glanced up at him again. Her internal temperature rose as she clenched her jaw and bared her teeth.

"I am not blind. And this is not how we did things on Rubrum."

"Who are you to tell me what we did or did not do on Rubrum?" Barber's voice climbed in pitch as he circled Melody. "I lead our research cell for a good reason. Do not question my decisions!"

Melody's eyes trailed Barber as he paced around her. Her nerves quivered even as her arms and legs stiffened. She glanced at his hand but saw no visible weapon. Good. Barber did not need anything to assist in channeling his rising anger.

"What if we just allow them to depart in peace?" Melody didn't let herself break eye contact with Barber for even a second while she spoke. "What they know about us is limited. We can lower the barrier and let them go onto another place. They will be none the wiser."

"Do you think it really is that simple?"

"Should it not be that simple?"

Barber stopped in his tracks. His eyes widened again. He thrust out a long arm and wrapped his hand around the collar of Melody's long coat, pulling it tight around her neck.

Her muscles flexed involuntarily.

"They belong to us. Our survival depends on it. It is that simple."

Melody closed her eyes and lowered her head.

"You let those humans go and catastrophe will strike," Barber said. "They will return with an army to sweep us off this land. We cannot afford to go. We have progressed too far and invested too much into this vital project to allow such a scenario to unfold now."

Barber finally released his grip on Melody and abruptly turned away from her. He resumed his former position at the workstation.

"You may go, but I insist you stay sequestered within the observation center to conduct your research for now."

A fresh wave of anxiety hit Melody as she left the room and returned to the corridor. It seeped into her fingers and toes as she took a sharp turn into another corridor to her right. Melody tried to shake their images from her mind. All four humans who came to the barber shop bore cuts and bruises. Their clothing appeared disheveled. They complained of hunger and thirst. She saw neither the two males nor the two females before this particular sun cycle. None of the four attacked her with weapons or appeared to even possess a weapon.

Could Barber be wrong?

Certainly, humans already living in this place proved hostile when they first arrived from Rubrum. Melody observed a different reaction in these four. She did not detect a similar level of fear and distrust.

Melody stopped halfway down the corridor and faced a doorway flanked by thick metallic columns on either side. She opened a panel embedded in the right column. Buttons lit up as she pressed four in a rhythmic sequence. A red light above the doorway flickered and scanned her from head to toe.

"Bio code scan complete," The same electronic voice from outside the observation center spoke to Melody again. "You are now permitted to enter."

Melody entered a cramped room. The door whooshed shut behind her. She headed straight for a small bed in the corner and threw herself onto it. Melody would not permit herself to relax. She sat up and buried her face in her hands.

Home seemed so far away now. Not just in terms of spatial distance. It felt like her homeworld had been relocated to another lifetime. Everything seemed so simple back on Rubrum when she first volunteered for this assignment.

The day Melody learned of her selection to this research cell remained vividly imprinted in her mind as though it happened only a few sun cycles ago. She had stopped off at her dwelling to throw together a quick evening meal. Melody barely began carving up some fresh suca fruit when the com-link first lit up. Her face lit up in equal measure when the Rubrum Transition Council delegate delivered the news.

"It is my honor to serve in such an important cause," Melody said.

"No greater cause exists for Rubrum," the delegate replied. "Our survival as a civilization, and as a people, will depend on what you accomplish."

After the delegate finished delivering a series of important instructions, Melody gazed out at the sun hanging low on the horizon. Rays of red light bathed the eastern sky and washed over small black trees dotting the hills behind her balcony. It did not fully sink in for Melody during that exciting moment that this would also be the last time she gazed upon those safe and familiar hills.

Melody understood all too well what everything in her assignment entailed from a logical standpoint. Her heart was another matter. She could not stay. None of them could stay. Rubrum's sun made such a choice no longer possible. That cold fact hit

Melody with greater force when she dropped off her pet treema into the care of her sister Halilah.

Oarc, her treema, always seemed to know when something was amiss. The animal's gloomy eyes still burned fresh in her memory.

"I will depart for only a short time. Be a good little treema for Halilah while I am gone."

Melody stroked Oarc's furry head and neck. Her pained voice betrayed the confidence those words tried to project.

Tears she tried to hold back while talking to the treema finally burst forth when embracing her sister. Halilah mirrored her emotions. Their arms remained wrapped around one another until those tears finally dried up again.

"Please be safe." Halilah spoke to her with a tender whisper. "Our family has lost so much. I cannot lose you too."

A lump formed in Melody's throat. She also yearned to see their mother and father again. Facing the end of their world would seem so much less frightening if they faced it together. Melody lost count of how many times she cursed the micro asteroid bombardment that caused a lethal hull breach on her parents' ship.

She vowed to Halilah a similar fate did not await her amid the stars.

"I love you," she told her sister. "We will reunite in a new home far from Rubrum. I promise."

A deep sigh escaped Melody's lips as her mind returned to her room within the observation center. She and the rest of this cell were no closer to fulfilling to her promise to her sister than when they first arrived on this planet.

Melody stood up and walked over to a small workstation on the other end of the cramped room. She activated a display screen. A series of bright colored panels popped onto the screen. Melody touched a panel in the upper left corner and enlarged it. Six smaller screens spread across the main display screen. Each smaller screen showed an image feed drawn from a different section of the observation center.

Melody had not given much thought to checking in on the progress of their genetic research for some time. Environmental research became her primary concern ever since arriving on the planet. Recording atmospheric conditions. Tweaking their bio armor to work better in those conditions.

The bio armor proved too unstable for prolonged use. Melody never anticipated what differing levels of radiation and luminosity from a yellow star would do to the armor or to their own bodies. She could not fully shake the panic she experienced when that armor malfunctioned during their second sun cycle after landing on the planet.

Melody had never seen so many deep burns on another being before. The bio armor did not offer sufficient protection. A chemical reaction with the bright sunlight caused the armor to grow thin and expose skin underneath to harmful ultraviolet rays. The crew member inside the bio armor nearly died. Others who rescued him all suffered burns to one degree or another.

Her warnings fell on closed ears and minds.

"We must consider another option," Melody told Barber and the others shortly after the bio armor failure. "This planet is not suitable as a new home – even with bio armor in place."

Barber tilted his head and answered with a disapproving cluck of his tongue.

"Where would you have us go? Our people have combed this part of the galaxy. We have not found another place like Rubrum."

"The galaxy has countless stars and worlds. If we keep searching, we will be led to the right place."

"That phase is over. Now we must adapt to a new environment. Our survival depends on it."

Barber abruptly turned and marched out of the room before Melody had a chance to make any further protests.

From the end of that sun cycle until now, they tried to find a way to adapt their bodies to this planet. Melody assisted in rounding up humans inside the town who could provide crucial bio code samples. Since that time, environmental research occupied the bulk of her attention.

Until now.

Melody scanned the various smaller screens on the larger display screen. Each screen showed images of small containment chambers. A single chamber offered enough height and width to hold one adult human.

One corner screen revealed a husky humanoid in tattered clothing. Thick wisps of brownish hair covered visible portions of his head, neck, and arms. He turned so Melody got a clear look at his face. A thick brow, beady eyes, and a snarling mouth filled with jagged teeth greeted her. This husky humanoid crashed against the containment chamber wall and snarled again.

Melody jumped back from the display screen. Her heart pounded inside her chest.

To her knowledge, they placed a human inside this chamber for bio code extraction. This creature she now observed bore little resemblance to any people they captured in the town. It did show striking similarities to the same creature she saw stalking those four humans near the house with lethal lights. Melody dismissed that particular creature as some sort of humanoid subspecies at the time and fled before it caught sight of her. Now she wondered if she had been mistaken.

Melody glanced at the other screens. Three other chambers were occupied. Two remained empty. Within the occupied chambers, she witnessed other similarly shocking sights. Humans originally locked inside those chambers now resembled hybrids of other creatures. One stared at a sealed door leading to the corridor outside the containment chamber. It possessed a contorted face. The creature clenched its teeth together and its shoulders bobbed up and down as it panted. Melody saw traces of what resembled Rubrum bio armor growing out of one arm and the length of the neck.

"Barber would not sign off on an experiment of this nature," she told herself.

For all his faults, Melody refused to believe Barber would do something so dangerous and unethical. Bio armor was not designed to fuse with the body it protected. They grew it from the same genetic material as the host body, but Rubrum safety protocols dictated removable armor to prevent serious injury or death if it malfunctioned.

Still, Barber clearly ignored this protocol with their human captives. She could not deny what appeared on the screen before her eyes.

New movement near one of the empty chambers drew Melody's attention. Two guards marched a human child down the corridor. Melody studied the new prisoner. It resembled a young human girl. Tears stained both cheeks. Dirt covered her skin and tattered clothing. Both arms bore gashes and burns. One guard opened the chamber door. The other guard shoved the captive girl inside.

A third guard followed behind the others. This guard carried a small four-legged animal in his arms. Melody squinted and leaned forward. Orange colored fur covered the animal's entire body. It possessed a long tail and small pointed ears. Whiskers protruded from both sides of its face.

The animal growled and hissed while struggling with the guard. It bared sharp fangs and tried to bite the guard's arm. That attempted bite quickly earned a slap in the head.

Melody gasped.

The small animal reminded her of Oarc.

Some key differences existed between the two animals. Her treema was three times the size of this little animal. Oarc also had much longer arms and legs designed for climbing. Still, the tail and facial structure bore some pointed similarities.

If this animal indeed came from a similar species to a treema, then it posed no threat to their people.

Neither did the child.

Melody shut off the display screen and pinched her eyes shut. Her head pounded as images of the girl and small furry animal wormed their way inside her eyes and refused to depart again. She could not bear to watch whatever they planned to do next. Barber had resorted to doing unethical experiments, and one fact became obvious.

New leadership needed to take control of the research cell before it grew too late. It fell upon Melody to provide that leadership.

PAIGE'S EYES POPPED open. She sat up in her bed with a sudden jolt.

A horrific scream.

It sounded like the scream came from the basement where Todd confined the alien.

She charged down the hall in her bare feet. Paige reached the basement door at the same time as Jason. They exchanged worried glances. Jason bolted forward and flung it open. Paige grabbed his arm and matched his pace down the stairs.

Sunlight scattered into the basement through a crack between two boards on a window above the alien. It forged a direct path to the chair where the alien was bound. Sunlight struck the alien on the neck. Pale skin had already turned red and now started to blister and crinkle.

Paige darted forward without thinking and pulled the chair out of the sunlight. The alien's screams subsided. Thin lips mashed shut. Eyes locked on her. Paige couldn't tell for sure if the alien's eyes probed her body, but it felt like that's what was happening. She didn't feel a bit comfortable about it, especially since the added light inside the basement revealed those eyes belonged to a male alien.

"Why did you do that?" Jason tugged on her arm and leaned closer to Paige's ear. "You shouldn't get that close. Your brother told us these aliens are dangerous."

Paige turned to him and pointed to the alien.

"He was in pain. The sunlight was burning him. I couldn't let him suffer."

Jason's lips twisted like he had a comeback primed, but he simply answered with a curt nod.

"Why did you show me mercy?"

Paige's eyes darted back to the alien. His low voice, almost like a growl, felt more unsettling to her than Melody's voice from the previous night. She licked her lips and backed up a couple more steps from his chair.

"It felt like the right thing to do."

"I wonder if the other humans with you agree with your feelings."

"Do you really want me to ask them?"

The alien cracked a crooked smile that vanished almost as soon as it emerged. Brevity didn't matter. His smile lingered just long enough to send a chill through Paige's bones. It came off more menacing than happy or relieved.

"Why trap all of us in this Podunk town?" Jason blurted out. His brown eyes grew colder and harder the longer he stared at the captive alien. "What do you get out it?"

The crooked smile returned. It hung on his lips a little longer this time around.

"A new permanent home. In due time."

Paige's eyes widened. A lump formed in her throat. The barrier's purpose became clearer.

"You intend to take over Earth." Her voice trembled a bit as this awful revelation escaped her lips. "You have no intention of sharing this planet."

"Why should we? You are an inferior species. Our needs outweigh your needs."

Jason started forward with the intention of pushing the chair back into the sunlight's path. Paige caught his arm and held him back. She shook her head. It would do them no good to become a murderer like this alien and his kind.

They needed a solution, not revenge.

Paige stabbed her finger at him.

"You're not getting away with this," she said. "I'll see to it that we find a way out of here and then put an end to your fucking invasion plan."

She wheeled around and stormed up the stairs. Jason smiled, flipped the alien off, and followed on Paige's heels.

They reached the midway point when Paige noticed Todd standing at the top of the stairs with his arms folded. A splint poked out from under a sleeve on one arm. Paige wondered why she did not catch that detail during their reunion last night.

Todd frowned.

"Now you see what we're up against."

Jason nodded.

"Yeah, that alien's a definite ray of sunshine."

Her brother's expression didn't budge an inch at Jason's ill-timed joke.

"Do me a favor and just stay the hell away from that thing."

Paige's eyes drifted down to his arm again as Todd closed the basement door behind them.

"What's with the splint?"

"It's a long story."

"None of us are going anywhere."

Todd tugged on his shirt sleeve, so the cuff covered up the end of the splint again.

"Just a dislocation. It will heal."

Paige's eyes narrowed.

"Just a dislocation? You make it sound like this is something you do all the time."

"I've endured much worse."

He abruptly turned away and walked into the living room. Paige threw up her hands and unleashed a deep sigh. Why did Todd always have to be so evasive about everything? He couldn't blame it on serving in Afghanistan either. Paige remembered him acting the same way when they were growing up. Todd always approached conversations like he had been entrusted with guarding top-secret information whenever they talked.

It never stopped being annoying as hell.

She flopped down on the small sofa next to Jason. Paige made a point of snuggling up extra close to him when Todd glanced over in her direction. Her brother rolled his eyes and turned away. A small grin crept onto Paige's face. Seeing her public displays of affection always grossed him out – or so Todd claimed anyway. Ever since that time where he caught Paige making out with her high school boyfriend by the backyard garden. If Todd had only known what they did when he wasn't around to spy on her.

Heather and Rich finally sauntered into the living room. Rich squinted and stretched his arms behind his head. Heather pressed her hand against her mouth to stifle a yawn. They sat on the larger sofa across from the smaller one. Rich reached down and picked up one of the assorted gadgets strewn across the coffee table.

Paige wondered if Todd confiscated these things from his alien prisoner. They looked unlike any objects she had ever seen.

Rich turned the gadget over and over in his hands. Paige thought it stood out as particularly strange among the odd-looking objects. To her, it resembled a beater from a hand mixer with some obvious key differences. The handle resembled a revolver handle. It appeared almost as thick as the top and possessed a series of embedded buttons that activated and controlled the device. The portion reminding her of a beater featured four narrow metallic cylinders, one on each side. These cylinders originated from the top of the curved handle, folded over, and the ends joined in a central point atop the device. A single column connected the handle to the cylinders. Right in the middle, where column and cylinders met, Paige saw an opening roughly the size of a quarter.

"What is that thing?"

Heather leaned forward and snatched it out of Rich's hands. He instinctively reached out to snatch the gadget back, but she smiled and shook her head. Heather pulled her hand back behind her head to keep the device out of his grasp.

"Careful with that thing." Todd didn't mind barking orders at the college students like a couple of errant soldiers. "It's too dangerous for amateurs to be handling it."

Rich's patented smirk reemerged on his lips.

"Who put you charge?"

Todd walked over and ripped the device out of Heather's hand.

"Common sense," he said. "Someone around here needs it if we want to survive."

"Concocting an escape plan should be our primary concern," Paige said.

Todd wheeled around and faced the small sofa.

"How do you propose we do that, sis? I don't have a clue on how to bring down that barrier and that thing downstairs won't tell me a damn thing."

Paige sensed an extra twinge of hostility in how Todd emphasized the word "thing." This standoff had grown personal simply beyond the alien's unwillingness to cooperate. His cold tone felt unfamiliar to her.

"Don't you think there's some sort of alien headquarters where they can control the barrier?" Heather asked. "They probably have a switch or something like that to turn it on or off."

"Maybe it operates in the cloud," Jason said. "Everyone uses the cloud."

Heather raised an eyebrow and looked at him with a bemused smile.

"Even a bunch of aliens from a distant planet?"

Jason shrugged.

"Sure. Why not?"

Paige pressed her lips together and tried not to snicker. She didn't succeed. A grin broke out and spread across her face. Paige finally laughed, tilted her head up, and kissed Jason on the cheek.

Todd closed his eyes and pinched the bridge of his nose between his fingers.

"I've scouted practically the whole damn town." A sigh punctuated Todd's words. "If it's around here, I don't know where. They're good about hiding themselves during the day and you saw the other night how safe it is to be out after dark."

Paige's mind returned to the chained-up alien in the basement. His skin burned abnormally bad after a brief exposure to a little bit of sunlight.

"They don't seem to react to light very well," she said. "Maybe we could use that to our advantage."

Todd beckoned toward the porch beyond the boarded-up living room windows.

"Why do you think all these lights are hooked up to this house? I scoured for lights throughout this entire town, so I could keep every dangerous thing out there at arm's length."

Heather hopped off the sofa and approached the living room window. She traced her fingers along a tiny crack separating two boards functioning as a covering over the glass. A sliver of sunlight bounced off cracked red polish now barely covering her fingernails.

"Why put up all the boards?" she asked, turning back to the group. "If light hurts these aliens so much, you should do everything you can to flood this place with light."

"I didn't put them there," Todd replied. "This place was already boarded-up when I found it."

"Already boarded-up?" Rich punctuated his question with a sarcastic chuckle. "Did you kick a vampire out of here or something?"

Todd turned and glared at him.

"Don't be ridiculous. There's no such thing as vampires."

Paige pulled away from Jason. She leaned forward and tilted her head at her brother.

"So who was here? Why did you choose this particular house as a personal bunker?"

Todd stared at the same device he confiscated from Heather.

"I looked for a place with a bunch of supplies to keep me going while I tried to figure out how to escape from this town," he said. "This house had what I was looking for. Some doomsday prepper, or a Mormon, must have lived here. No one was still around when I showed up. Don't know what became of them. Don't really care at this point either."

"We've got a bunch of supplies," Paige said. "That's good. At least, we can hold out in this spot for a while until we hatch a workable escape plan."

Todd shook his head.

"Afraid not," he said, glancing at her. "We have five people here now instead of one. We're already running low on some essentials."

"Is there a Walmart around here? Maybe we could stock up on whatever is left over."

"I don't think that's a great idea."

"Why not?"

Paige didn't understand Todd's reluctance to go scavenge for supplies at a local store. If the aliens could not go out into the sunlight without getting severe burns, then this offered a perfect time to gather what they needed for the long haul.

How could they attack them – or even track them for that matter– during the daylight?

Todd did not answer his sister. He turned and peered at the boarded-up window. For a second, Todd blinked back tears threatening to burst forth. Then he drew in a sharp breath and quickly wiped the corners of his eyes.

"Too dangerous," he finally said. "We'll just ration what we've got and go from there."

Paige jumped to her feet.

"I vote we go gather up every single damn thing possible from the local store," she said. "More supplies for us, mean less supplies for them."

"She's got a good point." Jason rose to her defense as quickly as he stood up and wrapped his arm around Paige again. "If we can make things tougher on these aliens, maybe they'll feel more of an urge to let us go."

Todd's unblinking eyes fixed on Paige. His frown deepened. Paige marched up to the front door and grabbed onto the doorknob. She turned back and flashed a tight-lipped smile at her brother.

"I'm going out for supplies," she said. "You're welcome to join me or you can stay right here. Your choice. But I'll be damned if I'm gonna sit around and do nothing."

Todd looked down and away from his sister. He wanted to tell her the true cause of his reluctance to leave the boarded-up house. Sharing the details of his injury with her would be so liberating. Discussing Caroline's fate could feel therapeutic. So many words and emotions were trapped inside, clamoring to get out. Todd wasn't ready to open that mental door. He could not explain to his little sister why he didn't want her making a supply run.

"That's what I thought," Paige finally said, breaking the brief silence. "You just want to be in charge. I'm not a soldier under your command. Keep that in mind the next time you feel the urge to bark out orders."

The other three followed her lead and joined Paige at the door. She flung it open, letting sunlight spill into the room.

"You'll thank us later after we return with a bunch of supplies."

Todd didn't look up or respond to Paige's final declaration. He wanted to chase after her, but already felt the light weakening him. Todd could only pray her stubbornness didn't lead to a worse situation for Paige and her friends than what he already faced.

PAIGE SENSED SOMETHING amiss with her brother. She had no firm answers on exactly what thoughts dominated his mind, but Todd's body language revealed enough to arouse her suspicions that a deep trauma burdened him.

He still shared no specific details on what happened to Caroline. Todd also looked weathered and battered when Paige reunited with him. His disheveled hair, crow's feet, and stubble covered face spoke volumes concerning the hell he endured. Much more was going on below the surface than her brother showed a willingness to reveal.

Paige resolved to get to the bottom of it.

For now, her primary concern involved executing a successful supply raid. Paige gave little thought to whether aliens guarded strategic buildings or put them behind a barrier like the one hemming in the town on all sides. She just wanted to take some sort of action. Paige prided herself on being a woman who made her own choices and took control of her own fate. Her parents did not agree with many of those choices, but they had to learn to let go of the handlebars and let her steer the bicycle on her own.

Paige mostly tuned out chatter from her friends as she surveyed both sides of the main road. With a small town like Travis, if they were going to track down a store, canvassing the main road offered the best bet for finding one. She should have waited long enough to ask Todd where she could find the local supermarket. It was too late now. Paige wasn't about to turn around and go back to ask for directions. It would only give her brother a second chance to argue her down until she finally gave in and stayed inside the boarded-up house.

The entire street gave off an eerie vibe. Conditions mirrored what they experienced a day earlier. No cars were parked along the sidewalk on either side. No breeze swayed branches or budding leaves in the trees. No random dogs barked, or cats meowed, or birds chirped. Every building they encountered had blinds or curtains drawn behind the windows. Paige never visited an actual ghost town before, but she imagined this is how those places looked and felt to a new visitor.

"What's on your mind?"

Jason slipped his hand into her hand. She clasped it tight. Her eyes blinked more rapidly. Paige didn't look at him because she couldn't stop herself from glancing all over the place.

"This whole town is too quiet. Everything feels dead around here."

"It's creeping me out too."

Paige finally glanced over at Jason. He rubbed his cheek as his eyes also darted all over the place. This unnatural calm felt almost as bad as what the group experienced before Randall's death. No one needed or wanted a reminder on how that eventually turned out.

"I vote we load up on supplies and keep going until we find an alien we can reason with," Rich said. "Maybe we can talk them into letting us go."

Paige gnawed on her lower lip and exchanged a worried glance with Jason. Rich did not interact with the alien prisoner that morning. He didn't grasp how combative and uncooperative that alien acted, even after Paige rescued him from the sunlight. As much as she wanted to believe Rich's suggestion had merit, what they experienced with the aliens so far told her any attempted negotiation would not play out in their favor.

Jason put Paige's thoughts into words.

"I don't think they can be reasoned with. That alien in the basement stared at us and talked to us like we were insects."

"They can't all be that bad, can they?"

"Are you willing to take that chance?"

Rich lowered his head.

"No. I guess not. I just wish we could do more than what we're doing. I feel helpless."

"So do I," Jason replied. "We all do. We're just gonna have to be resourceful and come up with a way to outsmart these bastards."

The group continued past the town square and turned down a horizontal street joining the main road in front of the square. They followed this new street for another mile or so before finally catching a glimpse of what they hoped to see.

"About damn time," Heather said. "I was starting to wonder if this worthless town had a supermarket."

The supermarket appeared much smaller on the outside than the one Paige usually shopped at a few blocks away from the McNeese State campus. Abandoned carts were stacked in or around various cart returns in the parking lot. It wasn't the only thing out of the ordinary. Cars and trucks varying in shape and size dotted the parking lot from one end to the other. Most vehicles displayed Texas license plates, but a few came from other states. Some vehicles were totaled in similar fashion to the semi they wrecked a day earlier. Broken glass. Shredded tires. Missing headlights.

It resembled a makeshift junkyard.

"This explains why we haven't seen vehicles on the streets," Jason said. He shielded his eyes from the sunlight with his hand as they darted around the parking lot. "It looks like every car or truck in town has been towed here."

"Why would the aliens do that?" Heather's expression matched her confused tone. "It doesn't make any sense."

A few ideas burrowed into Paige's head. Maybe the aliens deliberately disabled all these vehicles to prevent escape if the barrier failed. Perhaps they tried to cover their tracks after taking over the town. She didn't vocalize any of her thoughts to the others because Paige didn't think they would make any sense aloud.

"Beats me," she finally said. "At least now we know where to find a vehicle when we finally make our escape."

"Yeah, if any of these junkers still work."

Paige glanced at Jason and smiled.

"We can always fix one up."

Rich laughed.

"Definitely. Just like our car back on I-40."

Her smile morphed into a frown. Paige stopped and wheeled around to face him. Rich grinned at her and shook his head.

"I know. I know. Piss off, Rich!"

His words, delivered in a mocking tone, stole a favorite retort resting on the tip of Paige's tongue.

When the group reached the automatic door at the front entrance, the glass door did not slide open. The motion sensor had been deactivated. Heather popped forward and tugged at the door. She could not pull it toward her.

Heather turned and glanced back at the others.

"It's locked. Any ideas?"

"We gotta find something to break the glass," Jason said. "Look around for a heavy object."

Paige and Heather wandered over to a narrow island separating two rows of parking spots. Trees lined the island from end to end. Medium-sized round stones surrounded each tree. The two girls snatched up as many decorative stones as they could carry and returned to the entrance. Jason and Rich joined them pushing a row of shopping carts. Paige and Heather deposited the stones on the asphalt.

"Who's up for a little pitching practice?" Paige asked. She reached down and grabbed a stone again.

Jason grinned and picked up a stone. Heather and Rich followed suit. They stood a few feet apart from one another and wound up their arms.

"Aim for the same spot if you can," Heather said. "It should make it easier to get some major cracks in that glass."

They all released their stones at the same time. The door vibrated from top to bottom as rock impacted glass. A massive vertical crack formed near the center of the door. Smaller horizontal cracks spread out like a series of veins originating from the point of impact.

The foursome picked up more stones from the pile and tossed them at the door a second time. A third wave of stones followed. Then a fourth wave. All aimed in the same area. The cracks deepened and spread in the glass.

"Let's see if we can break through the door now," Jason said.

Jason and Rich each grabbed an end of a shopping cart and hoisted it off the ground. They lifted it up and tossed it forward with as much force as they could muster. The cart slammed against the glass. Shards popped out and fell to the cement at a couple of different points of impact. They retrieved the cart from where it crashed in front of the door, backed up, and tossed it against the glass a second time with similar results.

Rich wiped sweat droplets from his brow.

"This is harder than I expected. The movies make it look so easy to break through glass."

"Try ramming the whole row into the glass," Heather said.

Rich and Jason both glanced at the rest of the carts and then at each other. Identical smiles appeared on their faces.

They both lined up the shopping carts in a straight line just a short distance from the door. Jason and Rich each wrapped their hands around the handle belonging to the closest cart. Both boys leaned forward.

"On three."

Jason began the countdown. Rich took a deep breath and gritted his teeth.

"One."

"Two."

"THREE!"

Jason and Rich gave a simultaneous hard push forward. The row of shopping carts popped up onto the cement and the first one slammed straight into the glass. This time, Paige heard a large crack. Glass popped out around the point of impact. Shards rained down on top of the carts near the front. Small holes formed in a couple of spots.

Paige glanced back at Jason and Rich. Both boys rested against the end cart.

"Ram it again!"

They did as she ordered and gave another push. More glass cracked. Heather and Paige joined them and pushed from the sides. All four grunted. Every muscle tightened in Paige's arms and shoulders as she gave a forward thrust. Her feet started to slide on the asphalt.

At last, a welcome noise they all wanted to hear greeted her ears. A huge crash.

The glass door now had a gaping hole near the middle. A shopping cart on the front end dislodged a substantial chunk of glass. The cart itself became lodged halfway inside the newly created opening.

Paige turned to the others. A relieved smile finally burst across her face.

"Things are looking up. Let's hope there's still some useful supplies left in there."

Jason and Rich pulled the row of shopping carts back one final time. The front-end cart disconnected from the rest. It stayed lodged inside the door frame. Heather ran forward and yanked on the handle until the cart finally popped loose. She pulled it from the broken glass and pushed it off to the side. Her actions sent another cascade of fragments down to the ground. Heather kicked at glass around the hole and knocked more shards loose. Paige wanted to join her, but worried glass would cut her exposed legs to ribbons if she slipped.

Once she created enough space to fit around her slender frame, Heather crouched down and pulled herself through the hole. She stood, turned, and quickly unlocked the door from the other side.

"Grab some carts," Heather said, pushing the door open. "Let's get this shopping trip underway."

All four latched onto individual shopping carts and pushed them inside the supermarket. A shudder raced through Paige from head to toe when she reached the cash registers. Laying eyes on the aisles induced flashbacks to the convenience store from a day earlier.

Each aisle presented a chaotic mess. Boxes and cans strewn up and down the linoleum floor. End of aisle displays knocked over and scattered. No lights turned on in any part of the store. Some fixtures were completely busted. Others still held lights, but no longer worked. Cracked and broken glass peppered virtually every single door on the visible freezer cases.

"I'm getting a bad feeling about this place, y'all." The lilt in Paige's voice matched her trembling elsewhere. "Maybe coming here isn't such a good idea after all."

"I don't know if we have a choice," Heather said. "We need supplies and, honestly, no part of this town qualifies as safe under the circumstances."

"Let's each take an aisle and get only the most important things," Jason said. "We should fill up as many carts as we can push back to the house. It may take multiple trips, but it will be worth it."

Rich's face fell at the suggestion of pushing multiple fully loaded shopping carts back to their hiding place. Paige could tell he wasn't in a hurry to exceed his exercise quota for the day.

"Better yet, we could load up a truck out there and see if we can get it running," Rich suggested. "It beats the hell out of pushing around a shopping cart for a mile or two."

Jason stopped in his tracks. He folded his arms and looked at Rich with unblinking eyes.

"What? It's a good idea."

"Do you have a key to any of those vehicles?"

"We could hot-wire one."

"Do you know how to hot-wire a car?"

"Um … I think so."

Rich hesitated with his answer. Paige suspected he didn't know the first thing about it, but Rich wasn't about to admit that fact to Jason.

Jason turned away and slapped his hand down on the shopping cart handle again.

"Tell you what, if you can find a truck in one piece and hot-wire it, we'll act on your suggestion."

"Piss off, Jason."

Rich turned and stormed down the nearest aisle with cart in hand. A crooked smile crossed Paige's lips as she witnessed the argument. The tone in Rich's voice didn't suggest it, but she figured he got a little satisfaction from turning Jason's favorite comeback against him.

Paige chose an aisle with a hanging sign listing various household supplies. Cleaning products, detergents, paper towels, toilet paper, and other related items. Disappointment crept over her. Bare shelves peppered most of the aisle. It appeared the place had been cleaned out at some point in the not-too-distant past. Containers for many items were broken and their contents had spilled out. Those chemical puddles had long since evaporated. Discolored splotches dotted the tile like de facto chalk outlines marking their demise.

Without warning, a can clattered against the floor. Paige almost jumped out of her shoes. She glanced down one end of the aisle. Her eyes darted to the other end with the same speed.

"My bad," Jason called out. "I tried to drop too many things into the cart at once."

Knowing where the unexpected noise came from brought relief. But it also caused a rising irritation within Paige. With all they had endured, even the smallest out-of-place noise made her jittery now. She continued pushing her shopping cart down the aisle and stopped in front of an unopened bulk pack of toilet paper.

Another metallic thud echoed in her ears.

Paige jerked her head up. Her eyes darted around a second time, trying to identify the noise's source.

"Can you stop dropping things? You've got me on edge over here."

"That wasn't me," Jason replied.

Paige licked her lips. Who else made that noise? She tiptoed ahead of the shopping cart and peaked around the shelf at the end of the aisle.

"Rich? Heather? Did y'all drop something or bang into something?"

"Not me."

Rich popped his head out from a couple of aisles to her right.

"I didn't do anything."

Heather's voice conveyed trepidation that matched her elevated volume.

Paige's throat tightened. Tremors started to overtake her hands. She drew in a sharp breath and her fingers wrapped around the front end of the shopping cart.

"I don't think we're alone in here."

Her words came out quieter than Paige intended. She barely managed more than a whisper. But the others still caught everything she said. Silence overtook the group while they tried to trace the source of the new noise.

Paige stood perfectly still and closed her eyes. She tried to slow her breathing. It came in quick shallow bursts, matching the intensity of her heart thumping against her ribs. This was turning into a replay of what happened to them at the convenience store. She just knew it. A monster lurked, hidden away somewhere down an aisle. Paige convinced herself it was a certainty. Where was this unseen creature watching them? Did it crouch down in the shadows, waiting to pounce on them like a cat sizing up a mouse? Did this mean one of them – or all of them – would share in Randall's fate?

Paige tried hard not to let these questions flood her brain, but she couldn't stop herself.

"I can see you. You better come out here."

Her eyes popped open again.

Paige wheeled around to her left. Heather stood in front of an aisle near the middle of the store. She fiddled with a lock of hair and her mouth hung open. A few seconds later, an unfamiliar man emerged from the aisle. Jason followed right behind him, twisting one of the man's arms behind his back. He forced him to drop to his knees before Heather.

"I'll make this simple." Jason leaned over the man's shoulder while pressing the subdued arm against his spine. "You tell us who the hell you are and what the hell you're doing here."

"You're one of them."

"Do I look like one of them?"

The unfamiliar man cast his eyes to the ground. He refused to glance at Jason or at Heather. She took a few steps forward and stuck her fingers underneath his chin, lifting it up.

"Do any of us look like one of them?"

"Please don't hurt me."

"We're not here to hurt you –"

"Maybe we will hurt you."

Paige tried to project boldness and toughness in her voice as she interrupted Heather. The tremors gripping her hands made her feel like she wasn't totally succeeding. Paige drew closer to the stranger. She kept her eyes trained on him the entire time.

"How do we know you're a friend and not an enemy?" she asked. "Why are you here alone in an otherwise abandoned supermarket?"

He raised his free arm in front of his face, using it as a fleshy shield.

"I'm a traveler who got stranded here. My name is Andrew. I'm from Amarillo. Please let me go!"

Paige studied his face for a moment. Andrew's eyes bugged out and bounced from person to person. His chin trembled and short rapid breaths escaped his lips. She responded with a slight scowl and glanced over at Jason. He shrugged.

Paige leaned in closer, forcing Andrew to focus on her alone.

"Can we trust you? If we let you go, will you promise to help us?"

Andrew answered with vigorous nods.

Jason finally relaxed his grip on Andrew's arm. Andrew wrenched it free. He rubbed the limb for a moment and stared at Paige and Jason. Anger instead of fear now flickered in his eyes, then melted away as he took a deep breath. Andrew finally rose to his feet and gazed at his surroundings.

"It's a nightmare being hunted like an animal," he said. "I can't tell you how many hours I spent inside this store, just hoping and praying they wouldn't find me."

Paige gave him a sympathetic nod.

"We're going to find a way to put an end to this nightmare."

ANDREW IMMEDIATELY JOINED efforts to load shopping carts with food, water, toiletries, and other essential supplies. Still, his presence added to an unsettling feeling enveloping Paige like fog before a rainstorm. Andrew barely said a word and, whenever Paige glimpsed at him, his eyes were darting all over the place. She started wondering if his earlier horrifying encounter with aliens left him mentally unhinged.

"A new traveler has joined us in our quest to battle alien invaders. What strategies can Andrew share in aiding our fight against them? What secrets can we learn now that he has joined us?"

Paige cracked a smile at Rich going into narrator mode. She glanced up and peeked around the shelf. He pushed a full shopping cart with one hand while holding out his smartphone with the other hand. The battery must be hovering near zero by now. They left so many things behind with the car on the side of I-40 – including phone chargers. Rich had no possible way of posting to his channel with no signal inside the town. Paige didn't begrudge him shooting videos anyway. They had to find small ways to keep their sanity and ease tension amid these circumstances.

Andrew exhibited a wildly different reaction to being on camera. He glanced up from his cart as Rich approached. A scowl crossed his lips. At once, he swung his cart around and rammed it hard into the other cart.

Rich stumbled backward and the phone squirted out of his hand. It clattered against the floor. He glared at him and picked up his phone.

"What the hell, dude? You got a problem?"

"Don't record me with that thing."

Rich examined his phone. A couple of new minor scratches covered the phone where it struck the floor. Fortunately, the screen protector absorbed most of the impact. He glared at Andrew.

Rich stabbed an index finger at him.

"If you break my phone, you're buying me a new one. So chill or it's gonna cost you."

"We'll see about that."

Andrew let go of the cart and approached Rich. He suddenly lunged forward and took a hard swipe at the smartphone. Rich pulled it away and held the device behind his head. They were only a step or two away from an all-out fistfight. Paige realized if she didn't step in to put a stop to the escalating confrontation, their temperatures would crank up from simmering to boiling.

"Knock it off!"

She marched up to Andrew, grabbed his shoulder, and yanked him backward with visible force. He spun around to face Paige and crunched his hand into a fist at the same time.

"I've never hit a woman before –"

"You don't wanna start. Take my word for it."

Paige pressed her lips together and narrowed her eyes. She stood as firm as a concrete pillar in front of him, not flinching for a second. Andrew returned her hard stare. Heather and Jason ran over to see the cause behind the commotion. As they approached, he finally relaxed his hand and let it drop to his side. Paige glanced down at it.

"Smart choice," she said, staring back up at him. "Now cool your hot head."

Jason clasped Paige's shoulder. She turned and faced him.

"What's going on over here?" he asked. "I don't think we should be drawing any undue attention to ourselves."

Paige pointed at Andrew behind her.

"New guy here decided to try and break Rich's phone because he didn't want to be filmed. I told him to chill."

"I have a name, you know," Andrew replied.

Paige didn't even bother to look at him.

"Yeah, I'm sure you do. And I don't really care what it is at the moment."

Jason smiled and brushed his fingers through a lock of her hair. It produced the calming effect he intended. Paige's frown dissolved. She took his hand in hers and brought it down to her lips. Paige planted a gentle kiss on his knuckles.

Jason turned and glared at Andrew.

"Why fly off the handle like that? Rich's videos are harmless fun."

Andrew cast his eyes down at the ground again and kicked at a front wheel on his shopping cart.

"After what I've been through, nothing in this place seems like harmless fun."

"What happened in here?" Jason's tone softened a bit. "It's obvious there was some kind of struggle."

"I came into town after it all went down. People here panicked." Andrew waved his hand to indicate people inside the store itself. "Some loaded up what they could grab and fled for their lives. They didn't even stop to pay."

"Why did you stay?"

Jason's question was the same one Paige thought to ask. If he had a chance to flee from this place, why not take it?

"Where could we go? They cut off all the roads out of town."

Paige and the others exchanged knowing glances with one another and nodded. They understood more than they ever wanted to understand about the predicament he faced.

"Those of us who remained behind locked the doors and prepared ourselves for a fight or a siege," Andrew said. "We had plenty of food and water on hand. So we figured we could wait them out, until the police or the military discovered what was happening and came in to rescue us."

Heather glanced sideways at Paige, Jason, and Rich. Paige noted her skeptical frown.

"Why hasn't the military shown up?" Heather asked, facing Andrew again. "It seems like they would be all over something like this by now."

"I don't think they realize what's going on," he said. "Everything happened so fast. We didn't last a whole week before the invaders penetrated this supermarket."

Andrew swallowed with difficulty and slammed his eyes shut. He panted for a minute as though his memories were growing too painful to share.

"We were betrayed," he finally said. "Our efforts to contact the outside world proved futile. We sent out a small group to scout and discover if help was on the way. Only a few returned around sunset the next day and they came back changed."

"Changed?" Jason repeated the last word with rising concern in his voice. "Changed how?"

"They had been branded. These people were all now acolytes of these invaders. And they turned against us."

Paige's heart started thumping harder again. She took a deep calming breath, trying to soothe her fraying nerves.

"What … did they do ... to you?"

Hesitation permeated Paige's question. She wasn't certain she wanted to know the actual answer. The thought of human traitors helping aliens both frightened and disgusted her. As painful as it was to hear, though, they needed to know exactly what they were up against.

"They let the invaders in through the back entrance. Everything that followed was awful."

Paige's mouth gaped open as Andrew detailed a turbulent battle he witnessed between aliens and humans inside the supermarket. Screams. Blasts from energy weapons. Explosions. Merchandise scattering everywhere. Bloodied bodies smashing against the floor. His words painted a vivid and nightmarish picture within Paige's mind as he recounted each harrowing moment of that ordeal.

Andrew opened his eyes and turned his head toward the back of the store.

"When all seemed lost, I crept away and hid inside a stock room. I arranged several boxes into a makeshift barrier, so they couldn't see me."

Rich gave him a sideways glance.

"No one came looking for you?"

Andrew snapped his head around to stare down Rich a second time.

"Of course, they looked for me!" he said. "I hid myself well. I don't know how many hours I stayed in that same spot, praying they wouldn't see me. When it felt safe to come out again, daylight had returned, and I found out I was the only one left in here."

Paige looked at him with unblinking eyes.

"How long have you been in here?"

Andrew shrugged and glanced down at the floor.

"I honestly don't know. I lost my phone, and I don't have a watch. The invaders cut the power long ago. I've been too afraid to leave."

"You can leave now," Heather replied. "We'll take you with us."

"Take me where?"

Andrew raised his eyebrows and his lips curled into a frown. He tugged at a cuff on his long-sleeved shirt.

"We've got a safer place than here," she said.

Paige walked over to Heather and tugged on the sleeve of her blouse. She motioned her to draw closer with her index finger. The two girls withdrew a few steps from the others.

"What is it?"

Heather leaned in closer to Paige and shaded her lips with her hand.

"I don't trust him." Paige's voice also dropped to a whisper. "His story doesn't add up to me."

"What do you mean it doesn't add up?"

"Why didn't the aliens come back to search for survivors? If they went to all the trouble of invading this store, it seems like they'd also take whatever time they needed to wrap up loose ends."

Heather pulled back and shot her a sideways glance. She frowned and shook her head.

"Your brother isn't the only one equipped with survival skills, Paige."

"I know that."

"Do you? We aren't exactly screening job applications here. We need all the help we can get."

Paige hung her head, sighed, and answered with a slight nod. As much as she hated to admit it, their small group needed whoever they could recruit to make putting their escape plan into action easier. Even if some additions rubbed her the wrong way.

Jason snapped his head toward girls.

"What are you two saying?"

"Nothing," Paige said.

She raised her head again and stared at Andrew. Jason looked at him, then back at her. His eyes filled with worry when he saw that same emotion rested within her own.

"It's gonna be fine," he said. "Let's just get these supplies out of here and meet up with your brother again. We'll get everything figured out and be out of this town before we know it."

Jason rubbed his arm as he said these words. His tone sounded hesitant as though he didn't quite believe what he was saying. To Paige, those words felt manufactured for the sole purpose of reassuring her. She wanted his words to accomplish that purpose. Paige yearned to believe things would not grow worse. Accepting such a notion grew more and more difficult after considering all they had endured up to this point.

Paige kept her eyes locked on Andrew as each member of the group pushed a full shopping cart out of the store. Jason tried his hand at hot wiring an SUV in the parking lot. It appeared to be in working condition from the outside. No smashed-up body or missing parts like many of the other cars and trucks. Getting the engine to start, however, ended up being easier said than done.

After hearing nothing but clicking sounds for the fourth time, Jason pulled his hands out from under the steering wheel and threw them up in frustration.

"Damn it!" His cheeks reddened and his eyes narrowed as his voice grew louder. "I thought for sure it would turn over that time."

Paige frowned. Jason's tinkering with wires didn't produce a peep from the engine. They checked the battery, starter motor, and alternator. Nothing appeared broken or out of place. It didn't matter. The vehicle refused to start. Those aliens found a way to disable every single vehicle in this parking lot.

Heather glanced ruefully at the SUV and then down at the cart before her.

"I guess this means we'll have to push these shopping carts all the way back," she said. "I hoped for a different outcome, but we don't seem to have other options."

"At least we know where all the vehicles are kept now," Paige replied. "We can come back here later and work on getting a few running."

She cast her eyes skyward. Clouds partially hid the sun, but it still hung high in the sky. Quite a bit of daylight remained, but it wouldn't be wise to press their luck. Getting these supplies back to the house and reuniting with Todd took priority over fiddling with other vehicles in the parking lot.

Paige glanced back at the rest of the group.

"We better go," she said. "We've still got a ton of prep work ahead to get us through the night."

They lost one shopping cart before even making it out of the parking lot. Both front wheels on Rich's cart locked in place when he reached the edge of the lot. Rich kicked the wheels and pushed on the handle, but the cart refused to budge.

Heather crouched down and peered at the front wheels. She poked at one with her index finger.

"What in the hell happened to this sorry excuse for a shopping cart? This isn't a car that ran out of gas or blew a tire."

Jason tried to push on the handle after Rich stepped away from the cart and got the same result.

"Must be an anti-theft device kicking in," he said. "I've heard about them. The front wheels lock up a certain distance from a store to keep people from stealing carts."

Heather shot a frustrated look at him.

"That's perfect. How are we supposed to get supplies out of this place?"

"The old-fashioned way," Jason said.

He walked over to the front of his own cart and dug his fingers under the top row of metallic wires forming the body of the cart. Heather frowned and joined him on the other side. She latched onto the handle, and they lifted the cart off the ground. Jason and Heather carried it a short distance and set it down on the sidewalk.

Rich ran back toward the supermarket and returned a minute later with an empty shopping cart. Paige helped him unload his disabled cart while the others lifted and carried the remaining carts over to the sidewalk. Finally, Rich and Paige snatched up the newly loaded cart and set it down next to the others.

"Let's see if we can avoid any more surprises for the rest of the day."

Paige didn't blame Jason for sounding cross. Getting supplies also drained her patience and energy. Pushing a shopping cart brimming with whatever Paige could shove inside presented a larger chore than she anticipated. Sweat dripped from her brow and muscles tightened throughout her shoulders and arms as she pushed it forward. The cart's misaligned front wheels didn't help. It caused the cart to pull to her left instead of traveling in a straight line.

Metallic clanging from the baskets as they rolled along broke up the usual eerie silence permeating Travis. Nobody engaged in extended chatter during the long walk. All five put their focus into getting the carts to their destination. When the group finally reached the front door of their makeshift bunker, only one thought permeated Paige's mind. She wanted to collapse on the long sofa and settle in for an afternoon nap.

Paige flung the door wide open.

"We're back. And we come bearing gifts."

Her voice reverberated through the living room. She cracked a weary smile as her brother emerged from a back bedroom. It melted into a worried frown as soon as Paige noticed his pained expression.

Todd clenched his teeth as he tried to disguise a limp. A large damp spot showed on his jeans on the affected leg – around the mid-calf area. Her eyes darted from the leg up to her brother's face.

"What's wrong?"

He drew in a sharp breath and blinked slowly. The pain seeping onto his face retreated below the surface again a few seconds later.

"It's nothing I can't handle."

"Did something happen to your leg?"

"I'm fine, Paige."

"You don't look like you're fine."

His eyes narrowed and an annoyed frown deepened on his lips.

"I'm fine. Let it go, okay?"

Paige scowled and rubbed her hand down the bridge of her nose. She threw up her hands.

"Whatever. I don't want to deal with this right now. How about opening the garage door, so we can put away the supplies?"

Paige marched back through the front door. She crossed the front yard as Todd raised the garage door. The entire door made a rickety sound as it lifted off the cement pad. Jason, Heather, Rich, and Andrew stood on the other side, resting on the handles of their shopping carts.

Todd's brows pulled together, and his eyes melded into a steely glare upon seeing Andrew. He ducked back inside the kitchen door. A few seconds later, Todd reemerged toting a shotgun. He cocked the gun and raised it to his shoulder.

"Who the hell are you?"

Andrew shrank back from the cart and raised his arms. Paige gasped. She sprinted across the lawn and planted herself in front of him and his cart.

"What are you doing? He's here to help us."

Todd squinted at her. He quickly shifted the barrel a few degrees to the right to aim around his sister. Paige mimicked the barrel movement and shook her head.

"I'm not letting you shoot him."

"You're making a big mistake. We can't go around trusting every random person who pops up in this town.

Jason sidled over next to Paige. He folded his arms and stared at Todd.

"He's not an alien," Jason said. "Any human survivor who wants to join with us and help us escape is welcome as far as I'm concerned."

Todd bit down on his lower lip. Unblinking eyes stayed locked on Andrew. No one dared to move an inch. Finally, Todd lowered the gun and let the stock rest against the cement.

He stabbed an index finger at Andrew.

"Fine. I still want eyes on him. Trust is earned."

Jason glanced over his shoulder and waved Heather, Rich, and Andrew forward. They pushed their carts into the garage. Paige and Jason dropped back and grabbed the others. Once everything was inside, Todd lowered the garage door again.

"Who else is starving? Raiding an abandoned supermarket works up your appetite."

Rich snatched up a can of chili and a box of crackers from his cart. Multiple nodding heads greeted his question. The rumble in her stomach made Paige feel like she hadn't eaten in several days. She started up the stairs behind her brother and her friends. At once, an object clanked against the cement floor. Paige turned back and spotted Andrew stooping down to retrieve something from under one of the carts.

"You joining us for lunch?"

Paige didn't look at Andrew when she posed the question. She tried to catch a glimpse of whatever he was searching for under the cart. His eyes darted from the cart to her. He pulled back his hand and stuffed it in his pocket.

"You bet. I'm really hungry. Haven't had a good meal in a while. Hard to cook anything in a supermarket, you know?"

Paige lowered her eyebrows and gave him a sideways glance. She stepped aside and motioned for him to go through the door.

"After you."

Andrew shuffled past her while keeping his hands shoved in his pockets. It seemed like he was hiding something in there, but Paige lacked the energy to stop him and go into interrogation mode. Maybe taking her brother's advice and watching Andrew closely should be her plan going forward.

TODD SENSED PAIGE didn't trust the newest addition to their group either. Observing the way that she looked at Andrew in the kitchen told him as much. It only made her defiance feel even more perplexing. Her inability to see the danger posed by bringing an outsider into their sanctuary drove him crazy. Paige should have outgrown her stubbornness by now. It wasn't a helpful trait in their current situation.

"We can't make him a prisoner!" She said, jumping up from her chair and throwing her arms out. "He hasn't done anything to us."

Todd glanced behind his shoulder and pushed the door closed.

"Can you keep your voice down? I want this private discussion to remain private."

Todd rarely took his eyes off Andrew while the group ate lunch. His face stayed glued to his food most of the time and he made little eye contact with anyone else. Todd's efforts to pry more information out of the newcomer went nowhere. Andrew found a way to deflect his questions with one vague response after another. Eventually, Paige and her friends told him to knock off the interrogation.

Todd acquiesced and kept silent through the rest of the meal. He still couldn't shake the feeling that things didn't add up with this newcomer. That's why Todd removed all the alien gadgets from the living room as soon as Andrew arrived on the scene. For the same reason, he drew Paige to the other room where they could talk one-on-one. He needed to help her understand the possible danger that Andrew presented. But his warnings did not seem to be getting through to her like he hoped.

"It isn't easy to tell an enemy apart from a friend," he said. "I learned that the hard way in Kandahar."

Todd walked over to his sister and placed a hand on her shoulder. Paige answered him with an unblinking stare.

"Look around," she said. "We're not battling terrorists or insurgents here. This isn't a war zone."

"That's exactly what this is." Todd's voice grew firmer and more forceful. "We are fighting for our survival here. These aliens have seen to that."

"He's not an alien."

"Battle lines and sides aren't always clearly drawn. If you'd experienced what I've experienced, I think you'd understand why I feel the way I do."

Images barged into Todd's mind. A crowded street bustled with cars. Tall modern apartment buildings lined either side of the street. A checkpoint loomed ahead. Two Afghan soldiers stood guard in the middle of the road, stopping cars, and talking to drivers as they approached the checkpoint.

It seemed no different from any ordinary Kandahar afternoon. That all changed in a hurry.

Todd didn't see which direction the suicide bomber came from. He felt the blast wave. A huge ball of flame ripped through the second truck in the convoy. Smoke billowed upward. Shards of glass and metal flew everywhere.

The truck had become a charred heap of twisted metal.

Screams.

They poured in from all directions. Terrified civilians. Dying soldiers. Pelting his ears like a shower of hail.

He burst out of the third truck in the convoy and crouched down while scrambling across the ground toward the burning vehicle immediately ahead. Todd panted. His eyes darted in all directions. One bomb had gone off. He couldn't be certain that was the last one waiting to explode.

"This is all foreign to me. I'll admit it. But don't treat me like a dumb kid."

Paige's words jerked his mind from Kandahar back to Texas. Todd blinked rapidly and drew in a deep breath.

"I don't think you're dumb. I just want to protect you. You're my little sister. If anything happened … God, I wouldn't forgive myself."

Paige's face softened into a half-smile. She sat in the chair again and clasped her brother's hand on her shoulder.

"I'm not a little girl," Paige said, glancing up at him. "I know you love me and worry about me. The feeling goes both ways. But you also need to trust me more often."

Todd pulled his hand away and glanced back at the bedroom door.

"I do trust you. I don't trust Andrew."

"He does seem kind of nervous and shifty, but I think he would have done something to us at the supermarket if he truly was a bad guy."

"What makes you so sure?"

Paige shrugged.

"Just a hunch. More a feeling than anything else."

Todd continued to stare at the door. His eyes locked on it like he saw something more there than the painted oak paneling or copper knob.

"We had an informant we trusted in Kandahar," Todd finally said. "Fed us intelligence on where to sniff out Taliban cells. It all ran smoothly until someone got to him."

"What happened?"

"He led our convoy into a trap. As we neared a checkpoint, a suicide bomber came out of nowhere and attacked the second truck."

Paige's eyes widened and her mouth dropped open a little.

"Two soldiers were killed in the explosion. Two others lost a leg and were sent home."

Tears formed in Todd's eyes as images of their burned and mangled corpses flashed before him.

"I had no idea." Paige's voice dropped to a whisper. "I'm sorry you went through that."

"Surviving made me one of the lucky ones, I guess. Funny thing is, I never felt that lucky."

Todd turned back and faced his sister again. His eyes glistened with tears, and they started to roll down his cheeks.

"This feels like Kandahar all over again. I can't put my finger on it, but something about this Andrew character doesn't track for me."

Paige stood and walked toward the door. She stopped and rested her hand on the dresser top.

"I told Jason to keep an eye on him. I don't know what more we can do. I didn't feel right about leaving him at the supermarket all alone."

"What was he doing there?"

"He told us he got stuck there when the aliens attacked. Hid in a storeroom until they were gone. I think he may have been the only survivor."

Todd rested his hand on his chin. Caroline shared Paige's same sympathetic outlook when they first encountered living residents in the town. Memories of their relieved smiles flashed into his mind.

"We thought we were the only ones left!"

A gray-haired man peeked through a slightly ajar door. Caroline talked Todd into knocking on the door when she saw movement behind the curtains. Todd parked the SUV alongside the curb and approached the house with a lug wrench in hand. He held it over his head, ready to strike like a coiled rattlesnake, as he walked up the front porch steps.

Now seeing the man before them, Todd let himself relax a bit. Dark circles surrounded the man's eyes. His hair, shirt, and pants were all equally disheveled. Todd lowered the lug wrench. The man opened the door wider.

"I don't recognize you," he said. "Are you visitors passing through town?"

Caroline painted on a smile to disguise the worry Todd knew gripped her.

"That's the plan. We got into a bit of a jam trying to leave. We were hoping to find someone who could help us."

The man with bags under his eyes screwed up his face into a deep frown and drooped his head.

"That isn't us. We're the ones who need help."

Todd peered past his shoulder and into the room behind the man. A woman stood a short distance behind him. She had equally disheveled gray hair and a tattered dress to match. Her eyes kept bouncing back and forth between Todd and Caroline. The woman's unrelenting stare started to make Todd feel uncomfortable.

He shifted his gaze back to the man.

"What's your name?"

"Clyde. That's my wife Desiree."

"Maybe we can work together. There's four of us here. We can put our heads together, figure out what's going on around in these parts."

The muscles in Todd's face tightened. His face advertised his concern as he glanced back at Caroline. Her suggestion was well-meant, but he didn't know anything about these people.

"Actually, I think we should –"

"Look around. We don't really have options," Caroline said, cutting him off. "Beggars can't be choosers, honey."

Todd didn't really have an argument that came to mind to counter her suggestion. Clyde motioned for them to come inside.

Each breath from Todd's mouth pushed outward with increasing speed. He hesitated in the doorway and glanced back at his wife again. Caroline urged him forward with an abrupt wave of her hand.

"I shouldn't have gone in."

Todd drifted back to the present where his words were. Paige tilted her head and narrowed her eyes.

"Shouldn't have gone in where?"

"Into that house. That's where things took a turn for the worst."

Paige's breathing quickened.

"What happened?"

Images from those far-off events unfolded in Todd's mind like they happened only a few hours ago. Clyde and Desiree invited them to share a small dinner as evening approached. It wasn't much. Canned soup. It didn't matter in the end.

Both Caroline and Todd devoured the soup like it had been served a signature dish at a five-star restaurant. Neither had a bite to eat since setting foot in Travis. Clyde and Desiree made small talk about life in the small town and peppered Todd and Caroline with various questions. Todd felt reluctant to share any details. Caroline possessed no such inhibitions. She laughed and flashed her trademark smile while sharing one story after another. Being open was just a part of her nature – something Todd loved about her from their first date.

"What do you plan to do?"

Desiree's inquiry as she gathered up empty bowls seemed innocuous enough. Todd wasn't sure what they could do, but he also didn't want to clue the older couple into his growing concern about being stuck in Travis.

"Keep testing the perimeter," Todd finally said. "There's gotta be a weakness in this magnetic field holding us in this place. I just need to find it."

"I think it's escape proof," Clyde replied. "We're meant to stay here, period."

Todd leaned forward and locked eyes with Clyde.

"What happened in this town? We told you what Caroline and I saw at that cafe. Something's going on around here and we need answers."

Clyde fidgeted with his water glass. He looked up at the ceiling.

"I don't know where to start."

"How about at the beginning?"

Todd did not understand why Clyde and Desiree were being evasive. This marked his second attempt to ask about the cafe and the town itself. Both times, the older couple acted like suspects angling to get out of an interrogation room without incriminating themselves. It didn't track for him and made his suspicions about them rise.

Clyde finally made eye contact with Todd again. He stood and cleared his throat.

"It's getting late. We can let you stay here, but we need to lock up before –"

"Before what?"

"Before –"

Clyde let out a gasp. A pained groan followed. He doubled over. One hand clutched the other.

Caroline jumped to her feet.

"Are you okay? What's wrong?"

She ran over to get a better look at him. Clyde lurched forward as Caroline reached out to touch his shoulder. He flung his arm backward.

A menacing growl escaped his lips.

"Don't touch me!"

Clyde whipped his head around and his eyes took on a wild stare. Foam dribbled from the corners of his lips. Hard bone-colored lumps bubbled up under the skin on each side of his chin. The old man raised his hands. Both grew gnarled before their eyes. Other hard knobs formed on the back of each hand.

Desiree screamed.

Todd jerked his head in her direction. She slammed her hand against the wall. The plaster crumbled around her fingers. Massive lumps, mirroring those appearing on Clyde's face and hands, sprang up across her own arms and hands. Her face grew contorted. One by one, her teeth fell onto the floor.

Todd grabbed his wife by the arm and pulled Caroline backward.

"We better get the hell out of here."

Desiree let go of the wall. Both she and Clyde lurched forward. He extended his hand toward Todd and Caroline.

"Stay! Help us!"

A claw like horn burst through the back of each hand. Similar horns escaped Clyde's chin. New jagged teeth emerged in Desiree's mouth. The knobs covering her also began to burst.

Clyde panted and growled. He lunged at Caroline. Todd reached over and snatched a glass off the table. He broke the end of it against the table edge and jabbed the remainder in Clyde's face.

The old man let loose a gruesome scream. He clawed at the glass shards sticking out of his eye and nose. Blood dribbled down the front of his face. It bore a darker shade of red than any blood that Todd had ever seen.

Todd and Caroline bolted for the front door. Desiree dropped down and started galloping on all fours after them. Caroline flung open the door and Todd slammed it behind them before Desiree could reach the doorway. He grabbed a front porch patio chair and shoved it tight under the knob.

Paige's eyes grew as big as saucers while Todd recounted the events that unfolded.

"Did that woman – Desiree, is it? – break through the door?"

"I looked back and saw it cracking and splintering as she rammed her body against it on the other side." Todd shuddered as he answered Paige's question. "Caroline and I lucked out and made it to the car. It taught me quick to not trust any 'people' I found in this town."

"Why did they change like that?"

"I don't really know. All I know is the people still left in this town who I've encountered aren't exactly human any longer."

Todd opened the door and stepped back out into the hall, before turning to look at her one more time.

"We need to keep a close guard on Andrew. He needs to earn my trust. I don't hand it out like free candy bars to trick-or-treaters."

Paige's urge to argue or dispense a snappy comeback vanished. She closed her eyes and simply nodded. Todd turned and ventured out into the garage again. The other four packed away supplies harvested from the supermarket. They had started clearing the last cart when Todd entered the garage. Paige followed a couple of steps behind him.

"Nice of you to show up."

Rich stood and brushed dirt from the cement floor off his pants at the knees. His smirk flashed annoyance rather than the usual smug happiness.

"We all gotta pitch in around here," Todd replied. "My job is to make sure the lights around here keep working when the sun goes down."

"Let me guess: You're the only person in West Texas smart enough to turn on a light switch."

Todd sighed as he opened the garage door. The sun hung low on the horizon. Twilight approached. He marched out to the driveway.

"Cut the sarcasm." Todd glanced back over his shoulder and glared at Rich. "If you want us to find a way out of this place, then you better shut up and listen to me."

Rich snapped a sharp salute.

"Aye, aye. Captain."

Paige matched Todd's glare and pressed a finger to her lips. Rich flashed a smirk and shrugged. He returned his attention to the cart behind him.

Todd rounded the corner of the house and knelt in front of the generator. He checked the propane level. The fuel reservoir remained half full. Making it through the night didn't pose a problem. Keeping the lights going for several days in a row required tracking down more propane. Todd closed his eyes and rested his hand against the generator.

How long could they hold out in this place? How much longer could he stave off the changes trying to overtake his body? Time did not favor them. No fuel meant no lights. He didn't want to think about what came next if they lacked a protective barrier around the house.

Todd stood up again and returned to the garage. Paige closed the door behind him. Todd switched on the generator. Exterior and interior lights around the house sprang to life.

Andrew stared at the circuit box and chewed on a fingernail.

"Do you really think this is enough to stop the invaders?" Concern swam through his eyes. "We couldn't keep them out of the supermarket. There were tons of lights there."

"It works well enough," Todd said. "They hate the light. It does bad things to them."

The group filed back into the kitchen. Andrew brought up the rear. Metal clatter against the floor after Todd passed the refrigerator. He turned and saw Andrew stooping over.

"Don't freak out. I just dropped my keys."

Todd nodded and turned away again.

Andrew's eyes followed him until he disappeared into the living room. Once Todd was gone, Andrew straightened up. He opened his palm and pressed his hand against the refrigerator door.

When Andrew pulled his hand back again, a small oval metallic object remained behind. A tiny dark crystal ball, no larger than a marble, sat in the center. Shiny metal, resembling stainless steel, surrounded the small crystal.

Andrew pinched his lips together and pressed the ball. A small light flickered for a second and then it returned to normal. A triumphant smile crept from one corner of his mouth to the other.

"Let's see how well you're protected now."

MELODY LET HER eyes linger on an image of her and Halilah exploring the Vallia Ravine together. She paid little attention to the console vibrating against her fingers as the image flickered across the screen. It offered one of her few remaining connections to a simpler time. One she yearned to see return.

Oarc loved it whenever they took walks in the ravine. He scurried up and down one black tree after another as they journeyed along the bottom. His energy seemed limitless. Oarc never strayed too far from Melody or Halilah. Every few minutes, he dropped to the ground and bounded over to both sisters. When Melody scooped Oarc up in her arms, he immediately licked her cheek. Halilah always laughed whenever he did it. Feeling the sensation of his bumpy tongue against her skin made Melody squint and grin at the same time. It offered a truly amusing sight. Melody simply rubbed his furry head and snout and let Oarc jump down again, so he could scamper around and climb trees a little longer.

Melody almost felt pebbles crunching beneath her feet and could almost hear the small brook bubbling and churning as it wound through the trees. Melody wondered what the ravine looked like now. She wondered if spring had arrived on that part of Rubrum yet. Did trees and flowers still bloom? Or had her planet settled in for its predicted scorching and permanent summer?

Some days, Melody wondered if her parents were the lucky ones. Their souls found peace while she remained behind to face an onslaught of heartache and horror. Melody missed their light in her life. She missed sweet, beautiful Halilah. She missed Oarc and all his exuberant playfulness.

Melody pressed a small button on the bottom of the simularium console. The image faded away from the screen. She could not think about it now. Many tasks must be done before any reunion with Halilah and Oarc took place.

She took a seat at the workstation on the other end of her room. Melody enlarged two screens monitoring separate chambers containing the human girl and the small furry animal captured one sun cycle earlier. The girl rested on a rectangular platform jutting out from the wall. Her head faced the wall, keeping Melody from seeing the girl's face. The little animal curled into a ball on the floor inside the other chamber. It also concealed its face from Melody's view.

A narrow column of lights flanked either side of each chamber door. Both columns stood separate from the door itself. They resembled miniature towers fixed to the floor. Four square lights were embedded within each column. On the default setting, these lights splashed the chamber with an ethereal red glow. Column settings could be altered to produce brighter and darker light waves across the light spectrum.

Melody studied each chamber as column lights started to brighten. Her eyes darted between the girl and the small furry animal. The girl stirred from her platform and cried out. She sprung to her feet and swung around, finally showing her face on the screen. The girl unleashed a scream mixed with a growl and lunged at a portion of the wall concealing an image recorder.

Melody jumped back in her seat. Her pulse quickened. Her room lay a safe distance from the containment chambers, but that knowledge did not make Melody feel any safer from what the screen revealed to her.

Changes to the girl's bio code were already set in motion. Patches of skin on her face and arms had grown discolored and leathery. Old teeth had fallen out. New jagged teeth took their place. Multiple bony protrusions pushed upward from the underside of her skin. These growths spread down the length of her arms and over her hands. Small spikes already emerged from a pair of ruptured bony growths.

The girl snarled and snapped at the wall. Melody finally turned her head away from the screen. She glanced at the small furry animal inside the other chamber. It stood on its feet now and paced the chamber floor. This animal did not mimic the girl's violent reaction. It simply repeated the same sound over and over.

Meow.

It struck her as a call for help. Melody wanted to do nothing more than fulfill that desperate request. The small animal needed help. Clumps of fur had grown matted or fallen out. One eye had turned cloudy. A front fang lay on the floor only a short distance from the animal.

Melody couldn't look at it without thinking about Oarc. She also couldn't watch the little girl without thinking about her sister back home. What if they were trapped inside these chambers? What if they were the ones subjected to intense bio code treatments?

We crossed a line not meant to be crossed with our research, Melody told herself. *This child and this animal are not a threat to us. What we are doing here is wrong.*

She knew she must reason with Barber and help him see the error of choosing this awful path. Melody switched off the screens and rose from her workstation.

This all had to end.

Melody marched down the corridor to a central laboratory. Barber glanced up at the door as soon as she entered the room. He stood hunched over a platform with another scientist from Nuba – her home city. A sedated human lay bound to the platform. Melody did not recognize him from among previously captured town residents. He must be a traveler from elsewhere, exactly like the four people who escaped from her custody earlier.

"Our efforts to suppress these inert bio code strands are not bearing fruit. Blending our bio code with theirs cannot happen until these side effects are eliminated."

Barber's expression remained stoic as he glanced at the scientist standing across from him. His tone summed up his latent anger and frustration. The other scientist furrowed his brow and concentrated his gaze on the human's closed eyes and lips. He avoided eye contact with Barber.

"We are working hard through each sun cycle to get it done."

Barber's long fingers pried open an eyelid. A blank blue eye stared back at him.

"Double your efforts," he said. "Every wasted hour on this planet means one fewer life saved on Rubrum."

"Maybe the time has arrived to accept failure," Melody said. "We should look for another planet. A better planet."

Barber's eyes zeroed in on her as soon she said those words. Melody could almost feel those black orbs blasting waves of hot anger into her face.

"There is no time!" His voice climbed into a self-righteous growl. "Our people must be saved now. Do you not understand this fact? We have all suffered great loss."

Melody licked her lips and stared at the floor. She couldn't form into words the once-dormant anguish washing over her anew. Did Barber understand the depth of pain she and Halilah endured after losing their parents? Who was he to lecture her on suffering loss?

"I can never get my wife and son back from the radiation blast that enveloped the southern plains," he said. "I must find a way to prevent the remnant of our people on Rubrum from suffering a similar fate."

Melody jammed her hands into her coat pockets. She dug her fingers into her palms. Barber did not need to see her forming fists. It felt good to do it, even if she had to do it away from prying eyes.

"We are chasing clouds," Melody finally said. "It is a foolish error to not consider another option."

A small smile washed across Barber's lips.

"Your own foolish error may soon take a turn in our favor."

Melody's eyes flashed with anger like a flame bursting forth from a candle. She hungered to pop a fist out of her pocket and slam it into Barber's face.

No.

She must show restraint. Her reward would be deeper trouble rather than lasting gratification. Melody closed her eyelids for a moment and opened them again only once the anger subsided.

"What do you mean?"

"See for yourself."

Barber removed his hand from the human's face and crossed the room in a long-legged stride. He turned on a screen at a workstation on the other end of the lab. Images from three different rooms popped up across the screen. Melody raised her eyebrows and drew closer to the workstation.

"A spy has infiltrated the ranks of the resisting humans." His voice took on a triumphant tone as if the battle already ended in their favor. "We have eyes and ears in their sanctuary now."

"What do you plan to do?"

"Whatever needs to be done."

Her eyes narrowed to crinkled slits as a slight frown surfaced on her lips. Barber could act evasive with his plans all he wanted, but Melody discerned his true intentions. He planned to destroy the one called Todd and the four humans she tried to help. Barber saw this little band of humans as a lingering threat to their efforts to adapt to the conditions of this planet and the sun it orbited.

Melody fiddled with a curl of her red hair.

"Will they not uncover the true identity of your spy? Humans on this planet know the difference between one of us and their own kind."

Barber smacked the edge of the workstation with his palm. It made the other scientist jump. Melody's throat tightened, but she kept her legs rooted to the same spot.

"Do you think I'm foolish? Of course, I know that. This is exactly why we did not change the bio code on every human in this place."

"I thought you did not trust them."

"They serve their purpose. I need to lure out all humans that resist our presence here. Those who do not resist will help us find those who do."

Melody snapped her eyes shut again and drew in a sharp breath. Did Barber truly understand the consequences his actions would produce? Billions of humans lived on this planet. Their cell had no ability to withstand the humans' collective wrath once all that had transpired in this place came to light.

"You do not agree with my actions." Barber's voice took on an accusatory tone. "You sympathize with these humans?"

Melody opened her eyes and shook her head.

"No. … I just think the hour for us to consider another path … has arrived."

She tried to hide the hesitation in her voice. Melody did not want Barber to discern her real thoughts and feelings about the situation.

"Such a decision is not yours to make," Barber said. "Our mission is clear. We must find a new home for the people of Rubrum at all costs."

"Is this particular cost worth it?"

Melody's eyes drifted from Barber to the other scientist when she posed this last question. The other scientist raised his arms and shook his head. He refused to meet her gaze and continued staring at the human bound to the platform.

"My thoughts are Barber's thoughts," the other scientist said. "He is our leader. We must value the wisdom that goes into his decisions."

A wry smile crawled across Barber's lips again.

"If only others within this same room thought as you think."

Melody frowned and turned her attention back to the screen broadcasting images from the house with lethal lights. She grew weary of seeing others in their research cell show willingness to accept his decisions without a second thought. Their blind acquiescence dug under her skin with the irritation of a larval cimea, days before it burst forth from the flesh.

"Our path is clear," Barber said. "We will cut off power to the lethal lights from the inside. Then, we will converge on that place when the sun retreats from the sky one sun cycle from now. All survivors will be brought to this place and undergo bio code experimentation."

Melody nodded without turning to look at Barber again. Her eyes remained fixed on the screen in front of her. Wheels turned inside her mind. Barber's single-minded quest to adapt their bio code to conditions on this planet must be brought to an end. He could not be reasoned with, so Melody had to forge a different path.

She turned and walked with deliberate strides to the lab door as Barber continued to talk to the other scientist. When he heard the whoosh of the door opening, Barber's head snapped toward the doorway and his eyes locked on Melody again.

"I trust you will do your part to help us tear down the final pocket of human resistance in this place."

Melody froze in her tracks. A tremor crept up her spine. Did Barber suspect her true intentions? Melody could not let him detain her before she even reached the corridor.

"It is my honor to serve."

She tried to mask her true emotions with a flat tone. It worked. Barber nodded and refocused his attention on the other scientist. Once in the corridor, Melody dropped the facade. She stormed to her room. A guard passed her on the way. Melody kept her head down and pulled out her communicator to make it appear as if she were engaged in research.

After the door closed behind Melody, she headed straight to her workstation. Melody opened a panel and retrieved two standard issue weapons. She ran a scanner over each weapon until hearing a small beep. Then, Melody jammed both weapons inside her coat pockets. She ran the same scanner over her communicator until the same beep registered.

Melody put the scanner down and a relieved sigh escaped her lips. The others could not track her devices now. This plan would not fail. Once Melody left the observation center, it meant no returning to her old life as she knew it. That didn't matter.

Only one thing mattered now.

She had to make it to the humans in the house with lethal lights before Barber and the others did. They needed to be warned about what lay ahead.

17

PAIGE COULDN'T BELIEVE her ears. She slapped her coffee mug down on the table.

"Do you even watch the NBA? The Pelicans aren't ever gonna be a playoff team if we keep trading away elite players."

Jason leaned back and gave a half-shrug.

"You gotta roll the dice sometimes. AD wanted out. Just look at the haul we got back for him last summer."

Paige shot a glance at Heather, hoping for some reinforcements on the point she wanted to make. She refused to let Jason get away with mimicking clueless fans she debated on Twitter. Heather held up her hands and shook her head. A small grin crept onto her face.

"I'm not jumping in on this one. You're talking to a person who wanted AD shipped out long ago. You're on your own."

Paige sprang off the big sofa and threw her arms out in an animated fashion.

"I don't blame AD for wanting to leave. Our front office didn't try hard enough to surround him with the right talent."

"What about Holiday and Randle? What about Cousins?"

Paige turned and glanced down at Jason with a bemused expression.

"Who else besides those guys? You can't build a playoff team with only a couple of good players."

"I'm just saying we got a chance to build something special with Zion. Who cares if the Lakers ended up getting AD?"

"They're gonna do the same thing with Zion."

"I'd say putting Holiday, Redick, Ingram, and Favors around him is a good start."

Paige frowned.

"Seems like all we ever do is start over. I'd like New Orleans to actually be an NBA title contender for a change."

Rich laughed.

"This is why I'm not so hardcore about basketball like the rest of you. It makes my life so much more carefree."

She pulled out her smartphone. It showed only a black screen now. With the power required to run all the lights, Paige kept her phone turned off and also kept it off Todd's charger to help conserve energy. She shook the phone at Rich.

"Maybe you should mix a little basketball into your YouTube channel," Paige said. "You might get some people who actually care about your videos."

He smacked his chest and slumped back against the small sofa. Rich protruded his lower lip and did his best to resemble a sad puppy.

"You really know how to hurt a person, don't you? Hitting me below the belt there."

Paige tried to suppress a smile forming in the corners of her mouth. It was not a successful battle. A broad grin finally popped to the surface.

"Tease a bee long enough and you get stung."

Jason and Heather both burst out laughing. Paige welcomed their laughter. It broke up the tension of being stuck inside until morning. The insane number of lights Todd installed outside the house chased away shadows from all sides. He even harvested headlights from cars and trucks and rigged them up to serve as additional spotlights. It didn't mean Paige felt totally secure. They had an alien chained up in the basement, other aliens attempting to track down any remaining humans in the town, and awful creatures hiding in darkness waiting for a chance to tear each human they encountered limb from limb.

While she continued laughing, Heather's eyes drifted over to the opposite wall. They stopped on a painting of a rustic house overlooking the shore of a small pond. Heather stopped laughing and her face scrunched up into a puzzled expression. She rose from the small sofa.

"What in the world is that thing?"

Paige turned and gazed at the same wall as Heather. Her eyes traced it from ceiling to floor. When she laid eyes on the painting of the lake house, Paige also caught the same peculiar thing that drew Heather's attention.

A small metallic object roughly the size of a quarter, affixed to an inside corner of the picture frame. The oval-shaped object appeared to have been built from stainless steel, except for a tiny green crystal embedded in the middle. Paige focused her gaze on the crystal itself.

It blinked.

The crystal emitted light tinged with a greenish hue. Paige and Heather approached the painting at the same time. Heather reached out and popped the object off the painting before Paige could touch it.

"I've never seen anything like this."

Heather turned it over in her hand and examined both sides of the object. She passed it to Paige, who mimicked her actions. Paige also pressed on the tiny crystal with her index finger. At once, the light vanished. When she pressed the crystal a second time, it returned.

Her eyes grew as wide as plates. She took the object over to Jason.

"Something really creepy is going on here," Paige said "Did someone bug this house? Are we being spied on?"

Jason rose from the large sofa and gave the device the same once-over as both girls. His face scrunched up as he tried to figure out what purpose it served.

"I can't tell if it's recording audio or video. It looks unlike anything I've ever seen."

Paige took the object from Jason's hand again. She studied it a second time, tracing her fingers over the smooth metallic surface. Paige held it up to her ear. The object emitted no discernible sound. She cast her eyes toward the hall leading out from the living room.

"I wonder if my brother encountered anything like this in Afghanistan. Maybe he has a better idea of what purpose this device serves."

Paige started down the hall, intending to pick Todd's brain. As she passed the kitchen, she noticed the basement door hung open a crack. She changed course and headed for the door.

"Todd, are you down there?"

Footsteps on the stairs and a low growl greeted her ears. Paige got no response to her question.

"Todd, answer me! Are you in the basement?"

"No. I'm in the bedroom at the end of the hall. What's up?"

His voice confirmed his current location. Paige's heart started pounding. She scanned the kitchen and then dropped back and poked her head in the living room. Andrew was the only member of their group not present.

What did he think he was doing?

She flung open the basement door and flipped on the light switch. It clicked. No light turned on. The footsteps fell silent.

Paige jammed the metallic object into her pocket. She yanked open a drawer under a nearby cabinet. From inside the drawer, she snatched up a flashlight and flicked it on.

"What's up?" Todd repeated his earlier question. "Is something wrong?"

"I'm not sure. I think Andrew might be trying to do something to the captive alien."

Paige hesitated at the top of the basement stairs. The only sound she heard now came from Todd's feet sprinting down the hall. Soon, he appeared from around the corner. In one hand, Todd toted the same hunting rifle he used to rescue Paige from the strange creature earlier. His other hand gripped a big black flashlight.

"Stay up here and let me check it out."

Todd cocked the rifle, clicked on the flashlight, and barged past her down the stairs. Staying put was a good idea. Still, Paige's curiosity tormented her as much as a fresh bite from a fire ant. She had to see for herself what compelled Andrew to go into a basement where he did not belong. Both Paige and Todd made sure no one breathed a word to him about the alien prisoner.

"What in the hell do you think you're doing?"

Todd's voice took on an extra dose of gruffness. Paige tiptoed from stair to stair until she obtained a better view of what was transpiring.

Her flashlight caught a glint of Andrew's eyes. They were locked in a steely gaze at Todd and his hands doubled into fists. He crouched at the bottom of the stairs, right in her brother's path. Instincts took over and Paige called out to Todd.

"Look out!"

Todd glanced over his shoulder and immediately scowled at her.

"Go back upstairs! I can handle this myself."

Andrew sprang from his hiding place. He unleashed a shout that echoed through the room. Before Todd could swing his rifle in that direction, Andrew threw himself on top of him. He slammed Todd against the stairs.

They tumbled to the basement floor. A jumble of arms and legs.

Andrew grabbed the rifle barrel and wrestled Todd for control of the weapon. The flashlight popped out of Todd's other hand as he tried to secure his grip on the rifle. It clattered against the floor. The beam shot out toward the opposite wall, away from the alien, Andrew, and Todd.

Paige stood frozen in place, for a moment, unsure what to do. She finally raced down the stairs and lunged forward.

"Get away from my brother!"

She raised and wound up her arm like a pitcher getting ready to toss a fastball. A second later, Paige brought the butt end of the flashlight down on Andrew's neck. He responded with a pained grunt and kicked her shin. Paige gasped and stumbled backward. Her flashlight rolled out of her hand and came to a rest against the opposite wall. The beam shot toward the stairs, illuminating the cement floor in front of the stairs.

Andrew thrust his elbow into Todd's leg. Todd unleashed an uncharacteristic scream and loosened his grip on the rifle. That provided the opening Andrew needed to wrench the weapon completely from his hands. Once he had sole possession of the rifle, Andrew swung it at Todd and drove the end of the stock into the side of his skull. Todd's eyes glazed over and snapped shut. He slumped onto the floor. Blood dribbled across his left ear from a fresh gash above the top of the ear.

Paige's breaths grew shorter and angrier. She struggled to her feet.

"I'm gonna break your neck!"

Andrew swung the rifle around and trained the barrel on her.

"You're gonna do nothing except sit there."

He drew closer to the chair where the captive alien remained bound. The alien laughed and flashed a contemptuous smile at all three humans occupying the basement.

"This is more entertaining than watching a pair of lycas fight," he said. "Please continue. If you succeed in killing one another, it will save me the trouble of doing it later."

Andrew grasped the chain binding the alien to the wooden chair.

"You don't understand why I'm here, do you?"

"Should I understand?"

"I bear the mark."

With those words, Andrew leaned forward and revealed a symbol on his neck. His shirt collar once concealed the symbol. It stood out as clear as day now before Paige's eyes. A horizontal semicircle intersected by two parallel lines had been branded into his neck. Each line bore a slight zigzag pattern.

The full impact of his words struck Paige with the force of a hard slap to the face. Joining up with them in the supermarket had been a carefully planned ruse. He was no victim, concealing himself in a back storeroom for survival.

Andrew revealed himself to be nothing more than a filthy traitor.

"You lied to us." Paige's voice softened to a near whisper as the full weight of her internal revelation settled on her. "You betrayed us."

"I am one with Rubrum," Andrew said. "You must follow the same path to survive."

He pulled out a gadget from his pocket. It resembled a tool, but Paige had never seen anything with similar craftsmanship before. Andrew slid his fingers through open holes on the gadget, so it wrapped around both sides of his hand. He pressed a button at the top with his thumb.

A thin metallic rod emerged from the underside of the gadget. It began emitting a red glow.

Andrew pressed the rod into the chain. Sparks flew between him and the alien as the tool sliced through metal. One link after another broke into two separate pieces. Paige bit down on her lower lip and anger flashed in her eyes. She had to get upstairs and warn everyone else before it grew too late. Didn't anyone hear the noise down here? Why had nobody else come to the basement door to check and find out what was happening?

"Something crazy is going on here," a familiar voice said. "We scoured other rooms and found more metallic objects. Heather gathered them all up."

Paige cast her eyes toward the top of the stairs. Jason stood in the doorway. She wanted to sneak past Andrew and reach her boyfriend before he started down the stairs. Andrew's possession of the rifle and additional alien weaponry turned such an idea into an unworkable option.

"Watch out!" Paige used all of her lungs to warn him. "Andrew is trying to free the alien. Don't let them get away!"

"What?" Jason's words escaped his lips as a near shriek. "Just what in the hell does that dirty bastard think he's doing?"

Andrew stopped his cutting. He swung around to face Jason. Now the rifle pointed at the top of the stairs instead of Paige.

"Killing you comes to mind."

This offered the distraction Paige needed. She sprang to her feet and tackled Andrew. The rifle popped out of his hands and slid across the floor. Jason sprinted down the stairs as they wrestled on the cement floor.

Paige punched Andrew in the jaw. He recoiled and kicked her thigh. She strained at the cutting tool, trying to yank it out of his hand. Andrew spit in her face. Spittle landed near her eye. Paige pinched it shut. Her arm kept drawing closer to the elusive tool.

At once, she felt a hand grasp her shoulder and wrench her backward. Paige fell and landed on her backside. She raised her eyes and chin and came face-to-face with the alien. Now free from his chains and chair, he towered over her.

"Beating you from head to foot – along with the one called Todd – will give me great satisfaction."

Paige threw up her arms to shield herself. The alien opened his mouth to reveal two rows of sharp teeth. He stooped down and picked up a segment of chain from the floor.

"No!"

Jason jumped off the bottom stair. The alien looked up at him and uttered a low growl. Andrew scrambled to his feet and dove at Jason. He rammed the cutting tool into Jason's forearm. The red hot rod seared his skin. Jason cried out and smacked it away. Andrew grabbed him by the shoulders. He spun Jason around and threw him against the chair.

Jason fell onto the side of the chair and knocked it over. Paige watched with horror as he rolled off the chair and struck his head against the floor. Her boyfriend stopped moving. A lump formed at the point of impact.

Andrew turned and handed the cutting tool to the newly free alien.

"Let's move," he said. "We need to get out of here right now."

"You aren't going anywhere!"

Both Andrew and the alien snapped their heads toward the top of the stairs. Heather and Rich charged down the stairs together. She brandished a butcher knife and he held a hammer.

Heather swung at the alien when she cleared the final stair. He dodged the knife and clotheslined her with his forearm. Heather dropped like a sack of potatoes on the cement. Andrew snatched up the rifle from the floor again. He shoved the barrel into Rich's chest as he dashed forward and drew back the hammer to strike.

"Hit me and I'll blast you into the next zip code."

Rich dropped the hammer and raised his hands. Andrew grabbed a segment of chain from off the floor and wrapped one end around Rich's neck. He kept the other end in his hand.

"Now you're going to help me shut off all the bright lights ahead of us, so my friend here has a clear path out of the house."

"Rich, no! We can't let them escape!"

Paige scrambled to her feet again. She stumbled toward the boxes lining the wall.

The alien spun around and pointed the cutting tool straight at her. Paige grabbed a can of dry rice from an open box and threw it at his head. She missed her target and the can struck the stair railing. The alien smiled and shook his head.

"Your aim is terrible."

He motioned for Paige to join Rich by the stairs. Paige finally raised her hands. Todd and Jason lay motionless on the floor. Heather let out a slight groan and her leg twitched, but she could not get up. Their resistance had come to an early end.

They were all prisoners.

SIGNS ANDREW HELD a grudge against Rich bubbled to the surface once the group exited the basement. Upon reaching a light switch inside the kitchen, Andrew yanked on the chain around his captive's neck and ordered him to turn the light off. He didn't relax his grip until Rich complied.

Tears streamed down Paige's face as she scowled at Andrew and the alien. How could a fellow human betray them to these awful invaders? Andrew himself referred to them in such terms back when they first encountered him in the supermarket. Now she understood his words and actions were all part of a ruse to win their trust.

She wiped away tears and scowled. Paige grew angry with herself for not trusting her initial instincts or listening to Todd. This situation could have been avoided if not for her eagerness to find additional help. Paige couldn't undo her lapse in judgment, but she wasn't going to let Andrew off the hook for his treachery either.

"When did you join them?"

Andrew glared at Paige.

"I don't owe you an explanation for anything."

"What did they offer you? It had to be mind-blowing for you to betray fellow humans."

"Shut up before I shut you up."

"I get it." Paige's tone grew icier by the second. "You're nothing more than just a run-of-the-mill coward."

"Enough!"

Andrew squeezed the trigger and blasted the light fixture above Paige's head. She ducked as glass shards rained down around her.

"The next one goes right through your pretty little blonde head."

Rich shook his head at Paige. He didn't say a word, but he didn't need to speak. The fear enveloping his eyes said enough. She realized antagonizing Andrew would do nothing to improve their situation. Rage controlled every part of his face now. Beneath it all, a small part of him had to know helping these aliens was insane. Still, Andrew made his choice without remorse. Paige grasped with silent horror that highlighting the inherent madness in his choice only opened a door for him to kill her and Rich. Anything to shut up college students he perceived to be entitled brats.

Paige knew she and Rich needed a miracle to escape their captors before meeting a horrifying fate. The same fate that fell upon countless other people who also became trapped in this town.

Andrew gave the chain another rough yank and forced Rich to open the door leading into the garage. No lights were turned on inside the garage itself, but it held a circuit box controlling the generator. The circuit box regulated electricity powering every outdoor light guarding the house.

"Turn off the generator."

Andrew waved his rifle at Paige and directed her to approach the circuit box.

Paige glanced back over her shoulder through the open kitchen door. She hoped someone in the basement would regain consciousness soon and come to their rescue.

"Please don't do this," she said. "Whatever they've promised you, it isn't worth it. We're both humans. This planet belongs to us, not these aliens."

A scowl popped to the surface on the alien's thin lips. He shoved the cutting tool at her. It missed striking her throat by only a few inches. Paige jumped back when the red metal rod in the center threatened to graze her skin.

"You would be wise to follow his path."

"I'm not really the follower type."

"Do you truly crave to see what fate awaits such a poor choice?"

The alien flashed an unsettling smile. Seeing his expression made Paige's skin crawl worse than the last time fire ants raced up her legs. Peanut, the family cat, made a mistake of disturbing a large mound nestled against a backyard tree. He escaped without a bite. She wasn't so lucky.

Paige bit down on her lower lip again and closed her eyes. She wanted to scream, cry, and make a run for the kitchen. It wouldn't do her any good. Rich was bound in a chain. A gun and an alien weapon were trained on them. Paige had no guarantee she could even reach the door alive.

"Turn off the generator," Andrew said. "I don't want to repeat myself."

He popped a fresh bullet into the chamber. Her eyes snapped open again. Paige drew in a deep breath and approached the circuit box. Exterior and interior lights around the house extinguished as she flipped corresponding breakers. Darkness consumed the entire house and yard when she finally shut off the switch feeding power from the generator itself.

"Now we wait for the transport to arrive."

The alien folded his arms and stood at the garage door with a satisfied smile spread across his face.

"Open the garage door."

Paige saw nothing more than a shadowy outline of Andrew's face in the darkness. Still, she had no doubt he kept the rifle trained on her – ready to enforce his order at a moment's notice. Paige crouched down at the door and dug her fingers under the bottom. A pale red tinted glow from streetlamps splashed across her face as she hoisted the garage door up.

At once, rustling sounds emerged from the bushes forming the boundary between the front yard and a neighboring yard. Her breaths grew shorter and quicker. Paige glanced over at Rich. Both lips trembled and his eyelids were pinched shut. With all lights turned off, any creatures lurking around the perimeter now had a free pass to unleash an attack.

Deep growls tore through the air. A tremor raced down her spine. Paige's eyes became glued to the bushes. She had no desire to discover what hid in the shadows, but she didn't dare look away either.

A new sound greeted Paige's ears. It came from the opposite direction. Her heart started thumping even harder. She forced herself to turn and search for the source of the new noise. A small vehicle emerged at the end of the street. It hovered several yards above the asphalt and emitted a distinct whoosh while closing in on their position.

"What in the world is that thing?"

Paige regretted posing the question almost as soon as the words left her mouth. She didn't really want to talk to Andrew or the once-imprisoned alien. Their words were nothing but poison to her ears.

Her feelings didn't really matter.

"It is our transport. Soon you will join others of your kind in undergoing bio code testing."

The alien sounded smug and boastful as he revealed the strange vehicle's purpose. Paige glared at him and an urge to spit in his face rose within her. Following through on that urge was a bad idea. She and Rich occupied a precarious position as unarmed prisoners. Their captors lacked a conscience and would not hesitate to discharge their weapons at the slightest provocation.

The transport braked and slammed to a halt above the driveway. It descended until the strange vehicle hovered only a few feet above the ground. Paige had never seen anything like it in her life. It resembled a rectangular box rounded and smoothed into oval curves at all four corners. Small windows adorned the front and back of the vehicle. Each one permitted enough light and visibility for the driver to see where they were traveling, but not much else.

When a passenger side door opened, rustling among the bushes intensified. At once, a creature sprang out and landed on the driveway. If it was human at one time, it no longer qualified as such now. This hulking creature turned and snarled at Paige and the others. It bore tusks resembling a smaller version of those found on a saber-toothed tiger. Patches of coarse hair covered the creature. Bony knobs peppered each arm. Some knobs had already burst open and revealed small spikes composed from a similar hardened material as the tusks. The creature possessed wild eyes. Tattered clothing hung off its body.

An alien emerged from the driver's side door on the transport. The creature growled and charged at the vehicle. It barely reached the driveway before the transport driver turned and raised a weapon. Paige recognized it as the gadget that reminded her of a beater. The transport driver fired her weapon.

A single laser bolt discharged from the hole where four cylinders converged in the middle. The creature howled and dropped in a heap before reaching the door. It rolled over on its right side and, after one final muscular twitch, no longer moved.

Paige crept closer to the spot where it fell. She stayed out of reach from a pair of outstretched arms and leaned forward. A quarter-sized hole occupied a spot in the creature's forehead. Wisps of smoke drifted upward from the hole. Vacant eyes stared back at her. Both eyes were still so human in appearance. It chilled Paige to the bone to think this thing had once been an ordinary person.

What had these aliens done to these people?

The former alien prisoner gave the transport driver a curt nod. "Your timing is perfect, Mara."

Mara smiled and returned the weapon to her pocket once again. She wore similar glasses and long clothing to the other alien Paige encountered a day earlier. Her short light brown hair, however, stood in contrast to Melody's long red locks.

"It appears you have procured more test subjects, Gregor. Barber will be pleased."

Mara rounded the transport and stopped in front of Paige. Only the slain creature separated human from alien. Even though Mara's eyes were not visible to her, Paige sensed those oval orbs scanning her from head to toe like she was nothing more than a piece of fresh meat.

Gregor turned and pointed at the house.

"The news only grows better," he said. "I successfully incapacitated the one called Todd and other humans in his service. The lethal lights have been deactivated. The whole town belongs to us."

He glanced over at Andrew and beckoned at him to move forward. Andrew jerked on the chain once again. Rich stumbled forward and fell to his knees. He clenched his teeth and clawed at the chain around his neck.

"Climb inside the transport."

Rich staggered to his feet and obeyed Gregor's command. Andrew sat next to him, never relaxing his grip on the chain for a second. They occupied a long backseat. An empty middle seat awaited Paige.

"Now you will do the same."

She refused to look at Gregor when he barked the order. A renewed urge to make a run for it swelled inside her. Paige knew better than to try to play the hero. This wasn't a movie. No doubt existed in her mind she wouldn't even make it back inside the garage before Mara gunned her down as fast as the creature who tried to attack the transport.

A long-fingered hand gave Paige a shove forward.

"I will not tell you a second time."

Her parents always taught Paige to pray to God in her hour of need. Such a thought made her angry now. How could they be so naive to think it worked? Paige prayed when she and her friends first became stranded and again when a creature tried to attack her only a few moments before her reunion with Todd. Both times, things eventually took an even worse turn. If God was there and cared about her situation, he had an odd way of showing it.

She closed her eyes and made the decision to stand her ground. Paige would not climb into that transport. Not while even a spark of life remained within her body.

"No." Her voice emerged as a frightened whisper. "I won't let you take me from here."

At once, Paige heard a rumbling whoosh from a second airborne vehicle. She opened her eyes again and spotted a new transport. It traveled from the same direction as the first one. Mara scrunched up her nose and lips in a puzzled expression as she turned to gaze at the approaching vehicle.

A pair of small holes opened at the front of the second transport. Small laser blasts – resembling the one Mara sent through the creature's head – followed a second later. One impacted the rear of the first transport. The other missed Mara's left arm by mere inches.

Paige threw up her arms and waved frantically at the oncoming transport.

"Don't fire! My friend is inside!"

Mara jumped into the first transport and sealed it behind her, trapping Rich and Andrew inside. The second transport unleashed another laser volley. It shattered the other transport's rear window as engines started up again. The first transport shot straight up until it hovered above the treetops.

Gregor stretched out his left hand toward the sky.

"Do not leave! Return to the ground at once!"

Paige took advantage of the distraction the second transport provided. She tackled Gregor from behind and wrenched the cutting tool from his hand. Gregor swung at her with his other hand. Paige stabbed the rod into his left palm. Smoke wafted out of his skin as the cutting tool punched a hole down into his bones. Gregor screamed and clutched at the injured hand as Paige scrambled to her feet.

She sprinted toward the open garage door. Laser fire continued between the two transports. Paige skidded to a halt in front of the circuit breaker. Gregor ripped the tool from his hand. An open sore spewing dark blood remained behind. He snarled and scrambled to his feet.

The first transport finally shook off the second transport and shot across the treetops until disappearing further down the street. Paige turned on the main breaker again and flipped the switch controlling the generator.

"Wait! Please wait!"

Her ears perked up at those words. They didn't belong to the formerly captive alien. The plea came from the vicinity of the second transport. Paige tilted her head and glanced outside the garage door. The second transport driver dashed across the grass toward the garage.

Melody was the driver.

Gregor stopped in his tracks and wheeled around to face his fellow alien.

"Traitor!"

Melody pulled out a weapon mirroring the one Mara used earlier and fired a single shot. The laser bolt punched through his ribs and dropped him to the cement. Gregor thrust out his right hand to trip her as she passed him. Melody crunched down on it with her shoe without breaking stride. Gregor moaned and clutched his ribs with his injured hand. Dark blood dribbled through his fingers and pooled on the driveway underneath his body.

"Now you can turn on your outside lights," Melody said. "Hurry."

Paige flipped on corresponding breakers. A loud hum erupted from the generator. At once, the string of lights around the house and yard sprang to life again. Floodlights above the garage splashed their beams directly on Gregor. The alien threw an arm above his head, trying to shield himself from the light. He let out a scream.

Melody retreated into the shadows at the back of the garage. Paige did not move from her spot near the circuit box. Every exposed part of Gregor's pale skin began to turn red and form blisters. He crawled toward the interior of the garage.

"Have mercy on me," the alien begged. "Please let me live."

"Will you help me rescue my friend?"

"I can do nothing for the other human."

Paige scowled at him. She backpedaled and pressed the button that automatically raised and lowered the garage door.

"In that case, enjoy your tan."

The garage door dropped from its resting place. Gregor screamed as it came down in front of him – inches from his face – and trapped him outside in the light. Paige stood and stared at the door in silence until the screams finally stopped.

"Why did you rescue me?"

She wheeled around and faced Melody. Paige couldn't see more than an outline of the alien, but her hand no longer held the weapon she used earlier.

"Helping you is the right thing for me to do," Melody said. "Barber must be stopped."

A relieved smile crossed Paige's face. She did not expect this turn of events. An alien ally increased their odds of escaping from this awful town.

"We need to revive the others and track down that transport," Paige said. "There's still a chance to save Rich."

"We must not spare any time," Melody said. "Barber will do unspeakable things to your friend. I can no longer reason with him."

She emerged from the shadows and joined Paige on the steps leading into the kitchen. Melody paused in the doorway after opening the door. She raised her hands above her head.

"What are you doing?" Paige nudged her from behind. "You're not our prisoner."

Todd stepped out from behind the door. He pointed a butcher knife straight at the alien's throat. Paige's face fell when she realized his intentions. Todd motioned for her to join Melody inside and slammed the door behind them.

"I'll make that call, Paige. Not you."

PAIGE'S PROTESTS WENT ignored by her brother. Todd wasted no time fishing some nylon rope out of a hall closet and binding Melody to a wooden kitchen chair. He did keep the kitchen lights turned off. It ended up being the only concession Paige got him to make. Todd refused to believe Melody meant to do no harm.

"She saved my life out there," Paige said. "We're wasting time in here."

Todd narrowed his eyes and stared at his new alien prisoner.

"I don't trust aliens. I'm not letting her out of my sight. And I'm definitely not letting her roam free."

"We gotta save Rich!"

Todd didn't respond. He tugged on the nylon rope, making sure it held snug against both chair and alien. Paige glanced at Melody and then back at her brother. She tapped her fingers against the wall and frowned.

"So, I guess you don't give a damn about Rich."

"I've got bigger fish to fry," Todd said. "If the aliens have your friend, he's as good as dead. Or much worse."

Paige buried her face in her left hand. She felt tears trickle through her fingers and down her knuckles. Todd never used to be so cold and heartless. Why did he change? Paige wiped away the tears and sniffed.

"I guess I'll go check on Jason and Heather," she said. "At least they're willing to do something besides sit here and wait for the end."

She stomped out of the kitchen and down the basement stairs with equal force. Heather stood over Jason with a flashlight in hand. His eyes started to blink at a rapid pace. He shook his head and his eyes drifted over to Paige.

Heather and Paige each grabbed an arm and pulled Jason to his feet. Jason squeezed both eyes shut and groaned.

"You wouldn't believe the headache I've got right now. I feel like someone drove a nail straight through the back of my head."

Paige squeezed his hand.

"You took a serious blow earlier. Can you see? Can you walk? Please tell me you can."

Both girls let go of his arms. Jason stumbled backward for a second. He clenched his teeth and thrust a hand behind his head. Paige latched onto his other hand again to keep him from tumbling to the floor a second time.

"I'll get back to you on the second question."

Once Jason was on more certain footing, he wrapped Paige in a tight embrace. His lips pressed against hers. Paige soaked in the kiss like a thirsty woman downing a glass of water. Jason pulled back and caressed a lock of her blonde hair.

"I'm so happy you're all right."

Paige smiled. Similar relief washed over her after finding Jason relatively unharmed. Before she said anything else, Heather's arms wrapped around her from the side.

"Count me in the 'happy you're all right' club."

Jason took that as a cue to embrace both girls at once. They stood in a circle and shared a group hug.

"I've got a wild idea," Heather said. "Let's all stay home for spring break next year."

"No arguments here," Jason replied. "A nice relaxing fishing trip to the bayou is the only excitement I crave now."

Paige laughed and nudged him, ending the hug.

"Didn't you tell me the best fishing in Louisiana is in Wyoming?"

Paige couldn't help ribbing Jason about his boast. He kept comparing everything to lakes and rivers in his home state during their excursion out to the Gulf of Mexico last summer. Jason shared endless stories of how fast he caught his limit on each fishing trip and boasted about all the cool wildlife he saw up close. He talked up Wyoming until it became a larger-than-life paradise in her mind. An outdoor nirvana. It didn't match the hype for Paige when she finally went out there with him.

"Hey, I'd settle for planting some bass in the rec center pool and fishing there at this point," Jason said. "I just want to get out of this hell hole."

Paige cast her eyes toward the basement stairs again. Thoughts of Rich sprang to mind. Where did the transport take him? What were the aliens doing to him now? Every answer Paige came up with for these questions only inspired fear to overtake her mind. She shuddered to think he could end up turning into a nasty creature like the one who tried to attack her at the alien transport.

"Rich needs our help," Paige said. "We were taken prisoner when y'all got knocked out. I escaped. He didn't."

Jason and Heather exchanged wide-eyed glances and stared at her.

"What happened to him?" Heather's voice took on a panicked note. "Where is he now?"

"I don't know," Paige replied. "The transport got away before Melody or I could free him."

"Melody?" Jason repeated the alien's name. "Odd alien chick Melody?"

Paige nodded.

"She arrived in another transport and saved me all by herself."

A puzzled look crossed Jason's face.

"Why? Don't get me wrong. We can use the help. But I'm not sure what's in it for her."

"I guess she doesn't like what her fellow alien, Barber, is doing."

Heather scrunched up her face.

"Barber? That still doesn't sound like an alien name to me."

Jason shrugged.

"I just assumed he killed the guy running that barber shop and stole their name."

They climbed the stairs. A sudden scream reached from the kitchen into the basement. Paige, Jason, and Heather all dashed through the door. They emerged into the kitchen just as Todd pressed a gadget against Melody's cheek. It resembled a long square rod with three uneven tines jutting out from the top. Clear glass bubbles topped each tine and each one glowed red. Melody's pale skin around each bubble took on the same hue.

Paige darted forward and smacked the gadget out of her brother's hand. It bounced against the hardwood and slid across the floor. Todd lunged forward to slap her. She caught his hand before it had a chance to even graze her cheek.

Both cheeks turned red with anger.

"What in the hell do you think you're doing? What's wrong with you?"

Todd scowled at her.

"We need information. This thing has it."

"This thing? I can't believe what I'm hearing. She's here to help us! Do you understand that?"

"Enemy combatants can't be trusted."

Paige tightened her grip on her brother's hand.

"Melody isn't our enemy. Taking her prisoner and torturing her isn't going to accomplish anything."

"Back off, Paige.

"No. You let her go."

Todd ripped his hand away from her grasp. He stomped over and punched the kitchen wall. A large crack formed where his fist met paint and sheet rock. Todd refused to look at his sister. His eyes remained fixed on the captive alien.

"What do you know about anything?" he said. "You're condemning us to die in this backwater hell hole."

He wheeled around and stormed out of the kitchen. Paige cast her eyes at Jason and Heather. They both stood frozen by the refrigerator, unsure of what to say or what to do. She directed them to a nearby drawer.

"Find a knife or scissors to cut Melody loose. I need to go have a long talk with my brother."

Paige followed on Todd's heels down the hall. She finally caught him as he entered the master bedroom and flipped on the light behind him.

"This isn't over, Todd. What in God's name do you think you're doing out there?"

Paige blocked the doorway, so her brother couldn't duck past her to avoid hashing this out.

"It's never over with you, is it?"

"This isn't about me. This is about my brother who apparently thinks torturing a prisoner is the cool new thing to do."

Todd slumped down below the foot of the bed. He rubbed the hand he slammed into the wall moments earlier.

"You wouldn't understand."

"I can't if you won't tell me."

Todd became glassy eyed as Paige stared at him. He dipped his chin to his chest and stared at the floor. Paige walked inside the room. She stopped at her brother's feet and crouched down. Paige tilted her head, trying to force Todd make eye contact. He kept shifting his eyes away from her.

A light switched on inside Paige's mind. It dawned on her what bred such fierce hostility to all aliens in his words and behavior.

"What exactly happened to Caroline?"

Todd raised his head and finally looked at her. Tears welled up in his eyes.

"These monsters stole her from me."

Images Todd buried from that night clawed out of their grave and took root in his mind again. Paige could visualize the scenes unfolding as he described them as though she lived through those moments herself and endured what he endured.

Finding shelter became a primary concern for Todd and Caroline once the sun dipped below the horizon. Todd assumed they wouldn't be safe sleeping outside in their locked SUV. Something unusual happened inside this town. A connection had to exist between the energy barrier, the scene of destruction inside the café, and their narrow escape from Clyde and Desiree. Suffocating silence and few signs of life only added to an unsettling feeling gripping him and his wife.

Caroline gazed out the passenger side window as streetlamps began to automatically switch on. Her eyes darted from lamp to lamp.

"How are we gonna make it through the night? I don't know if we can even find a safe place to stay in this town."

"We gotta keep trying. We'll find a way out of here tomorrow."

Caroline turned and stared at him. Her unblinking eyes and nervous frown told Todd her true feelings. She did not share his optimism in the face of what they already encountered in Travis.

"I endured plenty of tough situations in Kandahar," Todd reassured her. "God will open a door for us. I know it."

Caroline glanced down at the floor mat and then back in his eyes. She forced a weak smile.

"I hope you're right."

Her smile snapped back into a frown. Caroline leaned forward and squinted at the streetlamps. She reached out and grasped Todd's arm.

"Something's wrong with the lights."

"What do you mean?"

"They're all red."

"Red?"

Todd focused so much of his attention on finding shelter he didn't notice the streetlamps until Caroline pointed it out. Now it put him on edge worse than before. A red hue bathed the entire street. It looked like someone tried to turn each lamp into a blinker light or traffic light.

He stopped the SUV and parked along the street. A row of empty houses on both sides of the street greeted the couple. Todd cracked open his door and unlatched his seat belt. Caroline leaned over and reached out to him.

She kept her seat belt buckled.

"What are you doing? I don't think we should go out there."

Todd cast his eyes toward the front porch of one of the empty houses.

"It's getting dark, honey. We need to find a place to sleep for the night. These houses seem to be abandoned."

Caroline fidgeted with the small golden band on her finger.

"Are you suggesting we break into one of the houses? I don't think that's a good idea. We should just stay here inside the SUV."

"It will be okay."

She frowned. Todd offered his best effort at giving her a reassuring smile. He planted a kiss on her lips and let his own linger there for a moment before pulling away.

"I'll keep you safe. I promise."

Caroline rested her hand on the seat belt for a moment, unsure what to do. She closed her eyes, took a deep breath, and finally unbuckled the seat belt. Todd pushed his door shut and hurried around to the other side to open her door.

After Caroline stepped out, Todd grabbed a small flashlight from the glove compartment and switched it on. A bright LED beam splashed onto the sidewalk ahead of their feet. He gently closed the door behind his wife. Todd eyed the purse dangling off Caroline's shoulder.

"Don't suppose you have a hair pin or paper clip on you? That will make it so much easier to get inside one of these places."

Caroline swung her pursue up to her chest and plunged a hand inside. She drew out two bobby pins.

"Will these work?"

Todd smiled and nodded.

"Exactly what I was I looking for."

She clung to his arm after handing over the bobby pins. Her eyes kept darting between the porch and their SUV. Her grip tightened around Todd's bicep with every step they took toward the porch. He handed Caroline the flashlight when they reached the door.

"Hold it steady and shine it on the lock, so I can see where to insert the pins."

Todd tried turning the doorknob first. The door did not budge. He took the bobby pins and snapped one pin in half. He inserted the closed loop of the unbroken pin in the bottom of the deadbolt. Then he inserted the broken one near the top of the lock. Todd rocked the pins back and forth until the deadbolt retracted.

He swung open the door.

"Nothing to it. Let's see if we can turn on some normal lights around here."

A rumbling whoosh pierced the night air as Todd stepped through the doorway. He swung the flashlight around. Both he and Caroline cast their eyes toward the sky. Todd's mouth fell open. Caroline slipped her hand into his and squeezed his fingers like a vise grip.

A small rectangular ship circled above the nearest streetlamp. Todd had never seen anything like it. The ship resembled a flying metal box smoothed into an oval at all four corners. It sported running lights emitting the same curious red hue matching every streetlamp they encountered so far.

"What is that thing?"

Caroline's voice transformed into a trembling whisper. Todd didn't know how to answer her question. He read about UFOs and saw them in movies. Encountering the real thing was a whole different animal.

The small ship descended and touched down in the front yard, a few feet inside the fence. It hovered a foot or two above the blades of grass. Todd stepped back on the porch with Caroline. He dared not walk any closer to the ship. His instincts told him to keep a safe distance after what happened with Clyde and Desiree earlier.

Two doors opened on the passenger side. A single occupant exited from the ship through each door. Todd's throat tightened and his breaths grew shallower. They resembled people at first glance, but something seemed off about their appearance. Each "person" appeared tall, lanky, and possessed extremely long arms and long fingers on their hands. They had pale skin to the point of being albino in complexion. Their eyes were hidden behind shaded glasses, which only heightened the nervousness gripping Todd. Both individuals also wore long coats over strange looking uniforms.

"Who are you? Where did you come from?"

Todd squinted and stepped forward a half-step. The nearest visitor sauntered in a long-legged gait toward him and Caroline.

"I intended to pose those questions to you."

Caroline cast a worried glance at Todd.

"We asked first," she said, facing them again. "Tell us what's going on here. What happened to all the people? Why can't we leave this town?"

At once, the second individual drew out a weapon from his coat. He pointed it straight at the young couple. Todd had never seen any other weapon resembling that design. It reminded him of a hand mixer beater with a revolver handle.

"We do not wish for you to leave."

Todd's eyes widened upon hearing their cold calculating response. A second later, two laser bolts discharged from the weapon.

"Get down!"

He dove on the porch and jerked Caroline down with him. They crawled behind the rail and under a porch swing as more laser bolts blasted both rail and swing. Caroline let out a groan. Todd immediately whipped his head around to look at her.

"Are you okay?"

A grimace overtook Caroline's face.

"I think so. It feels like I got the wind knocked out of me."

Another laser bolt hit a post in front of Todd. A second one struck the rail again. Both blasts sent splinters and wood chunks spiraling skyward. Todd searched for some sort of weapon he could use to fight back. He spotted nothing except the flashlight that fell to the porch during their scramble to get under the swing.

Todd stretched out on his stomach and snatched up the flashlight. At a minimum, maybe he could blind their assailants. Todd flicked on the flashlight again and cast the beam into the nearest individual's eyes. She let out a scream and dropped to her knees.

That's a weird response to a flashlight, Todd thought. He used her reaction to his advantage. Todd scrambled to his feet while keeping the flashlight beam in the attacker's eyes. The second individual drew out the same weapon from his coat pocket as the first one. He raised it as Todd charged down the porch steps.

Todd swung the beam at him and flashed the second individual in the face. He howled, dropped the weapon, and clutched at his eyes. Todd got a good look at those eyes for the first time. Both were deep black ovals.

These individuals were not human like him.

Todd tackled the nearest assailant and threw her to the ground. He punched her face and grabbed her weapon. The second attacker staggered a few steps toward Todd before regaining his footing. A low growl escaped his lips. Todd pointed the weapon at him and kept pressing a series of embedded buttons on the handle.

A brief hum emanated from the device. A blue laser bolt instead of a red one shot out this time. It looked like a glowing marble. The bolt slammed into the second assailant's chest and tore a hole through his back. He gasped and fell forward onto the lawn.

The first attacker ripped open a coat sleeve, exposing her arm. Small spikes protruding from bony knobs covered the arm. She jammed the spikes into Todd's lower leg and raked her arm across his calf. Todd let out a scream. He kicked her in the face with his other leg and sent her tumbling backward. One spike snapped inside his calf muscle and squirted a cloudy fluid across the open wound.

Todd scrambled to his feet and spun around. He fired the confiscated weapon a second time. His attacker crumpled to the ground. Dark blood dribbled from a hole in her neck into the grass.

Todd fished the broken spike out of his lower leg and limped up the porch steps. Caroline remained curled up under the porch swing. Her breaths were labored, and she pressed her hand against her belly.

"What's wrong? Are you injured?"

Todd grasped his wife's other hand. His eyes filled with fear as he searched for the cause of her heavy breathing.

"I … can't … breathe. It hurts … so bad."

"Let me see your stomach."

Todd pulled her hand away. He gasped. Tears started coursing down his cheeks. Blood covered her hand and the midsection of her blouse. A laser bolt left behind a fleshy crater just below her ribs.

"Oh God. Caroline. No. Please, God. No."

Todd slid her out from under the porch swing. Caroline's cheeks became streaked with tears too.

"It hurts. I don't want … I don't want ..."

The pain afflicting his leg no longer mattered. Todd sobbed and cradled her head and shoulders in his arms. Caroline rested against his chest.

Soon, two heartbeats became only one.

Paige's eyes glistened with tears as the full impact of Todd's recounting of those traumatic events hit her. Her lips trembled and she swallowed hard. Even though she was not an eyewitness to what unfolded, Paige saw Caroline's tortured face in her mind as clear as anything else in the room.

Todd gazed into his sister's eyes. A flood of tears burst forth with a ferocity of water rushing down a swollen brook.

"I watched her die in my arms," he said in a tortured whisper. "Caroline died in my arms. I couldn't do anything to stop it."

Todd lowered his head and broke down into sobs. He collapsed to his knees. Paige also dropped to her knees and embraced her brother. Her cries echoed his own. They clung to each other until each tear dried and faded away.

PAIGE REMAINED AT a loss for words after leaving the bedroom. For the first time, she fully understood the hell Todd endured in this place. She questioned if her own inclination to trust Melody was premature. Sure, the alien rescued her from being hauled off like Rich. Did that mask some ulterior motive or agenda?

Rich!

He counted on them to rescue him, and she had done nothing. Paige wondered how much time passed since Andrew and the other alien spirited him away as a prisoner. After learning about Caroline's fate, she feared the worst for her friend more deeply than before.

They needed to act fast to save him.

Paige sprinted down the hall. This would be Melody's test. If she truly had joined their side, then she would have no problem helping them track down Rich and mount a rescue mission.

A loud thump greeted her ears. An angry shout followed. Paige rounded the corner and spotted Jason leaning against the refrigerator. A scowl adorned his face. His open palm slammed against the fridge door a second time.

"We can't just sit here and do nothing." Anger dripped from his words. "He's our friend. Don't you understand that?"

Melody stood free of the chair now. She cast her eyes to the ground, hesitant to look at either Jason or Heather in the face.

"I am afraid I can do nothing for him," she said. "His bio code will be altered long before we can infiltrate the observation center."

Heather gave her a puzzled look.

"Bio code? What do you mean by bio code?"

"Genetic material used as building blocks for life at a molecular scale."

Heather's mouth fell open. Jason buried his mouth in his hands. A queasy feeling gripped Paige in her belly.

"DNA?" Heather put into words the revelation that hit all three of them at once. "You mean those other aliens are going to tamper with his DNA?"

Melody answered with a solemn nod. Jason focused a determined stare exclusively on the alien.

"That settles it," he said. "We can't let those bastards haul Rich off to God knows where and do God knows what to him. We gotta rescue him now."

"How do you suggest we do that?"

Paige walked between Jason and Melody as she posed the question. She trailed her fingers across his forearm, trying to coax him into softening his stare.

"I want to help him as much as you. But we barely survived an attack from one alien and a human traitor. We're out-manned and out-gunned."

Jason pulled away from Paige and started to pace back and forth between the refrigerator and a nearby counter.

"We can't just leave him out there to die – or worse. He's my best friend, Paige. He's counting on me. He's counting on us."

"Don't you think I know that? I want to help him too. We just gotta be smart about it."

Jason stopped and wheeled around to face Paige. His lower lip jutted out like he held back tears, but his eyes burned hot with anger.

"I'm going after him. I don't care what anyone else says. I'm taking whatever weapons I can scrounge up and I'm mowing down every last alien until Rich is out of their grasp."

Paige pressed her lips tight and answered with an unblinking stare. Jason had every right to be upset. She did too. But he also wasn't being rational. What he wanted to do would turn into nothing more than a desperate suicide run. They needed to create a sound rescue plan. Even after several minutes of arguing, Paige couldn't convince him of that fact.

"Can't you fix DNA once someone has tampered with it?" Heather's question raised a solution Paige did not consider. "Don't you have the technology to undo whatever your fellow aliens are doing?"

Melody closed her eyes. A small smile flashed across her lips, and she nodded.

"Using a bio code splicer could work," she said, opening her eyes again. "There is a risk it would not undo every change. Still, it can potentially heal any major damage."

Paige snatched the gadget Todd used on Melody earlier off the floor. She turned it over in her hands, inspecting the design. If only they had a few more alien weapons. They could take the fight to the invaders and free Rich with minimal risk or effort.

The alien ship.

Paige's eyes lit up when she remembered it. Of course. They were approaching a rescue mission from the wrong angle. They didn't need to blast their way in through the front door. Melody knew how to go in and out undetected. She could fly them in her vehicle and sneak them into the alien headquarters. Once inside, they would snag Rich and use the vehicle to fly over the energy barrier to safety.

Piece of cake. It sounded so simple. Paige internally scolded herself for not coming up with this idea sooner. She turned and faced Melody again.

"We can take your ship parked outside the house and fly in there," she said. "The other aliens are less likely to notice anything out of the ordinary. It gives us the perfect way inside your observation center."

Heather smiled. Ebony curls bounced onto her cheeks as she responded with a vigorous nod.

"I like your suggestion. Once inside, we track down Rich, free him, and get the hell out of town."

Melody sat on the chair again and gazed up at the others. Her black oval eyes filled with concern.

"It is a daring plan. But you do not realize the risk I took in coming here. I stole that transport. They will soon scour this place in search of me. We must consider the larger picture."

Jason stomped his foot on the hardwood.

"Why are you here? If you don't want to help us, then hand over the transport and get the hell out of our way."

Heather marched over to Jason, grabbed his shoulder, and spun him around so they now stood face-to-face.

"Who's gonna fly her ship? You? You need to stop being a hot head about this."

"She's right," Todd said. "The alien is right too. We have bigger concerns to think about right now."

Paige cast her eyes toward the end of the hall. Her brother entered the kitchen with a noticeable limp. He sauntered over to the rest of the group, never taking his eyes off Melody.

"Who in the hell asked you?"

Jason brushed off Todd's two cents as quick as he brushed away Heather's hand. His reaction didn't surprise Paige. If he refused to listen to her or Heather, Todd faced even smaller odds of getting his attention.

"I'm rescuing Rich whether you want to help or not," Jason said. "He's my best friend. You want to sit here and hunker down like a pansy, be my guest."

Todd didn't even bother to look at Jason. He shook his head and grabbed a seat on a stool near the counter.

"Anyone who wants to join Mr. Heroic on a suicide mission, go right ahead. The rest of us will use our brains and figure out a workable escape plan from this shit-hole town."

Jason didn't have a comeback primed and ready to go. He leaned against the wall, displaying pouting lips, and sulked. There wasn't much he could say. None of the humans knew enough about alien technology to fly Melody's transport on their own. They couldn't infiltrate the observation center without her. She knew the other aliens better than they did. If Melody wanted to take a cautious approach, they needed to take enough time to figure out how to get in and get out in one piece. Jason just needed to cool down and deal with it, as far as Paige was concerned. She loved him, but sometimes he let his emotions cloud his judgment.

"Can we hack their communications?" Heather asked. "Figure out their weak spots?"

Melody pulled out the gadget Paige had seen earlier. She couldn't shake the thought it resembled a smart phone plug without the USB cord. Melody held the gadget out in front of her.

"My communicator can do what you are asking. I must adjust it, so the screen does not engage when activated. We do not want them to see us listening."

Her communicator lit up and emitted a loud beep. A small holographic screen projected from a port between the two tines at the top. Melody extended a long index finger and touched the screen. A menu appeared and she tapped on a line of text near the bottom. Words composing the text were written in a language with characters Paige had never seen before. The characters resembled a hybrid of cuneiform symbols and Arabic letters. After

Melody tapped on the text, the screen vanished. Another screen replaced it, showing only a pair of lines measuring audio output.

Paige shot her a puzzled look.

"How come you speak English when your communicator uses a different language?"

"Your language is not my birth language," Melody said. "We intercepted visual and audio signals when we entered the edge of your planetary system. These signals helped us learn how to speak your language so we could communicate with you. Everything I say, including my name, is translated into your language."

Heather cracked a grin.

"So, you basically watched TV and listened to the radio so you could talk to us?"

Paige found herself equally amused by that same thought. Did the aliens stream and binge any of the same shows as her? Did they tune in to catch the Super Bowl or the NBA Playoffs? What type of music did they stream in their spaceships? Pop? Rock? Hip hop? So many questions flooded her mind.

Todd didn't see the same humor in Melody's revelation as Paige and Heather did.

"In other words, you spied on us for God knows how long before deciding to attack us." His voice took on a cross tone. "You aliens are a bunch of cold and calculating bastards."

Melody gazed up at his eyes for a moment. She bowed her head.

"I am sorry for what my people did to you and your people. We took extreme actions in a time of desperation, and it left a stain on all of Rubrum."

Paige scrunched up her face at hearing that word.

"Rubrum? What's Rubrum?"

"It is what my home planet is called."

"Why did you leave Rubrum?" Heather blurted out the question silently forming on Paige's lips. "What's your purpose in coming here to Earth?"

Melody glanced up from the communicator a second time. Her lips parted slightly, and tears ran down both cheeks. Paige counted it as strange to witness an alien crying. She always pictured them as emotionless creatures, ruled only by cold logic, like characters she saw in bad sci-fi movies. Of course, talking to an alien at all felt surreal, like she would wake up from this dream any second.

"We came here in search of a new home." Melody brushed back tears with her hand. "Rubrum is dying."

"What do you mean it's dying?"

Todd sounded more suspicious than concerned.

"Our people lived under a fallen sun," Melody said. "The life cycle of that sun is drawing to an end. Rubrum is sharing that fate. The atmosphere grows thinner each day. Rivers and lakes are drying up. Plants and animals are perishing in large numbers."

"So why come here?" he asked. "Out of all the planets in galaxy to choose from, why this one?"

Todd stood over the alien as he questioned her. To Paige, it appeared her brother was trying to tower over Melody so he could intimidate her. Melody kept her eyes locked on the communicator. She refused to make eye contact with Todd.

"Many planets we cannot hope to reach in a lifetime, even with our fastest ships. We identified habitable planets close enough to make a wide-scale evacuation work."

"How many planets are we talking here?" Todd had entered full interrogation mode. "How many of your kind were you planning to transport from your dying planet?"

Melody closed her eyes and rested her free hand under her small chin.

"We sent research cells to a score of planetary systems. My cell was selected to come here. We hoped to eventually evacuate hundreds of thousands who remained behind on Rubrum."

Hundreds of thousands.

Paige exchanged worried glances with Todd. He showed the same fear on his face gripping every inch of her body. The sheer number Melody dropped blew their minds. These aliens had more than enough manpower to mount a successful full-scale invasion of Earth. Would the others make their way here sooner rather than later?

They could not let any of these invaders from Rubrum take over Earth – no matter what the cost.

"Earth is our home. We're not giving it up without a fight." Heather vocalized Paige's thoughts. "I feel bad for your people. I really do. But it's also obvious they don't want to coexist in peace with us."

Melody opened her eyes again. She let out a deep sigh and answered Heather with a sad nod.

"I understand and I expect nothing less. Our bodies cannot tolerate the bright harsh light of your sun. Our efforts to adapt have borne no fruit. We must go elsewhere."

Paige couldn't help feeling skeptical. She came to them alone. That didn't exactly offer a promising sign as far as she was concerned.

"Do any of the other aliens feel the same way?"

"They fear Barber," Melody replied. "Once he is removed as cell leader, I can take control and convince the others to leave your planet peacefully."

"Will they listen to you?" Heather asked.

"I believe they will listen."

"What makes you so sure?"

"Barber is not the only leader who resides within our ranks," Melody said. "Others in our research cell are aware of my status with the Rubrum Transition Council. My voice will be accepted as one belonging to a leader."

Melody stared down at the communicator again. Chatter flickered from it like voices on a ham radio. The voices spoke in an unfamiliar language. Paige did not know how to describe it. Some words almost resembled a Slavic dialect in their guttural tones. Others did not resemble a single thing from any languages she heard spoken before now.

"What are they saying?"

Paige turned to see Jason joining the rest of the group clustered around Melody. He finally gave up on his pout for the time being. The alien did not glance up or say anything to Jason. Static crackled over the communicator, blocking out voices for a few seconds. Melody tilted her head and shifted the gadget in her hands.

"What are they saying?" Jason asked again.

"Barber is calling for a gathering of cell leaders in the field," Melody said. "No details. They are simply ordered to meet in the town square before the next sun cycle starts."

"Is that a good thing?" Heather asked.

Melody nodded.

"It means we can sneak inside the observation center with minimal resistance and shut down the energy barrier that encloses this town."

Paige's heart skipped a beat upon hearing this news. A smile crept from the corners of her mouth and flashed across her lips. For the first time, she had hope. Shutting down the energy barrier meant one thing.

Home.

They could escape this horrible place and go home at last.

RICH HELD OUT hope for as long as possible. He kept telling himself a rescue was imminent. Paige escaped. She would rally the others. They would figure out a way to track him down before too much time passed.

Neither Andrew nor Mara, the transport driver, anticipated what unfolded outside the house. Rich discerned as much from their deep frowns and worried eyes. His heart pounded when the second transport arrived, and a laser blast hit the rear of the first one after Andrew shoved him inside.

The jolt from that laser fire sent both Rich and Andrew careening forward. They landed in a heap on the floor. Rich saw this as his opportunity to escape. He glanced over and noticed Andrew holding his forehead after it struck the seat in front of him. Rich pushed himself to his knees and tugged on the chain around his neck. His fingers dug at the spot where Andrew connected the links.

"Don't fire! My friend is inside!"

Rich's ears perked up at Paige's protests outside the transport. What did she think she was doing? The other transport needed to keep firing. It gave Rich the distraction he needed to get outside again.

With a final tug, the chain fell from around his neck. Rich gasped and groped at his throat. He couldn't see the bruise no doubt forming there. Still, a throbbing soreness from being choked by that awful metal for so long consumed his neck.

Rich stumbled toward the transport exit.

"Paige! Help me get –"

A hand reached out and yanked on his leg. It brought him crashing to the transport floor once again. Andrew wrapped his arm around the leg, just below the knee. Rich kicked at him with the opposite leg but could not find a good enough angle to land an effective blow.

"You aren't going anywhere, dude." Each word slithered out of Andrew's mouth to form a venomous sneer. "I'm not reporting back to Barber empty-handed."

At once, open doors on the transport sealed shut. Rich glanced up. Mara strapped herself into the driver's seat and activated the engine. A rumbling whoosh echoed through the interior. She cast her eyes back at the jumbled mess Andrew and Rich had become in the rear of the transport.

"Secure the prisoner at once," Mara said. "This will be a turbulent ride."

Rich tried to pull himself off the floor. If only he could reach the front of the transport. Few options remained where Rich saw himself getting out of this situation in one piece. Perhaps if he reached the alien, he could overpower her and force a crash landing. He liked his odds of survival better in that scenario than going back to wherever the transport was headed.

His efforts to push forward met stiff resistance. Andrew wrenched Rich's leg and dropped him to the floor again. At that same moment, another laser bolt smashed into the rear window of the transport. Glass shards exploded into the air and rained down on their bodies. Mara ducked her head to avoid shards that zipped toward the front of the transport.

The transport shot straight upward until it hovered above the trees. More shots followed from the other vehicle, but none of those blasts impacted their transport. A twisted smile formed on his lips as he continued to jostle with Andrew.

"You're so screwed." The fear consuming Rich earlier drained from his voice as he contemplated Andrew's fate. "All that effort to infiltrate our group and you still didn't rescue the captive alien."

Andrew didn't say a word. He simply grappled until he got leverage on Rich. Only a couple of minutes passed before Andrew wrapped both arms around his neck in a chokehold. Rich gasped for breath and clawed at the limbs. His vision grew grainier much like a low-quality video.

Finally, darkness enveloped his eyes.

When Rich regained consciousness again, he found himself laying on a metallic platform inside a chamber. Dull red light flooded the room. Rich sat up straight and at once clenched his teeth. He pinched his eyes shut and pressed his hand tight against his temple. A throbbing sensation spread through the inside of his skull. It felt like an invisible hand wrapped fingers around his brain and tried to squeeze it like an orange.

Once the throbbing subsided a bit, Rich opened his eyes a second time. They darted from end to end in the chamber as he surveyed his surroundings. Walls, floor, and ceiling all were made from some type of metal. No windows inside the chamber. No visible door. Aside from the platform, a pair of vertical columns were the only other objects present inside the cramped room. Each column stood about seven feet tall and featured a series of lights.

Rich squinted at the column nearest to the platform. He wondered what purpose the red light served. Every streetlamp in Travis also shone red. Todd went to great lengths to surround the house where they all hid with bright incandescent lights of all shapes and sizes. Rich knew those lights bothered the aliens. Actual sunlight did the same. Why? How come they seemed to cope with red light, but not other types of light? Rich wished he knew answers to these questions so he could use the information to his advantage. There had to be a way of escaping from this room and that sort of information might prove useful.

A metallic whoosh greeted him. His eyes opened wide again as a vertical crack formed in the metal wall behind the two light columns. It widened into an open doorway and revealed an alien standing in a corridor on the other side.

The alien approached Rich with long, measured strides. Piercing black ovals fixed on him and a stern expression greeted him. It made Rich feel akin to an object examined under a microscope. An object. That summed up nicely what he meant to the alien.

"So, you're working with the one called Todd?" The alien's words felt more like a statement than a question to Rich. "I assume there are more of you skulking around, concealing yourselves like a cimea nest deep inside a cave."

A defiant smirk popped onto Rich's face.

"I am the one called Rich," he said. "And there are more of us than you can count. The others are all coming for you. So maybe you should let me go now. While there's still time."

The alien pinched his lips together. He marched right up to Rich and seized him by the jaw. Fingers pressed into his jawbone as the alien tilted his head upward. He lifted off the platform a few inches.

"Listen to me, human. You are not in a position to make threats. Tell us how to permanently deactivate all the lethal lights, so we can round up the others."

Rich's smirk vanished. There wasn't a single way in hell he would betray his friends to a bunch of homicidal aliens.

"Figure it out on your own."

The alien slammed him back down on the platform. He wrenched his hand away from Rich's jaw. Pain shot through his tailbone and jawbone at the exact same moment. Rich grimaced and rubbed his jaw with his hand.

"Your defiance amuses me." The alien's tone revealed the opposite was true. "A few little lights will not protect you forever. We are close to adapting our bodies to live on this planet. When we do, it will belong to us alone."

The chamber door opened again. A second alien entered the room. The first alien jerked his head around to face the newcomer.

"What is it?"

The second alien bowed his head and quickly looked back up.

"Sincere apologies for disturbing you, Barber. We may have reached a breakthrough with one of our test subjects."

"Which one?"

"The small furry animal we captured following an earlier sun cycle. It shows an ability to withstand harsher light without the same severe reactions as the humans."

Barber glanced over at Rich. A victorious smile washed over his thin lips. Seeing his smirk made Rich shudder.

"It appears your defiance is useless," he said.

"We'll see about that," Rich replied.

"Believe my words when I tell you that the time will soon arrive when you and your fellow humans shall see no more sun cycles."

"Are you threatening me?"

"What do your ears tell you?"

Rich grew stone faced. It dawned on him what sort of "help" Barber would have offered if they had followed the alien named Melody to meet him. It also underscored the danger Rich now faced. If he didn't figure out a way to escape from this place, he would be a dead man.

Or worse.

"You're gonna kill me."

Barber didn't say a word. He turned and marched out of the chamber with the other alien. Rich stared at the floor for a moment and buried his face in his hands. What could he do? He didn't have the slightest idea of how to open the chamber door from the inside.

"Don't let them brand you."

Rich jerked his head up. His eyes darted around the chamber. No one else remained inside with him. Still, a voice as clear as each breath escaping from his mouth flooded the chamber.

"Branding lets them control your mind like a puppet on strings."

Rich sprang to his feet. The voice sounded low and weak. But it also didn't sound alien. A captive human in a neighboring chamber? Maybe they could work together to get out of this place.

"Who are you?"

"I lived in Travis before the invaders overran our town. I fought them in the supermarket. I lost."

Rich pinpointed the part of the chamber where he heard the other prisoner. He trudged over to the opposite side of the chamber and pressed his ear against the wall.

"How are you still alive?" Rich asked.

"I wonder about that same thing every day. I don't know the Good Lord's purpose in letting me rot in this alien prison. He sure won't tell me."

"Is there a way out of here?"

"Doors only open from the outside. I injured both legs in the battle with the invaders. I'm not mobile enough to overpower the guards."

Rich glanced down at his own arms and legs. Aside from a handful of minor gashes and bruises, all his limbs remained in working order. He faced no such obstacle.

"I can get us both out of here. Listen for the guards and alert me when one is coming."

Silence greeted Rich. He tapped on the wall with his index finger. No response. Rich tried kicking it with his foot.

"Did you hear me?"

A deep panting noise greeted him this time.

"Yeah … I can do it." The voice seemed more strained this time. "Be ready for them."

Rich sat down on the edge of the platform again. He leaned forward. His eyes were glued to the chamber entrance. Both columns streamed a steady flow of red light. Rich wondered if he could find some way to turn off the lights or at least change the color setting. It made him feel like he was stuck inside a laser grid with no way out.

He studied the nearest light column. It showed no visible buttons or switches. The aliens must control these lights from a separate room. Rich wondered if he could pry the lights loose from the column. If he had a tool, doing it might not pose much of a problem. Tugging at lights with his bare hands presented a whole different story.

"An invader is coming. I can hear them."

Rich sprang to his feet upon hearing the voice from the other chamber again. A shudder gripped him at the same time. The voice sounded much rougher than a while ago. Rich crept past the light column and pressed his back against the wall. His fist doubled up and he drew in a deep breath.

Rich heard footsteps down the corridor. Feet clomping against the metal floor. He turned his head so he could see the alien entering the chamber. A metallic whoosh followed. An alien stepped through the open doorway holding a bowl.

"Feeding time."

Rich bit down on his lip and worked to disguise his breathing from his visitor. When the alien stopped between the light columns, he made his move. Rich sprang forward and delivered a hard jab to the alien's ear. He staggered sideways and banged into the near light column. The bowl popped out from the alien's hands. A gray chunky soup splattered across the floor as the bowl went airborne. It clanked with a thud against the floor several feet ahead of the alien.

The alien slumped to his knees. Rich grabbed him around the neck and rained blows on the alien's head. After getting in half a dozen punches, Rich released him from his grasp and the alien sank to the ground. Bruises formed around the right eye and on the right cheek.

Rich darted through the open doorway. His eyes scanned the corridor in both directions.

No sign of other aliens.

"How do I open your chamber?"

"It scans you … I think."

Rich's face crinkled into a look of disgust. This revelation would have proven more useful before he knocked out the alien. He certainly didn't think letting himself get scanned was a good idea.

"Give me a second."

Rich backtracked inside the chamber. He grabbed the alien by the armpits and dragged him outside. Then, Rich propped him up in front of the neighboring chamber. A small sensor flickered above the door. It activated upon detecting the alien and Rich. A small red light washed over the alien's face and body. Rich did his best to not let the light touch him. He wasn't sure if he succeeded or not.

An electronic voice spoke once the red light vanished. The chamber door slid open with a whoosh, vanishing into a slot in the wall. Rich held the unconscious alien out in front of him, treating him like a makeshift shield, as he stepped into the doorway of the chamber.

A lower level of red light flooded this chamber than what he experienced. Rich glanced to the side and quickly saw a reason for it. Someone or something shattered lights on one column. A recent occurrence judging by the looks of it. Only one column still supplied light to the room. The prisoner occupying the chamber had his back turned toward Rich. He stood hunched over with a hand pressed against the wall.

"Come on. Let's hurry and get out of here before more of them show up."

"I don't know how … I can repay you."

The prisoner's voice sounded rougher and lower than it did through the wall a few minutes earlier. He turned away from the wall. Rich got a good look at him for the first time.

His heart started pounding anew. Rich's eyes grew as wide as plates and his grip tightened on the unconscious alien.

"What the hell are you?"

The prisoner looked less human than any human Rich had ever seen. Clusters of small holes peppered his arms and face. The sort of holes you expect to see in a honeycomb or a strawberry, not a human being. Each hole held a partially visible spore. The man's face appeared craggy and leathery between the holes. He bore jagged teeth and a pair of chin horns.

All ingredients for a living nightmare.

Rich stumbled backward out into the corridor. He slipped and fell on his butt. The unconscious alien tumbled down on top of him. Panicked heaves gripped Rich's chest as he became pinned under the full weight of the alien's body.

"Don't leave me here," the prisoner said.

At once, he lunged forward and charged toward the corridor. Rich slid out from under the alien. His last foot kicked away from the alien as the prisoner dove on top. He crunched into the alien's neck and growled like a wild animal. The alien's eyes bolted open, and he screamed as he struggled to push off the mutated human.

Rich scrambled to his feet and took off down the corridor. A red light washed over him as he turned a corner. An alarm sounded through the corridor while an electronic voice repeated a warning in an alien language. Rich trapped himself in a virtual maze. He didn't have the slightest clue where to turn or where to run.

How was he going to get out of here?

A pair of aliens popped out in front of him, brandishing weapons. Rich turned to go down a different corridor. Another alien emerged out of a room behind him. Rich had his answer.

He wasn't going anywhere.

PAIGE STUDIED THE image projected from the alien communicator. It showed Melody standing in front of a ravine with a second female alien and a large furry animal. Paige traced the outline of the animal with her finger. She had never seen anything quite like it before. The animal possessed long limbs, a thick long tail, a husky body, and a furry snout with deep big eyes and tufts of hair sprouting from triangular ears.

"Your pet looks like a cross between a dog, a cat, and a monkey to me," Paige said. She handed the communicator back to Melody. "It's so cute."

Melody smiled.

"Oarc is a wonderful little treema. A bundle of constant energy. We enjoyed so many fun times together."

"You must really miss him." Paige offered up that conclusion after seeing the way Melody gazed at that image from her home planet. "Our family cat, Peanut, got on my nerves while I still lived at home. But I ended up missing the little bugger more than I ever expected when I left for college."

"What do you miss about your cat?"

“There’s something comforting about having a cat curling up in your lap during the day and snuggling up against your legs at night.”

“Oarc is not the only one who left behind a hole impossible to fill. I feel Halilah’s absence in a much more profound way.”

“Halilah? Is she the other one in the –”

“She is my sister,” Melody offered an answer before Paige finished the question. “My only sister. The only family left since the death of my parents.”

Paige frowned.

“I’m sorry. That must have been tough on you.”

Melody nodded.

“I cursed their loss over many sun cycles. I went through torment, wondering if something could have been done to prevent the fatal hull breach that claimed them. Eventually, I had no choice but to accept their fate.”

“Where is your sister now?”

“She remains on my home planet for now. Only a small number of us were selected for research cells. The rest of our people planned to follow once a suitable planet could be found for settlement.”

Paige stared past Melody at the boarded-up living room windows. She wondered how it would feel to be separated from her family with scant hopes of reunion. In a way, Melody endured trials that mirrored what Todd had gone through in Travis. Both lost loved ones under tragic circumstances. Paige’s heart ached over learning Caroline’s fate. She didn’t want to experience the further pain of losing parents, or a spouse, or children. She didn’t want to endure the same level of pain her brother or their new alien ally endured.

“This is the last of it.”

A pair of backpacks dropped on the coffee table in front of Paige. She looked up. Jason stood over her with a determined look on his face.

"That didn't take long," Paige said. "The person who used to live here really did stockpile everything imaginable."

Paige grabbed the nearest backpack and unzipped it. She scanned the contents. It went far beyond a 72-hour kit. Flashlights. Knifes. Matches. Food. Water. Thermal blankets. Every possible bit of survival gear crammed inside. One thing seemed certain. Todd and Jason counted on not coming back to this place when they put the gear together.

Todd, Heather, Jason, and Paige all changed into dark clothing covering their arms and legs to match Melody's outfit. The group met up inside the garage, each toting a backpack. Paige swore she enlisted with some sort of special ops team with how Todd outfitted everyone.

"I'm going to shut off the lights for a minute for our alien here," Todd said. "Once the garage door is open, all y'all need to make a run for the alien's vehicle. I'll meet you at the transport once I've turned on the juice again."

He opened the garage door. Melody stood back in the shadows until Todd flipped the breakers. Darkness enveloped the driveway and front yard. Melody dashed out of the garage with long-legged strides. Paige, Heather, and Jason sprinted across the lawn behind her. They piled inside the transport while Melody activated the engines.

Todd did not immediately follow the others. He ran over to spotlights aimed at the garage door and the front door and activated motion sensors. Then, he raced back into the garage and flipped breakers back to their original position. Todd switched off all lights, except ones operating on motion sensors. He grinned when those lights flipped on as he closed the garage door and sprinted past the sensors.

"A little gift for any aliens or other creatures who decide to drop by for a visit."

A rumbling whoosh echoed through the interior. The transport shot upward until it hovered above trees lining both sides of the street. Paige stared down at the driveway and yard below. No trace remained of Gregor – the alien who Todd had taken prisoner – except for a smeared trail of dark blood across the cement and grass.

"The dead alien vanished." Concern rose in Paige's voice. "Do you think we're being watched?"

Todd leaned over and peered out the same window as her. He shook his head.

"A former human lurking around here got to it."

Heather recoiled when he said those words.

"You mean?"

"They had a midnight snack," Todd said.

Paige grimaced and pressed her hand against her mouth. Heather did the same. Jason's mouth simply dropped open. The thought of a mutated human chowing down on an alien still seemed sick and wrong, no matter how many terrible things the aliens from Rubrum had done in this town.

"Why don't we just fly this out of here?"

Jason's question broke an uncomfortable silence in the transport. Paige thought he made a good point. The transport hovered above the trees, and she saw it fly up the street earlier. Forget shutting off the barrier. Flying out of this place seemed like a smarter and safer option.

Melody did not bother to even glance back at him before shooting down Jason's idea.

"Your idea is flawed. This transport cannot serve as an escape vehicle."

"Why not?"

Heather and Jason blurted out the question at the same time.

"The barrier we put in place also extends over the top of the town," Melody said. "We cannot fly much higher above these trees without risking a collision."

Paige's heart sank at hearing the explanation. Of course, it wouldn't be that easy. Nothing was easy when it came to finding a way out of this damn town. At least, they were safer in the air than on the ground. No mutated humans could attack them here.

They only had to worry about evading other aliens en route to the observation center.

Melody shifted a lever forward on a center console. The transport zipped above the street. She leaned forward and placed her hands into two pads atop corresponding short columns. Each pad contained a hand imprint that molded to the size and shape of Melody's hands. If she moved either hand a certain direction, the transport shifted in the same direction. Paige found it fascinating to watch Melody steer the transport in this fashion. She had grown so used to seeing a steering wheel in other vehicles. It seemed strange to not see one now.

A voice crackled over a communicator embedded in another console at the front of the transport. The words were in Melody's native language. Worry flashed through her eyes when Melody glanced down at the communicator. She said a few words Paige didn't understand, but her voice sounded different than normal – like Melody was trying to disguise it. After exchanging a few more words with the other voice, Melody switched off the communicator.

The transport veered left and made a U-turn. Paige cast her eyes at Jason, Heather, and Todd. Their expressions matched the alarm she felt. What was Melody doing? Where was she taking them?

"What's going on?"

Todd's gruff voice broke the silence inside the transport.

"Barber wants all prisoners brought to the main town square." Melody's tone turned somber. "He intends to send a message to the last of the human resistance."

Fear flickered through Paige's eyes. Did she intend to turn them over to Barber after all? The others drew the same conclusion. Jason slammed the back of his fist against the transport. Heather sat on her seat; lips pinched tight in quiet shock. Todd lunged forward. Paige barely caught his arm. She pulled him backwards by the elbow to keep him from attacking the alien.

"You betrayed us!" His demeanor channeled his military days once again. "This was a ruse to round us all up."

Melody glanced over her shoulder. A frown washed over her face. Paige could tell Todd's accusation clearly bothered her.

"I am not taking you to Barber. We are going to try to rescue your friend and other captive humans. Do you not see that? Is this not what you wanted to do from the beginning?"

"I thought you said we couldn't do anything for Rich." Heather spoke up in a quieter than normal tone. "Aren't we still risking getting captured?"

"Our circumstances have changed," Melody said.

"In what way?" Paige asked.

"The prisoners will now be out in the open instead of locked in containment chambers. We can intercept and free the prisoners before the cell leaders gather."

Paige started to smile at her line of thinking until she glanced at Todd. His troubled expression made her renewed hopes turn to doubts.

"This feels like a trap," he said.

"It is our best chance to rescue your friend."

Todd looked down and closed his eyes while plunging into deep thought. He opened them again after a few seconds and gave a reluctant nod.

"I hope you know what you're doing."

The transport soon circled above the main town square. Red streetlamp light did little to illuminate the square's features. Paige made out a central stone plaza in the square. A giant statue stood amid the center of that plaza. Hip-high sandstone rock walls surrounded the statue on all four sides only a few yards away. The walls formed a square within a square. Lamps lined a path cutting north to south through the border wall. The path led to both the front and the back of the statue. Open grass, interspersed with some trees, surrounded the plaza and filled out the square. A wrought iron fence bordered the square on all sides, dividing it from sidewalks and roads.

Melody steered the transport past the main town square itself. It veered right toward an empty alley behind an abandoned drug store about a football field length from the square. No sign of human or alien activity surfaced near the drug store nor in the alley. The transport descended until it hovered a few feet from the ground. Melody engaged a magnetic lock to tether it to that spot behind the drug store.

"Remain silent and follow my lead," she said. "Secure your lights and other weapons."

On cue, Paige drew out a broad knife and a sturdy flashlight from her backpack. She placed those items inside her jacket and zipped up the backpack again. Paige tossed a strap over one shoulder. Todd, Jason, and Heather all followed suit. They exited the transport behind Melody. The doors sealed with a whoosh behind the group. All five skulked along the alley behind the drug store and made their way toward the town square.

Heather's eyes darted from side to side like she expected a mutated human or alien to pop out of the shadows at any minute.

"Everything is too quiet around here," she said. "It's freaking me out."

Paige couldn't blame her for feeling that way. The energy barrier enclosing the town made the whole place feel so devoid of life. Just hearing a random meow or bark or bird call would do so much to ease tension she felt from head to toe.

Only absolute stillness greeted the group.

The alley soon intersected with a road running in front of the square. Melody emerged from the alley and halted on the sidewalk. She glanced both ways. Then, the alien looked over her shoulder and beckoned the others to move forward. They all crept across the road and crouched down along the fence line. Melody pulled out a pair of binoculars, furnished from Todd's supplies, and surveyed the other end of the plaza.

Paige mirrored her actions. She peered at a square building standing on an adjoining square across from the plaza. Sandstone formed the exterior much like the stone wall in the plaza. The roof appeared flat except for a small dome rising near the middle. Narrow stone steps, flanked by a stone pillar on either side, climbed to a central door at the front of the building. Given the prominent location and fancy architecture, Paige assumed this used to be the Travis town hall.

Similar stone pillars ran parallel to the path leading from the building to the plaza. Pillars alternated with lamps towering over the path. These lamps also cast light tinged with a distinct red hue. Seeing red lights everywhere in Travis – except at the house Todd occupied – nagged at Paige.

"What's with all the red lights?" she whispered to Melody. "Did your people do this?"

The alien nodded without glancing away from her binoculars. Melody kept her eyes locked on the building and plaza.

"We forced captive humans to coat every light with a special substance. It created a filter that protects our skin from the light."

The domed building's front door opened. Several aliens and humans marched down the steps. Paige adjusted the binoculars to get a closer look. Metallic restraints bound each human's limbs. Similar metallic collars circled their necks.

One lone alien emerged from inside the building behind the first group. He glanced down at a gadget resting in his hand. Paige thought the gadget resembled a king-sized thumb drive. Four buttons ran down the face of the device.

"Barber is here."

Fear clung to those three words. Melody kept a firm grip on the binoculars, but her voice betrayed apprehension her body didn't show.

"Can you see Rich?" Jason asked.

"Your friend is the last human in restraints," Melody said. "I do not recognize the other two, but they are dressed in uniforms."

Todd snatched the other pair of binoculars out of Paige's hands.

"Thanks for asking. Rude much?"

She grabbed at the binoculars after they slipped out of her grasp and tried to rip them out of her brother's hands without success. Todd turned his shoulder to block Paige's hand with his body. He held up the binoculars and studied the uniforms on the figures in the distance.

"Combat fatigues," he finally said. "Army rangers from the looks of it. If soldiers are showing up, the Pentagon must have gotten word something bad is happening out here."

"Let's see if we can get closer and draw them away from Rich and the soldiers," Jason said. "If we create a distraction, a couple of us can free them."

Todd lowered the binoculars and shook his head.

"We need to stay back. Something isn't tracking right with this situation. This all feels more and more like a trap."

Once they were within her grasp again, Paige snatched the binoculars away from Todd. Her brother sighed.

"Feel better now?"

Paige shot him a sarcastic smirk.

"Much better. Thank you."

She peered through the binoculars again at the alien whom Melody identified as Barber. He pressed three buttons on his gadget in a sequence. Little yellow lights embedded in each collar began flashing. Intervals between each flash grew shorter and faster.

"I am afraid nothing can be done for your friend." Melody's voice started to tremble. "There is no gathering. This is indeed a trap."

Paige lowered the binoculars. They fell from her hand to the ground. She sprang to her feet at the same time as Jason and Heather. They charged toward the open gate into the plaza. Paige heard Todd drop a mumbled curse as she raced past him. He and Melody also jumped to their feet and followed hot on their heels trying to overtake the other three.

Lights on each collar turned red after a final flash. Each alien accompanying Barber stepped back from the humans. He pressed a fourth larger button below the first three on his gadget. At once, all three prisoners dropped to their knees on the cement path in front of the steps. Their faces contorted in pain.

Paige gasped and froze. Tears streamed down her face as Rich let out a horrendous gasp. Within a few seconds, the collar lights switched back to yellow. Each alien stepped forward again and unlatched the collars and restraints from around the prisoners.

Rich's lifeless head popped free from his body. It fell onto the cement path along with the heads of both soldiers. His face remained forever frozen in painful terror.

Heather stopped in her tracks and fell to her knees sobbing. Jason kept going. He reached the stone wall surrounding the plaza before Todd finally tackled him and held him down on the ground.

Barber walked down the stone steps, barely acknowledging the three detached heads on the ground as he passed. He approached the stone wall from the opposite side. Melody shrank from his gaze. Hiding didn't really make a difference at this point.

They were all visible to Barber now.

Paige trembled from head to toe but still gave Barber the best death glare she could muster. The alien seemed amused by their collective reaction to what they had witnessed.

"So nice of you to join us here," Barber said. "It saves me the trouble of tracking you down and terminating you before a new sun cycle begins."

ADRENALINE SURGED THROUGH Jason's veins. He threw Todd off his back and sprang to his feet. Paige reached out her arm and shook her head. Her boyfriend ignored the silent warning. She discerned the thoughts now consuming Jason. Rich had been his best friend almost from the time they met in the dorms during their first year at McNeese State. Now Jason witnessed his murder without being able to lift a finger to stop it.

He wanted blood. Barber's blood. His rage would not be quenched until that alien shared Rich's fate.

"I'm gonna tear you apart, you son of a bitch."

Jason unsheathed his knife with one hand. He drew out his flashlight and flicked it on with the other hand. Paige shot a frantic glance at her brother. Todd pulled himself to his feet. Before he could reach out his arm to restrain Jason again, he charged past the stone wall toward Barber.

Todd directed an angry glare back at Paige like she bore responsibility for Jason's actions.

"Your damn boyfriend is gonna get himself killed and take the rest of us with him."

When Barber spotted Jason waving the knife and flashlight, he ducked behind the stone wall. Paige heard Barber's voice a second later, shouting at the aliens behind him in his native language. Each alien pulled back their coat and drew out a weapon.

"Jason! Get down!"

He ignored Paige's pleas. Laser bolts streaked toward him. One punched a hole through the head of his flashlight. The light beam instantly shorted out. A second bolt struck him under his right shoulder.

Jason tossed the broken flashlight aside. He groaned and clutched his arm. Jason staggered backward before finally collapsing in front of the stone wall. Laser bolts smashed against sandstone above him. Jason dragged himself along the wall until he reached the other side.

An unsettling mix of howls and guttural growls pierced the air. Paige cast her eyes at a nearby tree. A creature perched in the branches. It hunched forward, ready to dive on her once Paige moved into the right position. Her legs grew stiff and locked in place. She wanted to scream at each limb to move. Both became rooted to the ground as firmly as twin tree trunks.

The creature plunged from the branch anyway. It hit the ground hard but shifted at once into a four-legged sprint, with eyes fixed on her. Paige saw the creature clearly now in the red light.

An altered human.

She screamed. Paige tossed up her arms to shield herself from this monster closing in on her. At once, a flashlight beam fixed on the altered human and moved with it, focused on the eyes. The creature wailed and turned its gnarled bony hands into a makeshift face shield. Paige glanced back. Todd pinned his flashlight beam on the creature. She finally recovered her ability to run and bolted out of the way before the creature slammed into the ground and stumbled to a stop several yards behind her.

All three aliens accompanying Barber reached the other end of the stone wall and fired more laser bolts. Melody and Todd had both drawn out beater weapons. They returned fire. Melody's first two shots hit the stone wall. Todd found his mark.

The nearest alien dropped his weapon. He clutched the middle of his chest and slumped forward. His body dangled over the top of the stone wall. The remaining two aliens kept firing laser bolts at the group.

Todd glanced back at Paige and Heather.

"Keep low to the ground. Whatever you do, stay behind the plaza wall."

Paige and Heather both nodded and ducked down as much as possible while still running. As they neared the wall, another altered human sprang out from the darkened grassy area off to the side of the path. It looked different than the other one. This creature had a heavy brow and sported patches of coarse hair across its bare chest and limbs. It also possessed jagged teeth and breathed loud enough from running toward her to be heard from the other end of the square.

"Look out!"

Paige tugged on Heather's shoulder. The creature closed in on her position. Heather swung her flashlight right at its head. The beam hit the creature square in the face. It growled and veered away from the bright light.

Heather turned and sprinted forward again. She reached the stone wall and dropped down behind it next to Jason. Paige made it to the wall only a few seconds after Heather. She crawled over to Jason. His chin had dipped to his chest. Jason clutched his shoulder where the laser bolt struck. Paige cried out and smacked his healthy arm.

"Are you trying to get yourself killed too? We just lost Rich. I don't wanna lose you too."

Jason gazed into her eyes and offered up a weak apologetic smile. It yielded to a grimace as a new burst of pain dug into his shoulder.

"I'm sorry. I didn't know what else to do. I couldn't let them get away with it." He shook his head as his voice quavered. "They murdered him. They murdered Rich right in front of us."

Fresh tears trickled down her cheeks. She planted a kiss on his lips.

"We'll make them pay. I promise."

Paige slipped her backpack off her shoulders. Heather unzipped a pocket and pulled out some gauze and tape. Paige removed a backpack strap from Jason's injured shoulder. She grabbed a small pair of scissors and cut away burnt and bloody fabric surrounding the wound. The laser bolt struck Jason just above his pectoral muscle. Heather pressed a gauze pad against the wound and taped it tight against the skin.

The white gauze began to take on a red hue. It hadn't stopped the bleeding. Paige hoped the gauze would at least slow his blood loss until they reached a safer spot where she could give Jason's wound a closer look.

A second alien screamed. Paige peeked over the wall as the alien staggered to the ground. Dark blood seeped from holes in his chest and head into a crack on the cement path. She cast her eyes at the other end on their side of the stone wall. Melody and Todd both crouched behind the wall now. One or the other intermittently popped up to fire a laser bolt before taking cover again.

Growls behind her grew closer. Paige spun around to see both altered humans back on their feet. They stalked toward her, Heather, and Jason like hyenas zeroing in on a fresh carcass.

She backed up against the stone wall. Heather did the same. The creature with the heavy brow lunged forward. It snarled. Paige swung her flashlight up above her head as the creature went airborne. Once again, the beam found a destination in the creature's eyes.

It grunted and shielded its eyes. The creature dropped to the ground right in front of Paige, landing only a few feet from her lap. Heather's eyes widened as the former human's head shot up and it uttered another growl.

"I don't know if a simple flashlight is gonna cut it with these things," she said.

Paige nodded and unsheathed her knife. Heather did the same. The surrounding laser fire finally died down. Paige didn't dare look over to see how Todd and Melody were doing at this point. Her eyes remained locked on both creatures pacing back and forth in front of her, Heather, and Jason.

The second creature lurched forward and took a swipe at Paige. It revealed a gnarled hand with claws. Small spikes protruded from bony knobs down the length of its arm. Paige gulped as the creature snarled and howled at her.

A laser bolt struck the creature in the side, cutting through ribs. It groaned and staggered to the ground. The creature dropped to its knees. Paige darted forward and shoved the knife into its belly. It snapped at her forearm with jagged teeth. Paige jammed her flashlight inside the creature's mouth to keep it from biting her. A muffled yowl greeted Paige. The former human gagged and clawed at the flashlight for a few seconds before finally sinking to the ground dead.

"Darkness gives them life," Todd said. "Light takes it away."

Paige rolled her eyes at his bad pun. She might have unleashed a snappy comeback under normal circumstances, but the image of Rich's head rolling on the ground without his body made her blood boil. This was not a time or place for cracking jokes.

While they took out the second creature, Melody and Heather teamed up to take out the first one. Heather blinded the creature a second time with her flashlight before it regained its footing. More howls greeted her, followed by swats at the flashlight. Melody crept out from against the stone wall. She swung behind the creature and fired a laser bolt.

It punched a hole through the creature's neck. The first creature let out a dying gasp and fell forward in a heap on the grass.

Paige turned her attention back to Jason. He rested against the stone wall, clutching his shoulder. His breathing grew heavy and labored. She knelt by his side. Jason clenched his teeth and looked up at Paige with a half-squint.

"I never knew getting shot would hurt this bad. Action movies make it look like no big deal."

Paige brushed her fingers through his red hair and gave his other hand a gentle squeeze.

"Don't try to move or speak too much," she said. "We'll get you out of here. Find a safe place and fix up your shoulder."

Todd stayed close to the ground and crept around the outside of the stone wall. When he reached the opposite end, he stood up straight and stamped his foot into the grass.

"Shit! One of the aliens escaped."

Melody gave him a concerned stare. She jumped up and ran around to the other side of the stone wall. Three dead bodies were splayed out on the wall or near the structure. Melody lifted their heads and studied their faces.

"Barber escaped." A hint of a tremor gripped her voice. "We must move fast."

Paige clasped Jason's hand tighter.

"Can you stand? Are you able to walk?"

Jason screwed his eyes shut and nodded.

"I think so."

Heather helped her pull Jason to his feet. He stumbled as soon as they let go. Paige caught his arm again and draped it around her neck.

"I've got you. Don't worry, sweetie."

They started walking toward the wrought iron fence at a deliberate pace. Paige wanted to move faster, but she didn't think Jason could handle a foot race back to the transport. Todd and Melody caught up to them halfway down the path.

Both wore grim expressions.

"I do not know when Barber slipped away from the fight," Melody said. "We must hurry before your window for escape closes."

"What's the plan?" Heather asked. "I think Jason needs some major medical attention. His shoulder wound is serious."

"There is some medical equipment inside the observation center," Melody said. "We may be able to repair the damage, once we arrive."

Paige heard a groan when they reached the fence. It sounded like Todd. She looked over her shoulder as best as she could while holding Jason up. Todd stood hunched over at the entrance. His hand rested on the fence. At once, he clamped his fingers around a fence post. Todd gnashed his teeth and screamed. Paige turned herself and Jason around. Her lips started to tremble, and fear flickered in her eyes.

Melody and Heather rushed over to the fence. Todd clutched at his calf with his other hand. Paige and Jason made their way back to the fence. She leaned Jason against the fence, so he could rest. Todd yanked up both pant legs. Paige slammed her eyes shut and jerked her head away as soon as she saw the condition of each limb.

Bony knobs had formed inside a reopened gash on one leg. Similar protrusions pushed up under the skin on the other leg as well. Paige had seen similar features on a former human they just killed.

Todd was changing.

Melody pushed on a bony knob with her long index finger.

"Bio armor. It has infected his bio code and is trying to grow inside his body."

A frantic expression washed over Paige's face.

"What? Can't you do something to stop it?"

"Not here."

Todd let go of the fence and sank to the ground. He yanked his backpack straps off his shoulders. It struck the grass with a soft thud.

"Open the … front pocket." Todd's voice grew strained while trying not to scream from the pain. "Take out UV … light. Burn it … Burn it."

Heather darted over to Todd's backpack and did as he instructed. She produced a UV flashlight and clicked it on. Heather focused the blue beam on bony knobs protruding from the gash. Todd screamed again and his fingers squeezed the iron fence post. One knob started to melt into a cloudy liquid under the beam. Melody followed suit and retrieved a large flashlight from her coat. She clicked it on and held the beam over another bony knob. They repeated the process until they cleared the wounded leg of knobs.

Melody used her cutting tool to open the skin above and below the bony knobs on the other leg. She and Heather also melted those knobs down to a liquid state. Tears streamed down Todd's face through the entire process. When they finished, Heather mopped up remnant liquid with gauze.

"How bad is it?" Heather asked.

Melody switched off the flashlight and stuck it back in her coat.

"If I can get him to the bio code splicer, I may be able to undo some of the major damage," she said. "The corruption to his bio code has progressed far. I am astonished he has not already become like the creatures we have slain."

"My faith and prayers kept me going," Todd said. His voice remained weak from treatment on his legs. "I fought the changes, as you call them, for as long as hope remained for me to escape this place."

"How the hell did this happen to your legs?" Paige's voice quavered as this question escaped her lips. "Why didn't you say anything?"

"It's a long story."

Paige wasn't in the mood to endure a new round of Todd's usual evasiveness.

"It's a long walk back to the transport and I need answers. Humor me."

Todd panted hard for a few seconds and finally pushed himself up onto his knees. He glanced up at her and shook his head.

"You've never been one to let things drop."

"Damn straight. Especially not this. Now tell me how you got infected with that bio armor stuff in the first place."

As they walked, Todd recounted to Paige how he fought two aliens on the night Caroline died. One wore bio armor. The alien's spikes gashed him, and one snapped off in his leg during the struggle. It splashed a cloudy fluid on visible bone and spread throughout the deep laceration in the flesh of his calf. Todd dislodged the wicked spike right after the fight, but the damage was already done.

He didn't feel any side effects at first. Todd focused his energy over the next few days on burying Caroline, finding a place for shelter from the aliens, and scouting the town while trying to figure out where they controlled the energy barrier so he could shut it down and flee Travis.

Todd only started to experience problems with the leg after he found a suitable hideout and rigged up extra lights for protection. He treated it to the best of his ability before ambushing the alien he now knew to be Gregor and taking him prisoner.

"I hoped the alien I captured would provide much-needed answers," Todd said, finishing up his story. His gait improved while he spoke as the pain subsided again. "I thought it would cooperate after a while. But that thing resisted my interrogation right up until you showed up."

"Why didn't you tell me about this before now?" Paige asked. "You could have turned into one of those creatures and we wouldn't have been prepared for it. You could have killed us all!"

She couldn't help feeling cross with Todd over this revelation. His stubbornness and evasiveness put her and her friends in danger for reasons known only to himself.

"I screwed up big time." Remorse gripped her brother's voice. "I got so concerned with not making you worry about my injuries, I never even thought to ask for help."

"We've gotta hurry," she replied. "We need to get you fixed up before you become one of those monsters too."

Paige felt an increasing weight on her shoulders as they walked through the alley again. By the time they reached the transport, Jason's feet began to drag on the asphalt. She started to lose her balance trying to hold him upright. Paige looked over at her boyfriend. His eyes were growing glassy. Jason's mouth dropped open and he let out a slight moan. He slumped over and then slid from her grasp onto the ground.

"Jason! Somebody help me!"

Paige dropped to her knees. She rolled him over onto his back and pressed her ear to Jason's mouth. No sign of breathing. She pressed her fingers against his wrist. No sign of a heartbeat.

"He's not breathing." Her voice grew more panicked. "I can't find a pulse."

Todd dropped down to the ground next to her. He started doing chest compressions over the breastbone.

"Breathe into his mouth!"

Paige leaned over and gave Jason rescue breaths at the proper intervals. Todd kept pressing his hands at a steady rate. More breaths. No pulse. Jason's eyes remained unchanged. Soon neither could deny reality any longer. All traces of life had vanished from those eyes.

Todd finally pulled away from Jason's chest. Paige looked up at her brother and sobbed.

"No! Please. Don't stop. Don't let him die!"

Todd peered at the shoulder wound. The white gauze pad had turned crimson and grown sopping wet. He peeked underneath the gauze and his face fell when he saw the full extent of the wound. Todd shook his head and closed both of Jason's eyelids with his fingers.

"Your boyfriend didn't have a chance. The laser bolt must have hit a vein. He lost too much blood."

Paige cried out and collapsed on Jason's face. Tears raced down Heather's cheeks as she dropped to her knees next to Paige. Both girls clung to his lifeless body in the alley.

Todd stood and wheeled around to face Melody. He shot the alien a stern glare.

"I hope you're getting a good look at the cost of your people deciding to come here. All of us have lost people we loved because of it."

Melody glanced at the two girls huddled over Jason. She closed her eyes. A deep frown crawled across her lips.

"If we are to survive as a people, it will be on a different planet. I give you my word."

A SOMBER MOOD gripped everyone inside the transport. What started out as a diversion to a potential rescue mission turned into a nightmare. Paige yearned to wake from the nightmare. She wanted nothing more than to pop up from her pillow in her off-campus apartment, hear the alarm clock playing peaceful tunes, and see sunlight peeking through slats in the blinds.

It amounted to nothing more than wishful thinking. Paige's current situation was all too real. She blamed herself for what transpired. Rich's execution. Jason's death following their aborted rescue attempt. None of these things would have happened if she had not dragged them into undertaking this spring break road trip. All a veiled excuse to search for Todd. She found her brother, but at what cost?

Todd slid over and put his arm around Paige.

"I'm so sorry. I know how much you're hurting right now."

Paige glanced up at him and rested her head on her brother's shoulder. A lump formed in her throat anew as she contemplated the loss he suffered prior to her arrival. Caroline also perished at the hands of these invaders from a planet she never knew existed before a few hours ago.

Where in the hell is Rubrum anyway? Paige wondered. *Why did these aliens see a need to travel from a distant place just to destroy a bunch of lives?*

"It's my fault," Paige finally said. "I talked them into coming on this road trip. We wouldn't be here dealing with this mess if it weren't for me."

"It's not your fault."

Heather's voice, though choked with emotion, remained firm. She looked up from the floor and locked eyes with Paige and Todd.

"No one is to blame except those aliens," Heather said. "I, for one, will not let Rich and Jason die in vain. Melody is free to go wherever she chooses. The rest of the invaders can burn in hell."

Paige could not have stated it any better herself. Their plight generated no sympathy from her at this point. Especially not when it produced monsters like Barber and his followers. Rubrum deserved no better fate than to be erased from the collective memory of the universe.

Melody sat in silence, piloting the transport. It zipped over treetops again. They approached a large warehouse on the outskirts of town. Paige shifted her gaze over to Melody. She took mental notes of how the alien steered the transport. At this point, Paige had to prepare for every scenario – including ones where she needed to fly the alien transport herself.

"Can't we just fly the transport out of here?" Heather asked. She studied Melody's piloting with the same intensity as Paige. "I know you said the barrier crosses over the top of the town too. But shouldn't your own vehicles be able to cross through the barrier?"

That idea lit up Paige's mind with a ferocity matching lightning stretching an electric finger across a darkened sky. Why didn't she think to ask this question before now? Of course, the aliens would make it possible to go inside and outside of the barrier. They wouldn't be so foolish as to trap themselves in here along with their human experiments, would they?

Melody shook her head.

"Your thought is not a correct one. The barrier changes the electromagnetic properties in all organic and non-organic matter. It prevents anything that enters through it from returning outside."

"Kind of like a bug zapper," Heather replied.

"A bug zapper?"

"Never mind."

A massive door at the front of the warehouse slid open as their transport approached. The warehouse struck Paige as having an odd appearance. It resembled a structure raised from the ground in an extremely brief time. Mismatched pieces of wood, metal, and stone thrown in a pot and blended together at a drive-thru pace.

Melody reached down and pulled a lever on the console. The transport began its descent toward a landing pad near the front of the warehouse. Her eyes remained focused on the landing pad. Melody had little margin for error since the ship took up so much space. Paige peered through the windshield at a giant metallic ship. It occupied the bulk of the warehouse's interior space and appeared large enough to stretch from end zone to end zone on a football field.

"How in the world did your people build such a huge spaceship?"

A mixture of awe and terror tinged her question. The ship resembled something straight out of a sci-fi movie, but the level of technology it represented scared Paige. Apart from Melody, the aliens from Rubrum possessed no moral or philosophical dilemmas using such technology to subdue the entire town of Travis.

"We assembled this ship and others in industrial shipyards on Rubrum," Melody said. "It needed to be large enough to function as an observation center on a destination planet."

"Just how many other aliens are a part of your research team?"

"The ship holds enough supplies and space for 60 individuals. That is the same number we brought to your planet."

Knowing exactly how many aliens showed up in the ship did nothing to put Paige at ease. Their numbers were large enough that pulling off this escape plan without a hitch would require more than a minor miracle.

The transport stopped a few feet above the landing pad. Melody engaged magnetic locks to keep it stationary. She scooted her seat around, so she could face Paige, Todd, and Heather.

"Follow my lead once we exit the transport," Melody said. "I have created an idea on how we all can get inside."

Melody turned back and reached down under the console. She popped off a panel and withdrew a pen-length rod. A clear crystal chamber composed the top third. A pair of embedded buttons adorned the middle third. The remainder formed into a hard plastic handle.

"What's that thing supposed to do?"

Todd eyeballed the new gadget and cast a suspicious glance at the alien.

"Watch and learn," Melody said.

She opened all transport doors simultaneously and signaled for them to exit the vehicle. Paige started to slide toward an open door when Melody held up her hand.

"Pretend your arms are bound behind you in restraints," Melody said. "It will aid in our ruse."

Paige glanced back at Heather and Todd. Heather shrugged and put her arms behind her back. Paige and Todd followed suit. They waited until Melody exited the transport and walked over to help them climb out as though actual restraints bound their wrists together.

Two guards approached the transport. They cast their eyes toward Paige, Heather, and Todd. Paige's muscles tensed up as the first guard drew closer. The guard's eyes trailed her from head to toe as if she suspected something about the situation was amiss.

The second guard walked toward Melody. His lips curled into a frown.

"You dare to show your face here? Mara and Barber both revealed your treachery to the cell."

"They are mistaken. I played a part so I could do what no one else could do."

The second guard laughed.

"And what part did you play?" he scoffed.

Melody turned and pointed to Todd.

"Have I not brought the one called Todd here? He is the last of the human resistance in this place."

"Barber informed us that you and these humans killed three of our own within this same hour," The first guard said. "Mara told us how you sabotaged a rescue mission in a stolen transport. We are not the fools you think we are."

"Lies. They attacked with brute force. I infiltrated with stealth."

Melody held her chin firm and stared straight at the guard. She did her best to sell the idea she took these humans as prisoners instead of joining forces with them to fight against her fellow aliens. Stern expressions on the faces of both guards told Paige they weren't buying it.

She didn't like the direction this conversation appeared to be traveling. These guards had no intention of letting Melody escort any humans inside the ship. The time had arrived to think of a Plan B. Visions of sharing in Rich's fate and Jason's fate danced in Paige's head. She exchanged worried glances with Todd and Heather.

The second guard glanced over at the first guard and waved her forward.

"We shall send for Barber and sort this out," he said. "Secure the humans and escort them to containment chambers at once."

Paige gnawed on her lip and doubled up a fist behind her back. She had no intention of going down without a fight.

Melody shared the same thought.

As soon as the second guard retrieved his communicator and activated the holographic screen, Melody raised her pen-length rod and jabbed the crystal end against the guard's neck. A little cloudy mist flashed through the interior of the crystal.

The second guard lurched backward. He clutched at his neck and gasped. Only a few seconds passed before his legs gave way and he collapsed in a heap.

"What did you do?"

The first guard drew her weapon and wheeled around to face Melody. Todd sprang forward and wrapped his arms around the guard's throat from behind their back. He forced the alien into a chokehold. She clawed at Todd's forearm but failed to dislodge him from around her neck. Soon the guard's hands fell harmlessly against her sides. Todd finally relaxed his grip and pulled his arms back.

Both guards now lay unconscious and sprawled out across the ground.

"This will be substantially more difficult than I first imagined," Melody said.

She stooped down and rifled through the second guard's pockets. A few seconds later, Melody produced a thin flat crystal. It possessed the same shape as a credit card, but only half the size. Melody also checked the first guard until she located the same item on her body.

Melody handed one crystal to Paige and held onto the other one.

"Insert this into a slot near each entry way," she said. "This will deactivate the bio code scan, so you are not locked out of any area inside the observation center."

Heather cast her eyes down at the unconscious alien guards.

"This feels like another trap," she said. "If your people already know you're helping us, they're gonna be on us faster than fire ants swarming a picnic the minute we're inside."

Melody drew closer to Heather and pressed her hand down on her shoulder. She tried to force a smile on her lips but couldn't muster more than a sliver of one.

"I will do everything in my power to keep the three of you safe. Your survival and escape is my only hope of convincing you that Rubrumians are not all like Barber."

Todd closed his eyes and sucked in his lower lip. He released it with a deep breath and opened his eyes again.

"I'll hold you to it."

Melody slapped metallic restraints around each guard's wrists and above their ankles. Paige and Heather dragged them to a quiet corner inside the warehouse. Todd stooped down and confiscated weapons from each alien guard. He handed one set to Paige and gave the other set to Heather. Now they finally had the same weaponry as Melody and Todd.

"Let's do this," Paige said.

They retrieved the backpacks from the transport. Paige, Heather, and Todd trailed a step behind Melody as she marched up to the outer door of the ship. Melody sidestepped an exterior red sensor light above the door and inserted her crystal into the slot. The light clicked off a second later and the door popped open a crack.

Todd stepped forward and pushed it open. He moved the outer door far enough to give them enough space to walk through single file. Melody retrieved the crystal from the slot.

"The corridors can be confusing for a visitor." Her voice dropped to a whisper as they neared the inner door. "I will take you where we can access a map showing the entire interior and we can decide our most effective strategy from there."

Melody inserted the crystal into another slot near the inner door and they repeated the same process. She stepped through first and paused. Paige peered over her shoulder. No activity in the corridor. The other aliens must not have detected their presence inside the ship yet.

Once she knew the coast was clear, Melody crept down the corridor. Paige, Heather, and Todd stayed within a step or two of her. Todd's eyes darted from wall to wall and up to the ceiling. He scanned the area for signs of cameras or other surveillance devices. Paige hadn't even thought of doing that until seeing him do it. A small swelling of pride touched her heart when she saw her brother's skills in action.

The group traveled only a short distance before Melody veered down a second corridor. She stopped in front of the third door on the right side. Melody retrieved the crystal from her pocket and jammed it in another slot. The red light above the door clicked off. This time, Heather stepped forward and pushed it open. Melody glanced back out at the corridor after they all entered the room.

"Seal the door behind us. We do not want to attract inadvertent gazes."

Heather pushed it shut again. Paige surveyed the room. Cold and sterile were the first descriptors that popped into her mind. The room featured multiple metal platforms serving as tables and workstations. She saw no photographs, artwork, or anything else that showed a semblance of personality or humanity.

Melody approached a workstation covered with gadgets of all shapes and sizes that Paige had no conception of before this moment. She activated a display screen. Soon, six smaller windows covered the screen. Each one showed a different section of their spaceship-turned-observation center. Melody touched individual screens to go from room to room.

She finally brought up an expansive circular room. A bank of connected workstations and screens lined the wall. A giant column anchored the center of the room. Two broad consoles stood a short distance from it. Each console featured an array of buttons, lights, levers, and panels. Paige's eyes were glued to the screen, studying every little detail.

Melody pointed to the same screen where Paige focused her attention.

"This is the main operations room," she said. "From here, you can control multiple key ship systems. It is also where the energy barrier surrounding this place can be shut down."

Todd wasted no time getting to the point.

"How do we get there from here?"

Melody walked over to the other end of the workstation. She punched a button on a larger version of her communicator – comparable in size to a tablet. The shape and design still reminded

Paige of her smartphone power cord plug. A holographic screen soon popped up above the communicator.

Melody scrolled through the screen until bringing up a three-dimensional layout of the ship's interior. Paige approached the floating image and thrust out her hand. She traced her finger down the length of a corridor. Heather and Todd hung back and simply stared in awe at the hologram.

A de-facto model of the entire ship. Every room. Every corridor. Nothing withheld from their sight.

Paige located the main operations room on the hologram. She crouched down and narrowed her eyes. The detail fascinated her. Every feature on the other screen was also present in the model but scaled down to fit within the image.

Melody tapped on tunnels located between decks.

"Access tunnels run above both main corridors leading to the operations room," she said. "You can enter the tunnels from inside this room."

Heather cast her eyes toward the screen broadcasting feeds from various parts of the ship.

"Isn't there a chance someone will see us?" she asked. "Y'all seem to have cameras and sensors all over the place in here."

"I can deactivate the sensors inside the access tunnels from here," Melody replied. "No one should notice the change right away because the tunnels are not a key section."

Melody walked over to a small cabinet and opened it. She removed clear masks that fit over both the nose and mouth. Each one possessed a breathing apparatus attached to the front. A small cylinder topped the apparatus.

"Put these on before you exit the access tunnel. This will protect you from the gas."

"Gas?"

Paige, Heather, and Todd all repeated the last word. Melody nodded. Paige exchanged worried glances with the other two. Their faces filled with the same worry clawing at her insides. This plan seemed to be adding new wrinkles by the second.

She didn't feel prepared for these wrinkles.

"I need to flood the room with a sleeping agent. It will subdue whoever is inside. We cannot trust anyone else in here to not turn us over to Barber and the guards at this point."

"Will these masks protect us?"

Todd took a mask from Melody. He traced over it with his fingers, searching for obvious design flaws.

"For a few minutes," Melody said. "Once you are inside, I will expunge remnants of the sleeping agent from the air."

Paige and Heather took the remaining masks. Melody crawled up on a platform and stretched her arms above her head. She popped a panel loose. It exposed a narrow square opening, leading straight into the access tunnels. Paige stared at the tunnel opening and glanced at the backpack hanging off Todd's shoulders. She didn't need measuring tape to figure out their gear wouldn't fit inside the tunnel while on their backs.

"We're gonna have to lose the backpacks," Paige said. "Fitting our bodies in that cramped space is gonna be hard enough."

Todd wasted no time vetoing that idea.

"We have to take at least one with us," he said, slipping the backpack off his shoulders. "Gotta put the masks somewhere while we're crawling."

"But –"

"We'll also need some of the gear with us inside that operations room."

"Well, how do you plan –"

"I'll go first and push the pack ahead of me. Not everything needs to be complicated."

Paige frowned. She never liked it when Todd cut her off. His smug know-it-all tone when he did it only made him more annoying.

Todd tossed the backpack up into the opening. Melody helped hoist him up into the tunnel. She then gave Paige and Heather a boost upward before replacing the panel behind them again.

CRAWLING THROUGH THE access tunnel turned out more uncomfortable than Paige anticipated. It ended up being as cramped as it appeared from the outside. That wasn't the only problem. Three people shoved into a tight space compounded the heat inside the tunnel. Sweat beaded on Paige's forehead and trickled down both cheeks.

"I'm cooking like a roasted chicken in here," she said. "Can we speed this up?"

Todd replied with an annoyed grunt.

"Pushing this backpack forward while crawling on my hands and knees isn't the easiest thing to do."

Paige felt tempted to ask him if he wanted to change places. Her task wasn't much easier. She had to hold the communicator Melody gave them out in front of her while crawling forward. Keeping the device steady wasn't the easiest thing to do with her hand continually bumping metal panels below. Each bump jarred the holographic screen and caused the image on it to flicker. They needed the screen to stay activated so Melody could show them where to turn and when to stop.

"How much farther is it?" Heather asked.

Paige repeated the question to Melody. She studied the three-dimensional ship model and compared the image to their current position.

"Make another left turn ahead," Melody said. "You should see a narrow tube in front of you. This leads directly into the main operations room."

Paige reached forward and gave Todd's right foot a hard tap with her fist.

"Did you hear that?"

"Turn left. Narrow tube. Yeah, I got it."

Todd held up his fist when he reached the tube a couple of minutes later. Paige stopped crawling when she saw his signal. She relayed the same signal back to Heather. Todd pulled the backpack toward him and unzipped the main pocket. He drew out the three masks Melody gave them earlier and passed two back to Paige and Heather.

Paige set down the communicator in front of her, being careful to not accidentally switch off the screen. Putting on the mask proved easier said than done. She banged her hand on the portion of the tunnel above her head while trying to position the mask over her nose and mouth. Then Paige banged it a second time while locking the mask in place.

"Keep it down back there. Don't you know the meaning of stealth?"

Paige couldn't see Todd glaring at her, but she felt it couched in his words. Seeing his lack of trouble in slipping his mask on bugged her. It robbed Paige of a chance at an easy comeback.

She picked up the communicator again.

"We've reached the narrow tube and put on our masks," Paige said. "Your turn."

Sweat dripped inside her mask while she awaited Melody's response. Those droplets crossed her lips and left a salty taste in her mouth. Paige squirmed and mashed her top lip and against the bottom one.

"Releasing the sleeping agent now." Hearing Melody's voice again came as a welcome relief. "It should take full effect within a minute of exposure."

Melody carried her communicator over to the workstation. She held the holographic screen up, so it showed the feed from the main operations room on the workstation display screen. A thick mist billowed into the room. Aliens started falling to the floor left and right. Two made a run for the exit door. They stumbled and fell after running only a few feet.

"You should be able to enter now," Melody said. "Alert me once you are inside and I will vent the remainder of the sleeping agent."

Paige tapped Todd's foot again and held up her fist. He nodded and pushed the backpack aside. Todd grabbed onto rungs and climbed down the tube. He opened a door at the bottom. Paige tossed the backpack down to her brother. He caught it and stepped through the door. She took her turn climbing down the rungs next. Heather followed Paige. Once all three were inside the room, Todd closed the door behind them.

"We're all inside now," Paige said, raising the communicator again. "You can vent the room."

Fans activated inside the room. The mist rushed toward floor vents and disappeared as fast as it emerged. Paige popped off the breathing mask and loudly exhaled. She wiped away lingering sweat from across her face.

"That felt like a damn sauna up there."

Todd removed his mask and dropped it back inside the backpack.

"Don't get too comfortable," he said. "That's probably gonna be our exit route too when we're done in here."

Paige broke out into an exasperated frown as she tossed her mask to him. Todd was right but she wasn't in the mood to hear him prove it.

Heather popped off her mask and set it down on a nearby workstation. She turned and glanced at an alien seated in front of her. The alien's eyes were closed, and her body slumped over the workstation. Heather lifted an arm, examined it for a second, and let the limb drop.

"What do we do about them?" she asked, glancing at Todd and Paige.

Paige looked around the room. Several aliens were splayed out on the floor or on workstations. All unconscious. They probably should tie them up or lock them in a secure area. Melody didn't give a specific answer for how long the sedation would last. Leaving aliens lying around the operations room could turn into a disaster if the sleeping agent wore off earlier than expected.

Paige glanced down at the communicator again. Melody's face appeared front and center on the screen.

"Is there an adjacent room, maybe a supply closet, where we can lock up these aliens?" she asked. "I don't really feel comfortable having them out here with us."

Melody held up her finger and did a head count of all the sedated aliens.

"A door leading to a supply chamber is on the opposite end of the operations room. I believe there is enough space to hold everyone in there."

Paige ventured to the other end of the operations room where Melody directed. She saw the door in question. The door had the same annoying sensor above it as all the other doors in this spaceship. These aliens apparently trusted one another about as much as they liked humans. Paige sidestepped the sensor, like Melody did with the earlier ones, to avoid triggering it. She fished the crystal card out of her pocket and inserted it into a column slot.

The sensor switched off and the door cracked open. Paige pushed the door open. This one stuck a bit halfway, forcing her to put her back into it. Todd and Heather each grabbed an alien by the arms. They dragged the aliens, one by one, inside the supply room. Shelves were filled with assorted items Paige couldn't begin to explain to anyone who had never seen them before.

Heather and Todd propped each alien against the shelves. They confiscated every visible gadget or weapon on their bodies.

After they dragged the last one inside, Paige sealed the supply chamber again. She hoped this bought them enough time to escape into the access tunnels if any aliens awoke too early.

Paige got her first chance to survey the operations room. A giant clear column stood in the center of the room. It matched the width of a pillar on an ancient Greek or Roman temple. The column stretched between disc-shaped metallic pads. One pad was bound to the ceiling, the other was affixed to the floor. A clear tube wound around a vertical metallic rod occupying the middle of the column's interior. It housed clusters of some blue substance she couldn't identify that flowed through the length of the tube.

Workstations lined walls on both sides of the operations room. These bore a similar design to the one Melody used earlier. Two stout rectangular consoles stood at the room's north end. Each console rose about waist high from the ground. Both consoles featured a large, embedded screen and rows of numerous digital buttons resembling app icons.

Paige plucked the communicator up from a workstation again. The screen flickered when she positioned it inside her palm.

"What do we do now?"

Melody glanced away from the screen on her end. She zoomed into the operations room on the three-dimensional ship model before her. Melody studied it for a few seconds before facing Paige again.

"Go to a right-hand console on the north end of the room," she said. "The barrier is receiving power from our antimatter engine."

Heather glanced back at the column anchoring the middle of the room.

"Antimatter?" Awe tinged her voice. "That's some powerful stuff. We talked about in one of my science classes. Just a little bit provides tons of energy."

Melody nodded.

"You must input a specific code to reroute power back to the ship and force the barrier to collapse."

"What's the code?" Paige asked.

"It is in my native language," Melody replied. "I cannot tell you. I must show you what to do."

Paige, Todd, and Heather converged on the console. Having Melody also inside the room would make things much easier. The console had so many different buttons on the main screen. Paige didn't have the slightest idea what function even a single button served.

"Look for a vertical column of three green buttons on the right side of the screen," Melody said.

Todd reached down to tap on the buttons.

"Wait!"

His hand froze above the screen.

"I apologize." Melody shot him a frown matching her words. "I meant the left side. If you punch the buttons on the right side, you will automatically open containment chambers on the lower deck."

"That would be a bad thing, I take it?"

Heather's hands weren't anywhere near that part of the console screen, but she backed up a few steps from it anyway.

"Indeed. Many altered humans are being held in those chambers."

Todd pivoted over to the other side of the screen.

"Stay away from those buttons for now," he said. "We've got enough other things to worry about."

Paige adjusted the communicator, so Melody saw the buttons on the other end of the screen. The alien instructed Todd step-by-step on the required sequence to input into the console. When he finished, the three buttons flashed from green to a yellowish-orange color. Paige glanced over at the column anchoring the middle of the room. A slot opened on the metallic rod's surface. The blue substance retreated from the clear tube and poured into this new opening. Once the last trace made it inside, the rod sealed shut again.

Two symbols popped up near the bottom of the screen. Both symbols were bathed in red. Each one flashed with the same intensity as blinking lights. A line on a graph, measuring energy transfer to the barrier, dropped until it vanished.

"The barrier is now shut down."

Melody's declaration registered like sweet music in Paige's ears. One word popped into her mind the moment she heard those words.

Freedom.

They lost so much in this awful place. Jason. Caroline. Rich. Such a heavy toll and horrific burden to be exacted. Their deaths were so senseless.

Now they could begin to set things right.

It started with getting Todd's DNA repaired. Ridding themselves of Barber and his minions would be the next item to check off their list. Melody also deserved a chance to go to a better planet and possibly reunite with her sister and her beloved pet.

"How do we keep them from powering up the barrier again once we leave this room?"

Todd's question pierced Paige's thoughts. It did feel a little too easy. She learned the hard way that nothing in Travis ever ended up being easy.

Melody placed the three-dimensional model of the ship on the screen for the others to see. Her long finger reached out and tapped the primary door leading into the main operations room. The image flickered for a moment after she touched the screen.

"I can lock out access with an encryption. It should buy us enough time to deal with Barber and others among my fellow Rubrumians who are aligned with him."

A slight smile crept over Todd's face.

"Do it. Then let's go take down that miserable son of a bitch."

Melody answered with an abrupt nod. She sat at the workstation again and clicked on a corner icon. A wall of text popped up in the Rubrum language. Paige set down the communicator while Melody started to type. She gathered up the backpack and tossed the masks inside again. Paige zipped up the main pocket and handed the backpack off to Todd.

A loud gasp came from the communicator. A whimper followed it.

Paige dashed over and plucked it off the workstation. Melody's breathing had grown heavier. She stopped typing. Her eyes were fixed on the door just out of view.

"They found me." Her voice dropped to a whisper. "They are cutting open the door right now."

Paige stared at the screen with widened eyes and raised eyebrows. Sparks flew toward Melody from the direction of the door. Grinding and sizzling from a cutting tool reverberated through the room. Someone was trying to punch a hole through the door to get to Melody.

"Get out of there!"

Paige wanted to shout her plea at the top of her lungs. It came out only as a loud whisper. She could not afford to draw unwanted attention to their location. Melody got the message. She dashed over to the platform under the panel leading into the access tunnels. Melody popped the panel loose a second time and set it aside.

Sparks continue to fly from the door. Melody jumped down and peered at the screen on the communicator. Her expression grew more panicked.

"My time is running out."

"No! Get out of there," Paige said. "You gotta fix Todd's DNA. You gotta help us escape!"

Her voice grew more strained with each word. Melody simply shook her head.

"Flood the antimatter stream into the ship's engine. Once it hits –"

A loud crash reverberated through the room. Melody stopped in mid-sentence and cast her eyes toward the door. Two aliens Paige did not recognize stepped into the communicator's visual range. Andrew and Barber followed a step behind. The group surrounded Melody at her workstation.

Todd and Heather heard the crash. They peered over Paige's shoulder. Their eyes grew wider when they saw what she saw.

"Did you think we would not notice you sneaking back in here with those humans?" Barber's tone became agitated almost as soon as he spoke. "What did you hope to accomplish?"

Melody refused to look at him. She stared at the feet of the guards standing before her.

"This is their planet. They deserve to be left alone in peace."

Barber glowered at her. The pale skin of his cheeks grew flushed, and he crossed his arms.

"Do you not care about the survival of our people? Rubrum is dying. We are doing what is needed to give our people new life."

"At what cost?"

"When the sun cycle begins anew, we shall be called heroes. Except for you."

Barber stabbed his finger at Melody, so the tip nearly touched her left eye.

"You will be remembered as nothing more than a traitor and a coward."

The heat rose under Paige's collar as she watched and heard everything unfold. Barber revealed himself as nothing more than a selfish monster. No better than human dictators they discussed in her world history class. Paige wanted to rush down the corridor and charge into the room to save Melody.

She knew she would never make it.

The communicator's screen flickered. Paige swallowed hard and exchanged worried glances with Heather and Todd. Barber caught a glimpse of the flicker out of the corner of his eye. He leaned down and looked right at the screen.

"I am pleased you will witness justice handed out. Let me show you what we do with combative humans and traitors."

Barber turned back and motioned to the guards. At once, the two aliens each grabbed an arm on Andrew. His mouth dropped open and he struggled to free himself from their grasp.

"Let me go!" he shouted. "What are you doing? I'm one with Rubrum."

"No." Barber's voice grew cold. "You are nothing more than a dirty human."

One guard pulled out the same type of collar used on Rich earlier and slapped it around Andrew's neck. Yellow lights activated on the collar. Barber pulled out the remote controlling the collar. He kicked Andrew in the back of the knee, forcing him to drop to the ground.

Paige and Heather both turned away and squeezed their eyes shut. Both girls loathed Andrew after what he did to Rich, but they could not bear to watch his execution. It only caused images of Rich's death to reemerge.

A scream ripped through the air.

When Paige finally opened her eyes again, the collar had been removed. Andrew's head lay on the floor. His body collapsed in a heap behind it.

Melody closed her eyes. Tears streamed down her cheeks. She knew her fate was sealed.

"We will survive and thrive here on New Rubrum," Barber said. "Our people will grow strong and healthy again. Everything will again be as it was in the generations before our sun fell."

He withdrew a weapon from his coat. It bore an identical design to the ones Todd and Melody used in their battle with the aliens in the plaza.

"You will not see these things unfold."

Barber fired two laser bolts.

Both energy blasts ripped through different spots on Melody's chest. She tumbled to the floor in front of the communicator screen. Paige and Heather cried out on the other end. Melody turned her face toward them one last time. Blood trickled through her open lips.

"Halilah," she mumbled. "Forgive me."

Those were the last words Melody spoke.

BARBER AND THE other aliens from Rubrum had to die. No other solution presented itself in Paige's mind. He slaughtered Melody in cold blood before their eyes without hesitation. He ordered Rich's execution and bore responsibility for the deaths of Jason and Caroline. They could not let Barber or anyone with him flee from Texas or Earth. Paige understood the task that now lay ahead for her, Heather, and Todd.

The aliens had to be destroyed.

Barber plucked Melody's communicator up from the workstation. He stared past their enraged faces on the other end and studied the room behind them. His eyes widened when it suddenly dawned on him where they had gone. Barber snapped his head around to face the guards.

"Get to the main operations room right now. Humans have tampered with our barrier. Do what you need to do and then restore it at once."

He glanced back at the screen. A smug smile crossed his lips. "We shall deal with you in proper fashion."

Todd snatched away the communicator from Paige and switched it off.

"I think I've heard all I want to hear from that alien bastard for the rest of my life."

Paige cast her eyes toward the primary door leading in and out of the main operations room. Goosebumps formed on her arms and legs. No one knew if Melody finished the encryption before Barber and his entourage interrupted her. They couldn't really risk sticking around to find out.

"What are we gonna do?" Paige asked, glancing at Todd. "We can't keep them out forever."

It bordered on an impossible situation to her. Then again, Paige knew her brother dealt with so many impossible situations in Afghanistan and in Travis before she ended up here. He always found a way out. Todd proved he was a survivor in every sense of the word.

Todd rubbed his hands down his cheeks. He stared at the column holding the antimatter in the center of the room. A determined expression washed over his face.

"We're gonna light the candle and watch this place burn."

Paige approached the console. She gazed at the control buttons for the containment chambers Melody identified earlier. The wheels started turning in her head and her face lit up.

"I've got it." Paige slapped her hand down on the console. "If we release all captive former humans, that will hold the aliens off long enough to set some sort of ship self-destruct in motion."

"That would give those assholes a taste of their own medicine," Heather said. "I bet those creatures would love nothing more than a chance to attack."

Paige pointed up at the narrow tube leading back into the access tunnels.

"After we set the self-destruct, we crawl through the tunnel again and climb out near the ship's exit. From there, we hop on a transport and fly out of here before the place blows sky high."

Todd picked up the backpack and handed it to Heather. He flashed a brief smile at Paige before his expression turned solemn again.

"I like what you're thinking Paige," he said. "You two better get into that tunnel and get to that transport as fast as you can. I'll stay here and make sure the explosion goes off without a hitch."

Paige marched over to her brother and grabbed him by the shoulders. Her blue eyes locked on his blue eyes like a pair of lasers.

"What do you mean? You're coming with us."

"No, I'm not. This is where we part ways."

Tears welled up in Paige's eyes. Her lower lip jutted out. Heather's mouth dropped open and she shook her head, silently pleading with Todd not to do what he was contemplating.

Paige couldn't stay silent.

"No. Todd, I just found you." Her voice became choked with emotion. "Please don't make me lose you again."

Todd closed his eyes and bowed his head.

"There's no other way, sis. My body is still changing, and we can't repair the damage now that Melody is dead. I don't want to turn into a monster."

"You'll never be a monster to me. Please. We can think of some other option. I've lost so much over the last few days. I don't think I can handle losing any more."

Todd opened his eyes and lifted his head again. He tenderly touched Paige on the shoulder.

"You're strong, Paige. Stronger than you realize. I need you to be strong and survive. For you. For me and Caroline. For Mom and Dad."

They embraced. Paige buried her face in her brother's neck and shoulder. Her tears soaked into his shirt. Todd's eyes welled up with tears as well.

"I love you," she whispered.

"I'll always love you," he said. "Never forget that."

Paige pulled away from the embrace, brushing away her remaining tears. Todd did the same.

He walked over to the pile of confiscated alien weapons on a nearby workstation and picked out ones they didn't already have. Todd tossed a weapon to each girl. This new weapon looked like a futuristic pistol. It featured a rounded molded plastic handle that wrapped around the fingers. The handle connected to a hollowed out metallic rod about the same length as a ballpoint pen. A clip latched underneath the rod at the midway point. It had four blue slots. A trigger hung down between the handle and the clip.

Paige and Heather each tucked the alien pistol inside their belts. Todd took a deep breath and approached the console. He punched all three buttons controlling the containment chambers. A few seconds later, an alarm sounded. Red lights bathing the room began to flash.

"There's your window," Todd said. "You better leave while you still can."

He picked up the communicator Melody gave Paige and tossed it to her. Paige caught it and put it in her pocket.

"Don't forget this. I've got another one for me among the stuff we confiscated from the aliens. Keep it turned on and let me know when you've reached a safe distance."

"I will. I promise."

Paige walked over to her brother for the last time and planted a kiss on his cheek.

"Caroline would be so proud of you."

Todd embraced her one final time. Paige lingered for only a few seconds before turning and sprinting for the door to the narrow tube. She used the crystal to open it and followed Heather up the rungs. Paige didn't dare look back at her brother before climbing out of his sight. She would only start crying again and there wasn't enough time left for that now.

The tunnel felt as cramped and hot as before. It didn't bother Paige as much the second time around. Her sole focus turned to crawling through the tunnel as fast as possible. Barber and the others were scouring the ship for her, Heather, and Todd. Releasing all those monsters may have thrown up some roadblocks, but

Paige imagined it wouldn't be enough to stop every single alien on the ship.

A mixture of hellish noises penetrated the access tunnel from decks above and below. Screams. Howls. Growls. Each one only put Paige and Heather further on the edge. Paige kept wondering if an escaping alien or altered human would barge inside the tunnel and block their escape path.

"My life was a whole lot better before I saw and heard all these things around us," Heather said.

Paige agreed wholeheartedly with her observation. Sitting in a classroom listening to a boring lecture or stumbling through a pop quiz didn't feel so bad in the grand scheme of things. Those problems were ones she would kill to have now instead of dodging aliens and mutated humans trying to kill her.

"If we get out of this alive, I don't think I'll ever complain about my classes, work, or anything else," Paige said. "It all feels kind of trivial now."

The two girls were careful not to simply retrace their steps. Popping out into the room where they first entered the access tunnels would only heighten their risk of capture. Neither Paige nor Heather had a desire to encounter the lifeless bodies of Melody and Andrew sprawled on the floor.

Both girls operated on pure memory at this point as they navigated the access tunnel. Paige took mental notes of the layout for the tunnels and called out directions to Heather whenever one tunnel intersected with another. Bringing it up on the communicator would have been easier in theory. Without Melody's help, however, Paige had no idea what to buttons to push or which files to access so she could see the tunnel schematics again.

If only time had allowed Melody to give me a crash course in reading the Rubrum language, Paige thought. *Our situation would be better in at least one aspect.*

"We've reached a dead end."

Paige cast her eyes around the tunnel. Heather's words didn't inspire confidence they would pop out near the ship's exit. Dim red light scattering through the tunnel made it tough to locate the exit tubes without outside help.

Heather drew a flashlight out of the backpack and clicked it on. The bright beam immediately enhanced tunnel visibility. Paige could now see they made a wrong turn somewhere along the way.

It didn't matter now. Todd counted on them to get to safety before he blew the antimatter engine.

"You're gonna have to blast a hole in the floor of the tunnel," Paige said.

"Are you sure that's a good idea?"

"I have no idea where we are, and I can't pull up the ship layout to know where to backtrack. We're just gonna blow up with the ship if we don't get out of this tunnel right now."

"Okay. Scoot back. If this blasts fragments, I don't want either of us getting hit."

Paige backed up on her hands and knees until Heather had enough room to do the same. She snapped her eyes shut and shielded her face. Heather discharged four laser bolts from her beater weapon in rapid succession. Smoke from the new holes wafted into Paige's nostrils. She opened her eyes into a half-squint. Heather tried to fan away the excess smoke with her hand.

The laser bolts punched four fist-sized holes through the tunnel floor. Heather reached down through one of the holes. Footsteps and a voice shouting in the corridor below immediately followed.

"Humans are in the access tunnel!"

Heather retracted her arm and backed up against the opposite wall. Paige pulled out the alien pistol Todd obtained for her earlier. She now had just enough clearance to fire it. Sparks flew as an unseen cutting tool sliced through a section of the tunnel ahead of them. It soon dropped out of her sight.

An alien popped into view.

"Thanks for the rescue," Paige said.

She and Heather fired their weapons at the same time. The alien gasped and collapsed back into the corridor. Both girls stuck their arms out and fired in all directions. Two more bodies hit the floor. Heather and Paige listened for signs of other aliens. Shouts, growls, and weapon fire reverberated deep in the corridor – all from unseen parts of the ship.

"Let's go," Heather said.

She jumped from the tunnel to the floor below. Paige followed suit. Pain shot through her ankle when she landed. Paige stumbled and her hand struck the floor. She caught herself before falling completely over.

"Damn! I think I rolled my ankle."

Paige gritted her teeth and pulled herself to her feet again. Both girls surveyed the corridor. Three dead alien bodies. No other signs of activity. They only needed to figure out where to go to exit the ship.

A loud sudden hiss greeted them from one end of the corridor. A small growl followed. Paige raised her pistol and wheeled around. Her face scrunched up in a confused expression when she saw the source of these new noises.

An orange cat.

"I guess they weren't just experimenting on humans around here," Heather said.

She kept her beater weapon trained on the cat. Paige glanced at the weapon and shook her head.

"I don't think it's a threat," she said. "It's disheveled, but otherwise looks like a normal cat."

Of course, normal was a relative term in this situation. The cat was missing a front fang and appeared to be blind in one eye. It also sported matted fur and bald spots on its backside and near its haunches. Still, no signs of body armor, horns, or other nasty features they found on altered humans.

"Here kitty, kitty, kitty."

Paige repeated the call a few times in a soothing tone. She lowered her weapon. The cat stopped hissing and growling. Flattened ears perked up and its tail grew less bushy. Finally, the cat called out to both girls with a sad meow.

"Follow us," Paige said. "We'll get you out of this awful place."

Paige was skeptical the cat understood her words. But it acted like it knew what she was talking about. The cat bounded up to the two girls and then darted past their position. After a few feet, it turned and looked back.

Heather shook her head in disbelief.

"Are we really gonna follow a cat?"

"Cats are smart animals," Paige said. "If one is running from that direction, then we know not to go that way."

They trailed the cat down the corridor. After making a couple of turns, Paige started to recognize her surroundings. She saw the interior exit leading to the outer door of the spaceship.

The cat had found the way.

Both girls sprinted ahead of their new feline companion to deactivate the sensor and open the door before it accidentally triggered a DNA scan. Paige inserted the crystal into the column and then helped Heather pry the door open. They repeated the process on the outer door and called to the cat. It trotted forward at a brisk pace.

Paige activated her communicator once they cleared the outer door of the ship. The screen came to life again. Todd sat on the floor in front of the column. He panted and sweat beaded on his forehead. That meant only one thing – the bio armor was overtaking his legs again.

"We're outside the ship," Paige said. "Headed to the transport now."

Todd nodded. He gritted his teeth and pulled out the alien pistol he kept for himself and the beater weapon. Her brother set both weapons by his side.

"Good."

A relieved sigh escaped his lips. Todd pushed off the floor and pulled himself to his feet. He snatched up both weapons and stood before the column.

"I will not permit you to escape." A low, ragged voice called out to Paige and Heather. "You will pay for the destruction you have caused among the people of Rubrum."

Todd paused and glanced back at the communicator screen. Both girls wheeled around and faced the ship's entrance. Barber now stood outside. His clothes were torn. Blood oozed from a deep gash covering one forearm.

The cat hissed as soon as it spotted the alien. It flattened its ears and backed toward Paige and Heather.

"This is our planet now," Barber said. "I will not let you undo what we have accomplished and drive us from New Rubrum."

"It's called Earth," Heather replied. "And you can't have it."

Barber flashed a beater weapon. Both girls were quicker draws. They had their weapons trained on him before he could raise it. Barber's eyes grew wider as he sized up the unfavorable odds.

"Back away from the ship," Paige said.

Barber lowered his weapon and did as ordered. Paige pivoted around until she had him facing the ship. She smiled when she looked up at the cracks in the warehouse walls.

Sunlight peeked through the cracks.

"I think you're about to get the worst sunburn you've ever had."

Paige turned to Heather after saying those words and nodded. Heather fired her weapon above Barber's head. The laser bolt struck the wall and punched a fist sized hole through wood and metal. A beam of sunlight fell directly on Barber's back and neck. He stood there in silence for a minute before a wry smile crossed his thin lips.

"We cracked the code during this past sun cycle," Barber said. "I know how to adapt our bodies to your sun now. This means all who remain on Rubrum can relocate here."

"We aren't letting that happen," Heather said.

"You cannot stop it. Your sunlight will no longer be lethal to our bodies."

"Cool," Paige replied. "Let's see how that works with a few holes in you."

Barber raised his weapon again. On cue, both girls opened fire. Barber was only a fraction of a second slower. But that was more than enough time. Heather and Paige each hit Barber with multiple laser bolts. When they finally stopped, holes riddled his body. Barber collapsed in an oozing heap.

Paige retrieved her communicator and showed Todd the Rubrum leader no longer posed a threat. He painted on a smile that did little to conceal sadness weighing down his mind and heart.

"Godspeed Paige. Please give my love to mom and dad when you get home."

Paige started to tear up again.

"I love you."

"I love you too."

Todd set down the communicator and aimed his weapons at the column containing the antimatter chamber. Paige switched it off. She did not wish to see her brother's actual death when that moment finally transpired.

Heather and Paige climbed into the same transport that brought them here earlier. Paige made sure to usher the cat inside as well. It deserved to escape from this awful place as much as they did. Paige powered up the transport and launched it just like she watched Melody do earlier.

A sensor activated the warehouse door as they approached. Paige pressed her hands into the steering columns and pushed them far forward. The transport zipped through the opening. It climbed above the warehouse and barreled forward.

At once, a bright blue-white flash lit up the dawn sky. Heather and Paige pinched their eyes shut. A loud boom followed as the blast wave spread out in all directions from the ship and warehouse. The blast wave rocked the bottom of the transport. Paige opened her eyes again and steadied it before the vehicle dipped below the treetops.

"If any aliens were outside that ship, I don't think they made it," Heather said.

Paige glanced down. The blast wave wiped what remained of Travis off the map. Buildings were leveled. Trees incinerated. It looked like a nuclear bomb had been dropped on it all.

"We can only hope," Paige replied.

The transport soared over the road leading out of town. I-40 loomed in the distance. Their situation had not improved. They still had a broken-down car along the highway. She also had no idea what powered this transport and how much fuel remained. Paige focused on flying to the nearest city and seeing if they could finally get help.

Those plans abruptly changed.

"Do you see that?" Heather asked. "It looks like a whole bunch of trucks and tanks turning off I-40 down there."

Paige glanced through the windshield at the military convoy. She knew better than to simply fly away. Maybe an alien from Rubrum could evade radar or sonar at the helm of a transport. Paige didn't dare try with her limited knowledge.

"Looks like we're sticking around here for a while longer," she said in a deflated voice.

Paige steered the transport toward a landing spot on the road leading to I-40. She engaged the magnetic locks. Paige and Heather both took deep breaths and exited the alien vehicle with arms raised above their heads.

PAIGE ADJUSTED HER long-sleeved blouse and pencil skirt one final time while standing before the office door. She hesitated to step inside. Her hand hovered over the handle, but she wouldn't let herself make contact and pull it toward her.

Paige grew weary of answering the same questions over and over. This had gone on for at least two weeks now. If this meeting existed for the sole purpose of letting another military and government official grill her for new information, she became convinced she would lose her mind and her temper. Paige had nothing more she could tell them about the aliens and everything that went down in Travis.

She took a deep breath and finally pulled the door open. Paige entered a small waiting room. A receptionist looked up from a desk at her.

"Can I help you?"

"I'm here to see General Daly."

Paige glanced over at an office behind the receptionist. His name was printed on the closed door in big black letters.

"Is he expecting you?"

She nodded.

"Tell him Paige Beck is here."

The receptionist glanced down at her visitor ID badge. She picked up the phone and alerted the general he had a visitor. After hanging up, the receptionist directed Paige to sign in at the desk and have a seat on a couch in the corner.

Paige fidgeted with a ring on her finger. Jason once gave it to her as a birthday present. He thought she would enjoy the ring since it was made with a sapphire gem. Paige adored it. Sapphire was her birthstone.

Now it served as nothing more than a reminder of a love stolen from her. Paige couldn't begin to count how many times she tossed and turned over the course of a night while longing for his touch and his warmth. She longed to talk to Jason one more time. Share one more joke or one more kiss.

Being on this base also felt akin to torture. Paige couldn't look around without also feeling the loss of her brother. Everything in this place reminded her of Todd and his military service. From there, her thoughts also naturally turned to Caroline. She longed for happier times when Caroline dished on some of her latest culinary discoveries or Todd went one-on-one against Paige in the driveway. She always won enough impromptu basketball games to keep his trash talk in check.

Paige pulled out her smartphone. She clicked on the YouTube icon and brought up one of Rich's videos. His absence also loomed large in her life. Paige didn't always appreciate those videos when he was alive. Now, making it through one without tearing up often proved easier said than done. She missed Rich – even when factoring in all his sarcastic comebacks.

"Ms. Beck. So glad you could meet with me on short notice."

Paige snapped her head up at the booming voice. Gen. Daly stood in the doorway. He sported a sharp blue Class A uniform and a robust physique that matched his voice. Paige sprang to her feet and offered up a salute.

"Please come in and have a seat."

Paige followed Gen. Daly into his office. An open file folder lay on his desk. Paige stiffened. She couldn't tell what information it contained from a distance but spotted a photo of herself on the top page. It raised questions in Paige's mind as she took a seat in front of the general's desk.

What did they know about her?

Should she be concerned?

"I've already told the military everything I know about the aliens and their planet," she said, crossing her legs. "I really don't have anything left to say that hasn't already been said."

Gen. Daly glanced down at the folder.

"It's all here. This isn't about what happened out in Travis."

"Then, sir, may I ask what it is about?"

"This is about preventing what happened in Travis from happening elsewhere on Earth."

Paige tilted her head and leaned forward. Her eyes narrowed as she took in the full implication of Gen. Daly's statement.

"I killed the alien leader, General. My brother gave his life to destroy their ship. Every single alien that came to Earth from Rubrum is dead."

"One threat has been eliminated. Many other extraterrestrial threats remain."

Paige jolted upright. A shudder raced through her body. Other extraterrestrial threats? She wasn't ready for that revelation. Adjusting to normal life again had been hard enough. Paige still had a full year of classes ahead of her at McNeese State. Finishing off the past semester had been an ordeal with all she endured.

"Why are you telling me this?" Paige's voice grew quiet yet remained forceful. "What exactly do you want from me?"

The general leaned back in his leather chair. His eyes zeroed in on her and his face took on a stoic demeanor.

"The White House has authorized the creation of a new agency to deal with these threats. The Earth Defense Bureau. I have been asked to head up the EDB and I want you to take on a leadership role within the agency."

Paige pressed her hand to her mouth. Her heart pounded inside her ribs. His request weighed heavily on her mind.

Leadership role? The Earth Defense Bureau?

There had to be someone else qualified to do it. Paige's goals always pointed to the classroom. She couldn't put down a good history book. The only thing she enjoyed more than reading and learning was sharing what she learned.

Paige didn't want to lose her dream.

"I'm a college student," she said. "I'm training to be a teacher. You're not looking at some military tactician, scientist, or tech genius here."

"You have what these other people don't have," Gen. Daly replied. "We can't duplicate your real-world experience, Ms. Beck."

"With all due respect, sir, there has to be someone else more qualified to do this."

Gen. Daly rose from his chair. He walked over to a nearby window and motioned for Paige to join him. She arose and approached the same window. Paige peered through the open blinds and gazed upon the grounds of the military base.

"You want to be a teacher?" he asked, stretching out his hand toward the window. "That's exactly what I'm looking for in the bureau. I want someone who can prepare us to combat other hostile aliens we encounter out there."

She turned from the blinds and faced the General again. He kept staring out the window.

"We learned that we're not alone, Ms. Beck. Protecting the Earth from other alien invaders is our top priority now. I need you to join us in this fight."

I need you to join us in this fight.

Paige mulled over his words during the ride back to her hotel room. The general seemed convinced no one else could do the job as well as her. Such an implication troubled Paige. She ended up in Travis by accident. Todd, Melody, and Heather all played as critical of a role in defeating the aliens. Could Paige assume the burden they wanted her to assume?

That's the first question she sprang on Heather during a video chat in her hotel room. Her response didn't fall in line with what Paige expected to hear.

"I hate to say it, but he's right."

"If he wants an alien fighter, maybe he should recruit Stray for this new agency."

Heather laughed. Stray lay on the bed behind her, curled up into a tight furry ball. He briefly raised his head at the mention of his name and then resumed his nap.

The orange cat was much healthier since his rescue from the alien ship. His fur grew back to a full thick coat again. Stray remained blind in one eye and had multiple missing teeth. But he was happy. Paige intended to give him a different name at first. Stray just seemed to fit. Much like the little sweater she bought to keep him warm while he healed.

"I don't think Stray here can communicate his knowledge to the military's liking," Heather said.

Paige lowered her head.

"I'm just worried. We got lucky in so many ways."

"There has to be a reason we survived, Paige. Maybe we have what it takes to keep Earth safe."

Heather's words struck a chord with her. Paige never used to believe in fate or other such nonsense. But now she wondered if her experiences in Texas prepared her to serve a greater purpose.

"No one should ever endure what we endured," Paige's voice took on a determined tone. "I guess it's up to us to see that it plays out that way."

Paige finally began to grasp her true purpose. She had to protect Earth from all aliens at all costs.

THE END

ABOUT THE AUTHOR

Being a storyteller is second nature to John Coon. Ever since John typed up his first stories on his parents' manual typewriter at age 12, he has had a thirst for creating stories and sharing them with others. John graduated from the University of Utah in 2004 and has carved out a successful career as an author and journalist since that time. His byline has appeared in dozens of major publications across the world. John's debut novel, Pandora Reborn, became an international bestseller on Amazon shortly after publication in 2018.

John resides in Sandy, Utah. Follow his author website, johncoon.net, and subscribe to his newsletter (johncoon.net/subscribe) for news and updates on upcoming novels and short stories. You can also connect with John on Twitter (@johncoonsports), Instagram (@jcoon312), and on Facebook (@jcoon).